Mistress of Hours

by Emma Elizabeth

First published by Emma Elizabeth 2024

First edition

Cover art by @FlavulousArt

Paperback: 979-8-9906805-0-0
Epub: 979-8-9906805-4-8
Kindle: 979-8-9906805-1-7

To all the women who have ever worried
they are too much (or not enough)

Content Warnings

DEAR READER,

Please note that while the romance contained within these pages is low-tension and kind, the fantasy plot is not. It contains dark elements that may be disturbing for some. Please take a moment to review the content warnings at the back of the book if you feel inclined (there will be some spoilers), and please feel free to contact me if there are any you feel I've missed.

Acknowledgements

I FIND, as I sit down to write this note, that this all feels rather surreal. I decided one day in October, 2023, that the thought of writing fiction made me uncomfortable. I thought that if it made me uncomfortable, that probably meant I should do it. Within an hour of actually letting myself imagine what stories I could tell, the idea for Mistress of Hours had sprouted from my mind.

By the time anyone reads this, it will be almost exactly a year since this idea came to me. It has been as uncomfortable as I expected in many ways, but I have also found incredible joy and purpose in this journey. For that, I am so, so grateful.

I would like to thank my sweet husband, William, who has read my (many) drafts and pushed me to make the world of Domhan na Rùin richer. He has supported me and believed in me, and I truly cannot say how much his partnership means to me. (He also created the incredible map you'll find at the front of the book. He is a man of many talents.)

I'd also like to thank my friend Sophie—your excitement, brainstorming plot points with me, editing and poking holes and cheering me on, gave me confidence to challenge myself throughout this process. Thank you to my friend Shak, for listening to my crazy plot rants over many cups of chai. Hollie, Kristen, Michele, Sarah—your enthusiasm for this little world I created, along with your feedback, made editing not just bearable but fun. To my wonderful beta readers: my story truly would not be what it is today without your help. I am eternally grateful.

I'd also like to extend a special thank you to the Author Alcove. I never could have guessed that I would find such deep friendships with you all over the past months, and it means more to me than I can say that you all had my back when I needed you most.

Flavia and Bo—you both made bringing this incredible cover to life such a special experience for me as a first-time author. I cannot thank you enough for your enthusiasm, your creativity, and your expertise.

Thank you to Emily for your thoughtful feedback and support. My characters really came to life because of your guidance, and I am so grateful to you for helping me make this story so special.

Thank you all, so much, for believing in me and being a part of this journey. And thank you, lovely reader, for giving my story a chance. I hope you love Evienne and her world as much as I do.

Name Pronunciation Guide

EVIENNE ELODIE D'AUCLAIRE: eh-VEE-en EH-low-dee Daw-clare

ORION DOEHLAN: Oh-ri-on Doe-lan

CECELIA CHANDELLE: Seh-see-lee-a Sh-an-del

JAC YARWOOD: Jack Yar-wood

SOLON LÙTAIR: Sol-on Loo-teyre

HESTIA BASILLE: Hes-tee-ah Bah-seel

DOMINIQUE MALINOIS: Dom-in-eek Mal-in-wa

LÉHIONA VASS: Leh-hee-oh-na V-ah-ss

ALDITH DU PONT: All-dith Doo Pon-t

BASTILLE DU PONT: Ba-steel Doo Pon-t

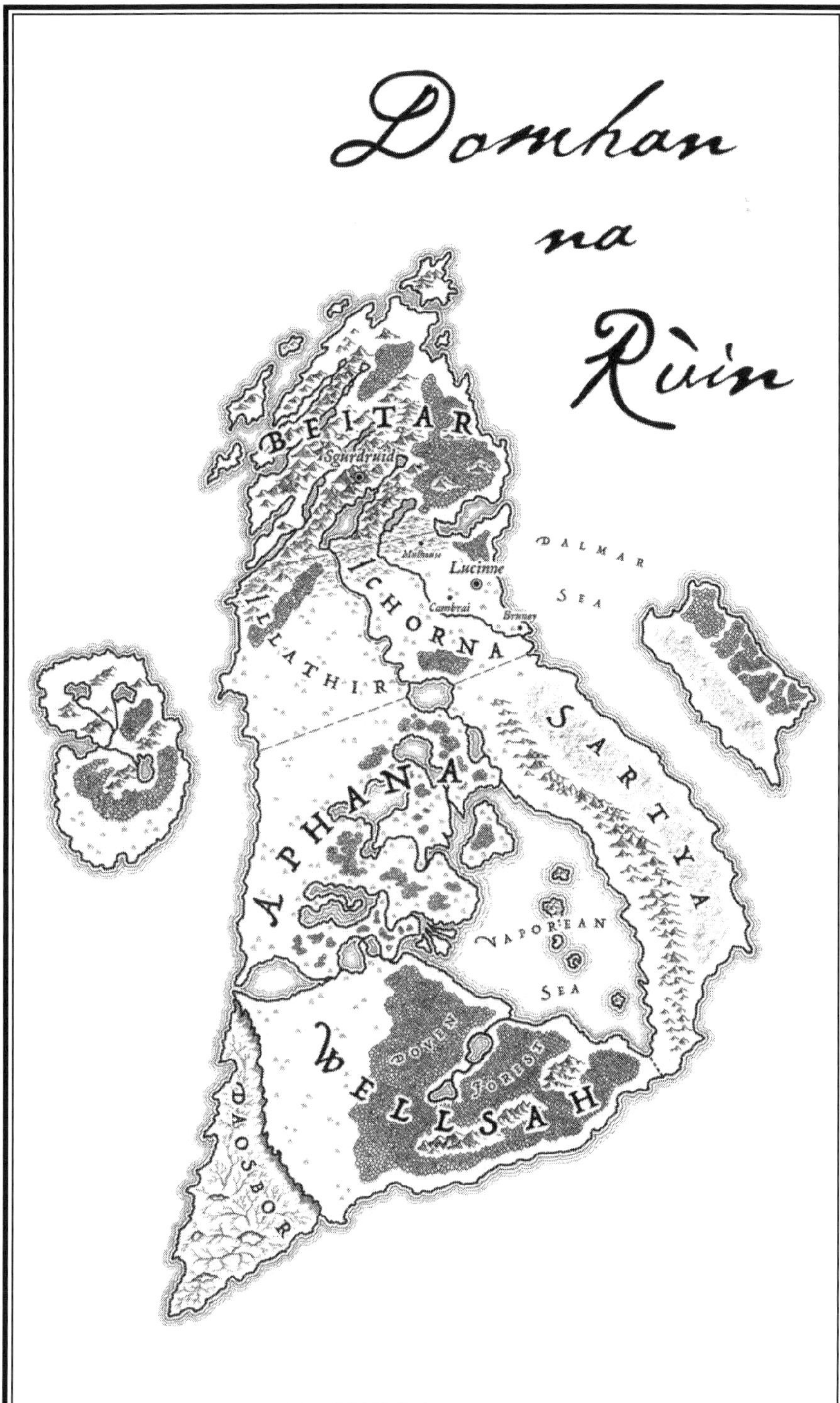
Domhan na Rùin
BEITAR
Sgurdruid
Lucinne
Cambrai
ICHORNA
ILLATHIR
DALMAR SEA
SARTYA
APHANA
VAPOREAN SEA
WELLSAH
DOVEN FOREST
DAOSBOR

Prologue

THE STONE WALLS of the catacombs bled their biting cold into the air. Bastille waited, his torch struggling to breathe in the closeness of the passage. The darkness was a leech, pulling every bit of light and warmth into its bottomless depths.

He had been to Sgùrdruid before but never to the catacombs. The place felt so ancient; it was a marvel that anyone was able to build this labyrinth of tunnels into the side of a mountain. The city sat far above, its inhabitants entirely unaware of what was to come.

Guilt weighed heavily on Bastille's soul, but he knew what he had to do. People across Ichorna suffered more and more each day because of their isolation. He had to do something to entice the rest of the world into trade with them. They were a small nation and not equipped with the resources to be self-sufficient. He was out of options; if he did not follow through with this, he would watch his people sink into ruin.

After seemingly endless moments, he heard near-silent

footsteps approaching. They were so quiet he thought he may be hallucinating.

The outline of a man appeared on the edge of the torch's glow, an apparition stepping out of the blackness.

The man was youthful, with a long, angular face and stern nose. His eyes appeared fully black in the dimness. When he spoke, goosebumps prickled Bastille's arms despite his thick cloak.

"I see you decided to follow through," the other man said in a voice that was eerily gentle.

"I must do what I can for my people, and I see no other options before me," Bastille answered with a sigh. His heart ached with the truth of what they were about to do.

"I still don't understand why you've offered this—it doesn't make sense," Bastille added.

"It is not for you to understand. You must only know the consequences for yourself and Ichorna. Do you want to do this or not?" the man answered, his tone growing harsher. "There is no room for indecision."

"Let's begin, then."

Chapter One

Evienne closed her eyes as the cold damp of the autumn morning settled deep into her bones. The air, laden with fog, hung suspended in her lungs; in this very moment, she felt the kiss of mist on her lips, the numbing bite of cold in her toes. She exhaled, her eyelids lifting slowly as time resumed its ever-forward march.

As the seconds drifted by, she felt her heart beating a steady rhythm. She surveyed her surroundings as her horse shifted beneath her. An inhuman snarl cleaved the silence, forcing her into intuitive motion.

The vicious point of her silver-bladed ring pricked her palm as she turned atop her horse, calling to the magic that coursed through her veins. Her blood was the spark, but her will fanned the flames of her power.

She faced down the massive beast then, with its spindly canine legs and grotesque, sallow face. Its smattering of black fur matched the depthless shade of its massive, empty eyes. Its teeth were bared, thin lips pulled back in a snarl.

Evienne didn't hesitate; her Regne du Sang, the most ancient and revered of the blood magics, was music to her. Without remorse, her power took hold of every drop of blood in the creature's body. With nothing more than a delicate twist of her wrist, she contracted the blood, and every bone in the beast's limbs snapped.

She pushed it down then, and when it lay prone on the ground, she gave one final tug on her magic to collapse the creature's skull.

Sounds of other mages locked in combat with these creatures, the Gevaud, surrounded her suddenly in an unwelcome din. It was not that they were unexpectedly loud—this was a battle—only they did not match the silence of her mind.

A pack of Gevaud had swarmed into the small town square. Evienne's fellow Sangviere now worked their blood magic to eliminate the threat, taking on the beasts one by one.

A scream pierced the air as a cluster of the creatures targeted a formation of mages on the opposite side of the square. Evienne watched, helpless from this distance, as they overpowered one of the Sangviere, taking him to the ground and ripping through his flesh with feral growls.

The other mages in his formation tried to defend themselves, one throwing up a glowing red shield of magic in an attempt to save her companions. They were not on horseback, though. Most Sangviere were not experienced enough to wield from a mount. Evienne knew they wouldn't last long. She urged her horse into motion across the square; this is why she was here, after all.

As she neared the group, now surrounded on all sides by the Gevaud, Evienne sliced a longer cut in her palm with her ring, blood welling as the dainty silver blade cut through her skin.

Her magic came to her in a rush now, and the lifeblood of the nearby creatures called to her. She felt their life force as if it were a siren's song. Her power hummed, and she closed her eyes to revel in the feeling of rightness. She seized the creatures' blood with her magic, taking hold of every drop that rushed through their veins, and pulled with all her might.

All at once, the six Gevaud that had surrounded the mages burst in a shower of red mist.

Evienne reigned in her horse, nodding in reassurance to the wide-eyed Sangviere who now stood before her in shock. Her breathing was heavy. Such a feat of Regne du Sang was not for the uninitiated—magic took a physical toll—but Evienne was the greatest Sangviere Ichorna had seen in hundreds of years. Her abilities were unmatched by any living mage.

Lou, the commanding officer of this unit of Sangviere, pulled up their horse next to Evienne's. They were out of breath as well; this was the largest recorded horde of the horrible beasts to attack since the so-called Gevaud Crisis began nearly ten years ago. The first Gevaud had been spotted in Ichorna about a hundred years ago, but they had started terrorizing people more recently. What had started as a nuisance had become more serious, with the Gevaud stalking and killing townsfolk if left unchecked. Sometimes, like today, packs of them would ransack a town in broad daylight. Lou waved to a medic, who rushed over from the edge of the square to tend to the fallen mage.

"I'm glad you were here today. What you just did certainly wasn't something we should leave to the novices," Lou said, still trying to catch their breath.

"I am glad I could help; the attacks seem to be getting worse every month. This is the most I've seen in one place," Evienne answered, surveying the chaotic aftermath of the battle. She was still out of breath, and her muscles had started to ache. The cut on her hand was already beginning to close though, the sharp pain turning to a dull throb. The healing spells she wove into all of her castings kept her palm from forming too much scar tissue.

Lou nodded, their face grim. "The people of Cambrai were able to get out in time. It seems like they were able to follow those evacuation protocols you set up fairly seamlessly. It's a good thing, too. Our casualties could have been significant if there had been a whole town of civilians here."

Evienne hummed her agreement as she and Lou watched the Sangviere working with the troop of guards stationed in Cambrai to clear the square of Gevaud corpses. Using her magic as she had today made her feel so alive, so connected to the world around her, but she was exhausted now—and hungry.

No matter how many times Evienne confronted them, the sight of the massive, mangy beasts unsettled her. Despite years of dealing with them, no one knew where they came from or what caused their attacks. Her patience with the unknowns had long since worn thin, but it seemed answers were impossible to come by.

After a few moments, Evienne turned to Lou. "Is there anything else I can do to help here?"

"I think we have things reasonably under control now that those horrible things have been dealt with," Lou said. "I know you must have things to do back in the city, High Sangviere," they added with a teasing smile.

"Lou, stop it, you know you don't need to call me that," Evienne answered with a small laugh. They had known each other for nearly fifteen years—ever since Evienne had arrived in Lucinne with no friends and no family in the city.

"Regardless, that is what you are, Evienne, and I know you're very busy. So, don't worry about us. We'll clean up and oversee the return of the townsfolk. I'll see you soon," they said and nudged their horse forward, making their way over to a cluster of confused-looking guards.

Evienne smiled as Lou retreated and turned her horse, Belle, toward the main road that led out of the town square. Belle's hooves clicked against the paving stones. She shook her black mane and shifted into a canter. Lou hadn't been wrong; Evienne did need to hurry back. She was meeting with the queens this evening. She had received the summons last night, and at this rate, she was going to be late.

It would have been easy to take the Rail Dellumine back to the city from Cambrie. The network of magic-powered trains now connected all of Ichorna, and there were special cars at the rear that accommodated passengers of the equine persuasion. But Belle had never enjoyed being herded onto a Rail car, and Evienne loved the hour-long ride back to the capital city of Lucinne.

As she rode, she felt some tension leaving her shoulders.

As much as Evienne loved Lucinne, the bustling city that had been her home for nearly two decades, her heart sometimes longed for her home to the north.

She passed one of the lookout towers that now dotted the land all across Ichorna and waved to the guard currently stationed there.

Evienne was proud of the fact that her system of lookouts manned by Ichornian guards had worked so effectively to warn of the horde of Gevaud roaming the countryside near Cambrai. She knew she had more work to do, but her contributions were helpful to Queen Aldith and, most importantly, to the people of Ichorna.

Her role was to oversee the Sangviere and advise the queens, with some special assignments as needed. She taught classes at the Academie du Sangviere and managed placing mages in various roles throughout Ichorna. It had been months since she had been on a defensive mission like the one today, but she had decided it would be best to be there as backup for the other Sangviere. She felt now that had been a wise decision; perhaps she was not supporting the other mages in the field as often as she should be.

When Evienne began her training as a Sangviere, she never imagined where the path would lead her. She had been friends with Queen Aldith—who had, at that time, been the crown princess—in school, but she did not anticipate ever rising high enough to serve as one of the Queen's closest advisors.

The countryside drifted by as Evienne let the brisk autumn air fill her lungs. The breeze nipped at her despite the thickness of the blood-red wool coat and black leggings that made up her uniform. She rarely wore it these days, but it was easier to ride a horse in this than in her preferred velvet gowns.

She always struggled with her feelings after an encounter with the Gevaud. She didn't have cause to use her Regne du Sang often, but she reveled in the call of this part of her magic in her soul. She knew this ability to control other living things was part of why Ichorna had been isolated for so long among the nations of Domhan na Rùin. She knew outsiders found blood magic to be abhorrent and unnatural; but when she used that magic, she felt connected to life itself, and it felt right deep in her bones. Wielding her Regne du Sang made her feel free in a way nothing else ever had, and she felt guilty for it. A lifetime of warnings about the dangers of blood magic pulled at her mind every day.

Lush, misty hills flattened into damp, empty fields, the smell of rich earth on the wind as Evienne neared Lucinne. The capital city was at the center of Ichorna, like a great beating heart.

She reached the gates of the city by dusk, weary and damp and absolutely starving. She knew better than to go on this sort of outing without packing food for herself, but she had forgotten, and now found herself in a bit of a silent rage. She would have to hold out a little longer, though—she needed to go straight to her meeting with the Queens.

As she rode through the city, rich sounds, smells and colors overwhelmed her senses. The scent of spices and warm bread found her, and her stomach grumbled.

The city had drawn her in from the moment she arrived as a child, feeling alone and unwanted and adrift. It was home now.

As she approached the palace, the main road took her beneath the Rail Dellumine overpass. The bronze cars, with their swirling filigree design, sped silently over the tracks.

The Rail system was the great pride and technological joy of Ichorna. Its invention a hundred years prior had been alluring enough to outsiders to finally draw them to reopen trade with Ichorna. Visitors and immigrants from across Domhan na Rùin now filled Lucinne. The web of infrastructure had expanded, with the Rail Dellumine reaching even the most remote villages and towns. This expansion had been Queen Aldith's sole focus in her first years as Ichorna's ruler.

Evienne nodded to the guards as she passed through the palace gates and made her way to the stables at the edge of the complex. Soon, the whole palace would be overflowing with foreign visitors. Queen Aldith had invited nearly every noble in Domhan na Rùin to Lucinne to ring in the new millennium. Evienne was curious about what the month-long celebration might bring, but she already felt a bit tired at the thought of all the events she would have to attend. As High Sangviere, she was expected to participate to keep an eye on things, yes, but mostly because Queen Aldith liked to show her off. Evienne and her magic had a bit of a reputation.

She left Belle in the capable hands of their stable master, patting the horse's flank fondly before stepping back out into the deepening twilight. She hurried across the main courtyard of the palace complex and entered the main building's labyrinthine halls, her steps quick.

Queen Aldith's sitting room was at the far end of a long hall and occupied the southeastern corner of the palace. The light in this beautiful room was soft in the evening, and Evienne paused in her hurry to take in the lovely shades of dusk.

Oddly, it was one of the only rooms in the whole palace that did not have Lucinne's characteristic stained glass. Instead, the room was all crisp white marble. Dramatic splashes of deep blue textiles dotted the room; the couches and chaise, the massive rug, and the impossibly long satin curtains all shared the midnight hue.

A small fire crackled in the hearth to combat the deepening evening chill. Evienne found her usual seat by the fire and waited for the queens to arrive.

Léhiona floated into the room a few moments later. The Queen Consort was arrestingly graceful. She always wore a menagerie of vibrant colors in fabrics that caught the air and billowed around her. Her presence in any space was captivating.

Her hair was the color of spun gold, her skin alabaster, and her eyes an unusual and striking violet. Léhiona was the most beautiful woman in all of Ichorna, Evienne was sure of it.

Léhiona's perfect rosebud lips spread into a smile at the sight of Evienne. The two had become fast friends almost as soon as Léhiona had arrived twelve years ago.

She had made her journey from Ichorna's northern neighbor, Beitar, as a teenager, continuing a centuries-long tradition of diplomatic marriages between the two nations. Just like the consort before her, Léhiona had made a vow of silence regarding her homeland that was magically enforced by Beitar's king before she came to Ichorna. Evienne thought the custom was bizarre, but it had been that way for as long as anyone could remember. The consorts came to Ichorna and had a fresh start, cutting all ties with their homeland.

"Evi, did you eat dinner?" Léhiona's voice fluttered through the space, catching on the hard marble in soft echos.

"I'll eat after our meeting," Evienne answered too quickly, and Léhiona's eyes narrowed.

"When was the last time you ate?"

Evienne grimaced, her dark brows tipping up in guilt. "Breakfast..."

Léhiona rolled her eyes, her chuckle flitting through the room. "I'll have something brought, and no, I will not hear any arguments about it."

Evienne smiled at her friend, slumping back into the cushions in acquiescence. The thought of food was too wonderful to put up a fight.

Léhiona moved to ring for the staff just as the massive wooden door swung open, and the human tempest that was Queen Aldith strode into the room.

She was a force of nature. No matter where she was going or what mood she was in, Aldith commanded every ounce of attention. She was fearsome to her enemies, and respected by her people. She had earned their obedience early and often, and now she commanded their fierce loyalty.

Aldith was crowned queen very young. Her father died

when she was just twenty-four, and Aldith had taken his place the very same day. Her mother—who had been from Beitar—followed the king in death soon after, falling victim to a mysterious wasting illness.

Six years later, and Aldith's wild mane of curls was still mostly black as night, but a few silver strands now peeked through. Her eyes were the darkest brown, her complexion sun-kissed. She always wore black.

"She forgot to eat again, didn't she?" Aldith's silky alto voice met Evienne's ears.

"Of course, but we'll rectify that momentarily," Léhiona called from the other side of the room.

Aldith approached and took her place across from Evienne, on the chaise. She and Léhiona always shared the reclining sofa during these meetings. Though theirs had been an arranged marriage, it was not a loveless one, from what Evienne could tell.

Aldith and Léhiona were opposite as night and day, yet somehow they seemed perfect together. Aldith's steel was tempered by Léhiona's grace. Though Aldith was Queen Regent, she respected Léhiona's opinions on matters of state more than anyone else's. Léhiona was more than a Queen Consort in practice, if not in name.

Once a maid had hurried in with a serving cart of delicious-smelling food and a steaming pot of tea, Aldith and Léhiona situated themselves on the chaise side-by-side. Evienne made herself a plate of tender beef and savory vegetables before sitting back in her chair and eyeing the queens expectantly.

"Beitar has sent word that they plan to send a delegation for the celebration of the new millennium in a few weeks, and we'd like you to keep an eye on them while they're here," Aldith said smoothly. Léhiona watched as her wife spoke, her impossibly long lashes brushing her high cheekbones.

Evienne froze with a bite halfway to her mouth, eyes wide. "Beitarans are coming? Did they say why?" Evienne's questions fell from her like drops of rain at the start of a downpour. She found herself glancing at Léhiona to gauge her reaction to Aldith's declaration.

"They didn't say why, but they are sending a nobleman, as well as his travel companion, a scholar from Sgùrdruid. I think perhaps their magic has finally all gone, and they're coming to ask for some sort of aid," Aldith answered, her face a smooth mask of indifference. Léhiona sat at her side, no apparent emotion on her lovely face.

It did not escape Evienne's notice how odd it was to sit here in front of Léhiona talking about the Beitarans as if she was not one herself, but one of the conditions of the marriage alliance with Beitar from centuries ago was that the consort would be magically bound into silence regarding anything related to their homeland. Léhiona could try to share, but speaking on certain topics would physically hurt her. From what Evienne understood, if Léhiona veered too close to a topic concerning Beitar, she would experience a searing pain in her sternum akin to the sensation of burning. It had never made much sense to Evienne to set up a diplomatic marriage and then bind someone into silence; they could not speak or act in the interest of Beitar because of the magical gag. The arrangement seemed to rather one-sidedly benefit Ichorna. Evienne didn't know what to make of it, but it wasn't her place to pry.

"What sort of aid could we offer? And if they knew they would need our help, why be so incredibly distant all these years?"

"Who knows what they want, but they are always invited to these sorts of things, so I suppose it was to be expected they'd eventually make an appearance. I'm just surprised to see them crawling to us in my lifetime. I suppose we'll have to wait for their groveling to start to learn more," Aldith mused. Evienne was taken aback at how brusquely Aldith spoke of Léhiona's homeland in her presence. Aldith had always been direct, but this seemed harsh even for her. Evienne stowed her unease at the display and attempted to stay focused on the conversation.

"Well all right, they're coming. Did they say when they will arrive?" Evienne was trying to process this information. The celebration for the turn of the millennium had been announced last year, and all of the important leaders across Domhan na Rùin had been invited to attend. Ichorna had hosted a similarly grand celebration at the last turn of the century, so it seemed it may become a tradition.

Everyone attending would gather here in Lucinne for a month of festivities. Diplomatic summits, balls, tournaments—all manner of spectacle—would take place during the final month of the year. Many had already responded to signal their attendance months ago, but a few last-minute changes to the guest list could always be expected. To hear about visitors from Beitar, though, was extremely unexpected—they would likely be the talk of the event.

"They're set to arrive in three days' time," Aldith answered. "We'd like to put you in charge of keeping an eye on them. Nothing too obvious—you can mask it as hostess duty or personal interest—but we are wary of their intentions. There is no one we would rather have to handle any threats than you."

"Of course, I'm happy to stay close to them. Thank you for trusting me with your safety and the safety of our people."

"Who else would we ask? They'll be flattered that the High Sangviere has taken such an interest in them. Who knows, maybe you'll enjoy their company!" Léhiona laughed a bit, her expression too pleasant to be natural, and rose from her seat to pour herself a cup of tea from the cart the staff had brought.

Evienne knew it likely wouldn't get her anywhere, but she had to ask. "Léhiona, are these emissaries people you knew before you came here?"

Even from where Evienne sat behind her as she added sugar to her tea, Léhiona's shoulders visibly tensed at the question. "I uh," she started before taking a deep breath. "I met Lord Solon once when I was a girl. He came to visit the court at Sgùrdruid for a season. The scholar, Professor Doehlan, I know nothing of."

Aldith snagged Evienne's gaze and pursed her lips, disapproving of Evienne's prying. Answering such questions could hurt Léhiona, and she was very protective of her wife's free and gentle spirit.

"Thank you for sharing, Léhiona," Evienne added, her face apologetic as she held Aldith's gaze.

Aldith quickly pushed the conversation forward. "We can't take any risks with so many members of Domhan na Rùin's leadership in attendance."

"Of course not. You have my word, they will have my undivided attention during the celebration. I'll work with the other Sangviere to delegate my other responsibilities temporarily," Evienne stated, her voice steady despite the adrenaline coursing through her.

She was to be responsible for the Beitaran visitors. She should feel nervous with so many unknowns at play, but all she felt was a sense of wonder and excitement. She would have to watch them, yes, but she would also get to talk to them. She would get to ask them about their people and customs in a way that no one really had for a generation. She wondered what they would be like.

Lost in her thoughts, Evienne's mind drifted out of the conversation, only focusing when Aldith called her name in question.

"Evi? Are you still with us?" Aldith's voice held a note of laughter.

"Yes, apologies!" Evienne smiled and laughed at herself. Her friends knew her well enough to expect this sort of thing; her mind wandered often.

"I was saying that Dominique will be increasing security around the Centrale Dellumine for the event, but I want you to make sure the Beitarans stay away from the facility. The last thing we need is those recluses stealing the technology that has finally coaxed the rest of the continent into trade with us," Aldith said coolly.

The mention of Dominique's name had the muscles in

Evienne's shoulders tensing. She knew her friends couldn't cut Dominique out of their lives because of what had happened between the two of them, but their tolerance of her still stung.

"Understood. I will ensure they don't get too close to any of our proprietary equipment," Evienne said, hoping that was the end of this conversation.

Aldith nodded; it was settled.

The way Aldith spoke about the Beitarans in front of Léhiona left Evienne uneasy; she attempted to regain a shred of normalcy. "Aldith, will Sylvain be joining us for the celebration?"

Aldith rolled her eyes and chuckled, her features lightening. "Yes, my wayward little brother should be here tomorrow morning, actually." She had a soft spot for her sibling. The now twenty-four-year-old prince was often away, traveling Domhan na Rùin and enjoying his total lack of responsibilities.

"I am glad to hear it. I am sure he will be the life of the party," Evienne said with a smile. Léhiona was smiling as well; she and Sylvain were very close.

"Right, I should begin making arrangements," Evienne said as she rose, setting her plate back on the serving cart.

"We will see you very soon, Evi." Léhiona turned her warm gaze to Evienne from her place on the chaise.

Evienne smiled at her queens before bowing slightly at the waist and turning for the door. Her steps carried her across the palace to her own rooms, where she promptly collapsed into the massive plush armchair by her fireplace which, thanks to the palace staff, already held a crackling fire.

She stared into the flames as she tried to gather her thoughts, her exhaustion finally catching up with her. She hadn't used her magic so extensively in quite some time, and it came at a cost.

She was grateful, though, to have gotten out of the city, despite the reason for her trip. Ichorna was about to host the largest celebration in a generation, so her duties would keep her here for the next month. She knew her assignment with the Beitarans would require a lot of meaningless conversations with nobles, and she already felt drained at the thought of it. Drained and excited.

She sighed, rising to change out of her uniform. With heavy eyelids, Evienne quickly washed—feeling more grateful than usual for the magically heated water the capital provided—and slipped into an impossibly soft black silk nightgown. Her position as High Sangviere came with healthy compensation, and she shamelessly enjoyed the nice things she was able to buy for herself, this incredible nightgown included.

Evienne settled into the plush pillows, closed her eyes, and was asleep in mere moments, letting the day slip away from her as she retreated into her dreams. Tomorrow's problems would be there for her when she awoke.

Chapter Two

Orion surveyed the rolling, foggy hills that surrounded him from atop his horse. He and his companion had stopped to admire the view behind them, to the north—the dramatic peaks of Beitar, their homeland, they were leaving behind. The craggy, ancient mountains seemed to shift suddenly into this landscape of softly rounded slopes. Orion found it unsettling after a lifetime amongst Beitar's peaks.

"I think I see Mulhouse on the horizon; we should try to make it there before nightfall," Solon said, interrupting Orion's train of thought. He nodded and urged his horse forward.

Mulhouse was a small but important town just on the border between Beitar and Ichorna. They would not be staying long—only passing through on their journey to the Ichornian capital of Lucinne.

"Are you ready to be the furthest away from home you've ever been?" Orion asked Solon.

"Are you? You're the one who's been dreaming of it your

whole life," Solon answered with a chuckle. "I just hope the food is good."

"I'm sure it will be; they're famous for their bread. Makes sense with all those fields," Orion answered.

"I intend to try at least one of every type of pastry I can get my hands on," Solon said. Orion smiled at Solon, who was about the same age as Orion's father. Solon was usually so formal with others, but Orion felt lucky to really *know* Solon. Their journey would be long indeed if Solon refused to engage in meaningful conversation.

Since the waning of Beitar's magic had begun a few centuries ago, the various kings had kept the people on a tight leash because a lack of magic made all of Beitar vulnerable amongst the other nations of Domhan na Rùin—each one a magical powerhouse in their own right. Journeys outside the borders were strictly limited to diplomatic trips once a decade. Even imports and exports were handled directly on Beitar's border and only at sanctioned trading posts. Orion, despite all his studies, could never fully understand their rulers' desire to remain separate. Protection alone did not seem reason enough for this total isolation.

He loved Beitar; would never tire of its wild, dramatic beauty. Its cold winds and shades of white and gray, a crackling fire in a massive hearth, the shadowy gothic halls of the university—it was home.

But Orion had spent his years dreaming of seeing the rest of the world. His love of folklore and magic had led him to devour every book he could get his hands on from the moment he could read. For the first time, he was faced with an opportunity not just to imagine, but to experience.

Orion could hardly believe he was about to set foot on Ichornian land.

The damp air seeped into Orion's heavy cloak as his dappled gray horse, Maisie, carried him down the southern side of another rolling hill.

Before he and Solon had departed, he had gone to his parent's home outside the Beitaran capital city of Sgùrdruid, where he lived and worked. Their cottage was perched high up the mountainside at the end of a winding road of steep switchbacks. The walk was nerve-racking, but the view was breathtaking.

Over dinner with his parents, Orion had explained the official reason for their journey: they would attend the celebration the Ichornian queens were hosting to celebrate the turn of the millennium. His father hadn't had much to say, only clapping his son on the shoulder and nodding in approval. His mother, on the other hand, had fussed over him, making sure he had enough warm clothes for the journey and had packed a basket of baked goods to send with him.

Orion was grateful to be on such good terms with his family; he knew many were not so fortunate. They had always been supportive of his dream to work at the university in Sgùrdruid, though they did not always understand his motives.

After a few hours of weaving around and over seemingly endless foothills, they came to the edge of Mulhouse. It was a hardy town made up of buildings of stone with massive exposed timber beams and thatched roofs lining the wide gravel streets. Despite its geographic significance as the northernmost town in Ichorna, it was not particularly affluent. Its people worked primarily harvesting lumber and tending sheep.

The two Beitarans made their way through town, catching curious glances from the townspeople as they went. They found the Inn on the southern end of the small town square. They left their horses with the stablehand, paying him well for his services, before entering the Inn.

He and Solon agreed they would prefer rest over conversation for the night, so they asked the innkeeper to send dinner up to their rooms. Orion peeled off his slightly damp clothes and laid them out near the small fireplace in his room to dry. He couldn't help but feel a pang of longing for his own hearth back home.

Sitting on the plush rug, he crossed his legs and let the steam from his bowl of stew brush across his face. He stared into the flames, feeling exhausted and something else—he felt on the precipice of something. That uncanny feeling, like a premonition, sent a wave of adrenaline through his veins.

Orion knew the true purpose of their trip—a truth that only he and Solon trusted one another with. He had no doubt they would not have been allowed to go if the king had even the slightest suspicion of what they planned to do, despite it being in Beitar's best interests.

He supposed the feeling was just anxiety. He was going somewhere new, doing something unprecedented; he only hoped that they would be successful. Beitar's magic hung in the balance.

Chapter Three

THE COOL MORNING light filled Evienne's chamber as she caught her own gaze in the full-length mirror. She hardly recognized the woman staring back at her. Her skin was as pale as it had always been, but her cheeks now wore a rosy glow. Bright hazel eyes met her stare, unmarred by the bruised purple that had haunted them in the past.

Her figure was full and soft, not wrung out with anxiety as it had been for so many years. She had been wasting away, but the woman before her now was *living*. She smiled at this version of herself, healthy and whole and completely her own.

She turned away from her mirror and paused to breathe and feel this moment. Today was another day she could live as her own person, find out more about who *she* wanted to be.

This room the queens had given her after her divorce from Dominique had been her haven these past three years. The whole room was a rich mahogany, with sculpted wooden trees lining the walls. They stretched up to the ceiling to create a canopy of carved wooden branches and leaves.

The warm wood of the room was accented by plush furniture in shades of green. A fireplace dominated one wall of the room, while a floor-to-ceiling bookcase covered the opposite wall. A massive rug in a shade of deep crimson spanned the center of the room. In one corner, a bronze door led to her marbled bathing chamber.

The queens had given her free reign to do what she wished with this space, and she had made it luxurious and comfortable. Evienne liked nice things and took joy in surrounding herself with objects that she had chosen for herself. After so many years of being dictated to, she made an effort to seek out things that she loved.

Evienne grabbed her bladed silver ring, slipped on her soft leather shoes, and set off. She groaned at the soreness of her muscles from yesterday's mission. She was grateful that blood magic didn't require extensive physical combat training, but it would be nice if her body didn't protest *quite* so loudly after a day of riding.

She was headed to the Academie du Sangviere to observe the young mages training for the upcoming tournament that would take place during the millennial celebration.

She arrived just as two young mages took positions across from each other in the training yard, and a professor signaled for the practice duel to commence. Both mages pricked their palms, calling to their magic. One summoned a translucent red shield that Sangviere were trained to use defensively, while the other launched an aggressive volley of razor-sharp darts made of red ice.

A Sangviere's basic powers manifested in ways that were unique to each individual; sometimes a blood elemental presentation, other times weapons of blood. The possibilities were endless, but these defensive and elemental summonings were the most common applications of blood magic. Only the most advanced Sangviere could master the ancient art of Regne du Sang. Evienne had felt the call of that deeper magic after only a few months of her training; it had always felt so natural to her.

While using one's own blood to perform the Regne du Sang to control animals was, to many, questionable enough, the Sangviere possessed a magic that was darker still. The Valsang was a forbidden art, and the only way to take control of the blood of another human being, Sangviere or not. The art of Valsang required the use of another human being's blood—any human blood other than the casting mage's would do. Because of this, and the moral ambiguity of controlling other people, the use of Valsang had been outlawed in Ichorna for centuries.

Evienne's mind wandered as she watched the duel, contemplating the moral implications of blood magic as she had many times before. She started, pulled abruptly from her thoughts, when she heard someone say her name; one of her fellow professors was asking if she would accept a student's invitation to duel. During these practices, novices could ask to spar with anyone, but it had been a long time since a student had tried their luck with her.

She took a deep breath and stepped into the center of the courtyard. The professor who was serving as the referee let Evienne and the young Sangviere take their positions, then signaled them to begin.

Evienne gave the student a moment to make a move, and they foolishly chose to go on the offensive, summoning a dagger of pure blood and rushing at her head-on. She let the student take a few steps as she pricked her palm—in a breath, she had summoned her scarlet fire to her hand. The next moment, she launched her flames at the other mage. They were forced to dodge, dropping to roll out of the way.

Evienne tracked their motion, whirling to her right to send a stream of crimson flames toward the student where they now crouched near the ground. They summoned a barrier to deflect the flames. Evienne didn't let up, allowing her fire to slowly consume the student's shield.

Finally, the student yelled, "I yield!" And Evienne immediately stopped the onslaught of her blood fire. The now-humbled student was out of breath, and inclined their head to her as she passed them on her way out of the dueling ring. "Thank you, High Sangviere," the student said reverently. Evienne smiled at them in acknowledgement.

As she took her place back on the edge of the courtyard, she realized the gaze of one of her fellow professors, Julien, was fixed on her from where he sat across the way.

Julien had been a few years ahead of Evienne in school, and they had dallied a bit in the years since Evienne's separation from Dominique. He was handsome enough; tall and broad with dark brown skin and eyes to match. He was kind, too. She returned his gaze openly, and Julien smirked at her. Perhaps she needed a distraction tonight.

NIGHT air danced across Evienne's damp face from the window by the bed she found herself in. She blinked slowly, drawing fresh air into her lungs, feeling seconds of her life drifting by.

Julien made some sort of burbling noise from where he lay next to her, signaling his deepening slumber. She slipped from the bed, as she always did after this sort of thing, dressed quietly, and left.

Evienne wanted desperately to find a love that felt safe, but she didn't know how to trust herself to truly love again after Dominique.

The dim halls of the palace floated by her bleary gaze. She loved sleeping too much to be traipsing around in the middle of the night like this, but moonlight trysts rarely occurred at six in the evening, as luck would have it.

She found the door to her rooms quickly, shuffling in and heading straight for the bathing chamber. A quick rinse would do; anything to get Julien's cologne off of her skin. It smelled nice, but she wanted to feel clean.

She could barely keep her eyes open under the spray of warm water, letting her mind drift, imagining a better encounter than the one she'd had this evening. What would it be like to take a lover that could satisfy her every want? Even Dominique had never really asked what it was Evienne wanted. Dominique knew her way around a woman's body well enough, but desire is the domain of the mind.

Sleep found Evienne quickly that night. In the darkness behind her eyelids, soft colors danced, never quite in focus. The flutter of wings filled her restless mind. The colors shifted into focus for only a second, revealing the downy wings of a great luna moth before a searing red light drowned everything out. Evienne gasped as she jolted awake. In the dark of her room, she thought she heard the echo of a scream.

She waited a moment, barely able to draw breath. Seconds slipped by, and no further sounds of distress met her ears. A vivid dream, then, just like all the ones before.

Waking up alone in a bit of a panic was nothing new for Evienne. Even when Dominique had shared her bed, Evienne was always careful not to disturb her.

She'd been having dreams like this for years. Not outright nightmares, but always tinged with an undertone of malice. Sometimes, the luna moth drifted through her mind; sometimes a mighty gray dragon.

A few times, a pair of piercing sea green eyes glowed in her mind's eye. One thing never changed, though. There was always the horrible red light.

She had tried to tell Dominique about the dreams once, but her then-wife hadn't seemed interested, telling Evienne that it was surely just some childhood daydream lingering in her mind. Dominique had always been dismissive of the things that really mattered to Evienne; she had her own idea of what should be important and held to it without remorse.

Evienne adjusted the pillows behind her back and sat up in bed, her legs still tangled in her sheets. She stared at the window, filled with dawn's earliest gray. Another day stretched its long hours before her, and she sighed.

She tried to live her life passionately, but lately she wondered at the path she had set herself on. The things that matter most in one's life change over time, and it had been a long while since she considered what truly mattered to her. She loved Ichorna, but the aggressive pursuit of technological progress and trade with the rest of Domhan na Rùin never struck her as all that important. She had just gone along because of her love of her magic, and because she heard all her life that this was a noble pursuit.

Her friends, Cecelia, Sylvain, and the queens; her mentor, Hestia; this was the tiny family she had made for herself over the years, and each of them mattered to her immensely.

The people of Ichorna mattered, too. Evienne had always seen all of the heartache in the world and felt it so keenly, so intensely, that it was almost too much. But her love for the people of this country had driven her to study to become a Sangviere in the first place. She studied and practiced so that she would be prepared to defend other little girls as alone as she had been. The emptiness she had felt when her father sent her away had slowly faded over the years as she filled her life with other things she cared about, but it still felt like a deep bruise on her heart. Evienne settled back down into her pillows, clutching her blankets under her chin. She tried not to think too much of Mulhouse and all she had left behind.

Her combination of aptitude and diligence landed her at the top of her class throughout her schooling. She had blinked, and suddenly, she was the High Sangviere of Ichorna. It was a title that had never been held by one so young before. Evienne was barely thirty; the next-youngest had been forty-five. She would serve either until she retired, or a new monarch took the throne.

She tried to fill her role with the confidence it deserved. The queens certainly trusted her—Aldith never would have chosen her if she had any reservations about Evienne's abilities.

Evienne was the strongest Sangviere Ichorna had seen in centuries. Her Regne du Sang was unrivaled. It had come to her disturbingly naturally, but it was her tireless study of the art that had truly set her apart.

As a girl, Evienne was thrust into this world because of her talent at school. Her father—the governor of Mulhouse—sent Evienne to a boarding school in the capital in a work exchange agreement when he no longer wanted to pay for her care at home. She was allowed to live and study, but she worked at the school in exchange for her room and board. Despite the relative comfort of her situation, the feeling of being unwanted by her family haunted Evienne to this day.

It was at school that she met her best friend, Cecelia, and Aldith. Dominique joined their cohort a bit later, when they were around thirteen. The four of them became fast friends, all talented in their own right. Aldith and Evienne had shown the earliest aptitude for the Regne du Sang, while Cecelia's study became more specialized in the physical magics used for archiving.

Dominique was interested from an early age in the blend

of science and magic that made Ichorna so unique in Domhan na Rùin. She was always at the Centrale Dellumine, learning about the capture of raw magic to be converted to energy to power the city.

As the light in Evienne's room shifted from dark gray to pale purple, her thoughts drifted through the life she had lived. Thirty years of days and hours and minutes, decades of feelings and trying not to feel, thousands of dreams and moments; what would today's hours bring?

Evienne slipped out of bed and dressed in a deep blood red gown. Its layers of chiffon and silk moved fluidly around her legs, while the bodice wrapped her curves in smooth overlapping layers that came to a point at her collarbone. The dress had a high neck and long, fitted sleeves. It was dramatic, but she loved it. Even if she didn't feel intimidating, she enjoyed dressing the part.

She left her silky hair down to fall in soft waves around her shoulders. Her hair had an unruly, wild curl to it naturally, but she took pains to style it into this smoother state every few days. Next, she darkened her eyes with a smudge of black liner, and dabbed a deep red stain on her lips, the color so dark it was almost black.

The woman staring back at her was fearsome, powerful, self-assured. She knew in her heart she was the first two of those things. It was the last one that needed some work.

Evienne set off through the halls of the palace with a lightness to her step; the mornings she met Cecelia in her study for breakfast were her favorite. She was so wrapped up in her eagerness to talk with her friend that she slammed right into a tall, willowy figure as she rounded a corner. She righted herself, readying to apologize, when she realized who she had run into—and was struck by an overwhelming urge to flee.

Chapter Four

"Evienne," the woman glared down at her from a substantial height.

"Dominique." Evienne felt the muscles of her shoulders tense and her breathing shallow immediately. She had no idea how she had ever felt anything but the physical need to run away in this woman's presence. She was beautiful, but only in the way that a poisonous flower was beautiful.

"You really should watch where you are walking. It's so unbecoming for someone of your rank to be so careless; what would Her Majesty think if she saw you bumbling around like this? What if I had been one of the visiting nobles that will be swarming this place in a few days?"

Evienne's lips tightened into a thin line. In these moments, she could never think of what to say to put Dominique in her place; it was always hours later that the right retort would come to her. Thoughts of this encounter would plague her for days to come, if the past was any example.

"Just like you, not to have anything to say for yourself,"

Dominique laughed derisively. "It's really so sad, *Vivi*. You had so much potential. If you hadn't left when you did, I certainly would have soon enough—it's hard to watch you flounder," Dominique spoke lightly, casually, despite her hateful words. Evienne couldn't help the frown that curled her lips at her old nickname. She had always hated being called that.

This interaction seemed to be the sum of their relationship now. Evienne knew that it had been abuse, she had gotten out, had risen above, had become more herself than she had been ever before; but it still stopped her in her tracks every time Dominique stood before her.

"Excuse me," Evienne said with more confidence than she felt as she stepped around Dominique to continue on her way. She didn't want to dignify Dominique's words with a real response.

She caught Dominique's searing blue gaze for a split second as she brushed past, and it was filled with loathing and resentment. Dominique had always thought she knew what was best for Evienne. It was only when Evienne realized what was happening and started to reclaim herself that Dominique's *love* for Evienne had soured.

Evienne felt air pulling into her lungs, focused on evening out her breaths. Every second that passed, every step that took her away from Dominique, had her feeling more settled in herself.

It was three years ago now that Evienne had woken up one day realizing that she had made herself so small in Dominique's presence, there was almost nothing left that was really *her*. That devastating revelation had been promptly followed by their separation. For better or worse, Evienne hadn't waited around for more of her soul to wither.

Evienne fought against the tightness in her throat as she walked. She was embarrassed that Dominique still had this effect on her. She had learned not to accept this sort of treatment from anyone, but her spirit still shrank away from this woman as if she were a branding iron poised to further mar her sense of self.

Evienne supposed their coupling always had a sinister thread running through it, now that she was able to look back on it. Time was clarity's greatest ally.

Dominique's earliest moments of control had been less nefarious—posed as preferences, suggestions. She had punished Evienne with subtle signals of displeasure when she stepped out of line. Time had shown Dominique's true colors, but by then Evienne was so focused on meeting her expectations to keep her heart safe that she didn't realize what was really happening. When she did notice it, it had been like waking up from a nightmare—sudden and disorienting.

The halls of the palace were bustling with people this morning. Everyone was preparing for the celebration. Evienne tried her best to avoid making eye contact with anyone; she wasn't in the mood to talk to anyone but Cecelia. She was trying desperately to cling to the person she was outside of that relationship, the person she had hammered and forged herself into these last three years.

Breathing in, locking down that version of herself that always surged to the front of her mind when Dominique was around, she focused on the scent of cloves on the air and the sharp clicking of her boots on the marble floor as she moved through the winding passages.

She was Evienne Elodie D'Auclaire, High Sangviere to the Court of Ichorna, and she would not allow anyone to make her feel small ever again.

These were the words she said over and over to herself when she felt her spirit wavering. Evienne knew who she was, who she wanted to be; but understanding who she had been helped her to be kind to herself in these fraught moments.

She pulled herself together as she wound her way through the dusty labyrinth that housed Ichorna's rarest tomes. Cecelia was the head librarian in Ichorna—all of the province's librarians reported to her in one way or another—so her study was here in the main library.

The study was warm and welcoming, just like Cecelia. A large, honey-colored sofa took up one side of the room while a massive oak desk dominated the other. Shelves of books were built into the walls, and light filtered in through the circular stained glass window across from the door. Its panes of yellow, orange, and red made the space feel like a flickering fire.

Cecelia herself sat curled with a book on the massive couch, her dark brown hair falling in a smooth curtain over the armrest. She looked up as Evienne entered, smiling as she laid eyes on her friend. Cecelia had the best smile, open and generous and always reaching her eyes.

"I'm so glad we could squeeze in one more cozy breakfast before the celebration," Cecelia said as she righted herself on the couch and slipped a bookmark into the crease between the pages. She gestured to the tray on the low table in front of the couch as Evienne took her seat. Evienne decided then that she wouldn't even mention her encounter with Dominique; it wasn't worth their time to dwell on it.

The tray was full of pastries, tiny quiches, and, most importantly, a steaming pot of tea. Evienne poured Cecelia a cup and then one for herself before grabbing a buttery pastry filled with chocolate and settling back into the downy cushions of the couch.

"So, tell me about your week. It's been a few days since we had time to catch up," Cecelia sighed as she nestled further into the couch, cradling her cup of tea.

"I suppose my week has been alright. We dealt with a massive raid on Cambrie the other day, but I'm sure you already heard about that. Too close to the city for my comfort, but it seems that's becoming a trend. There were so many of them. I feel there's more I could be doing to find where these things are coming from. After all these years I should have figured it out."

Cecelia worried her lip, her brow slightly furrowed as she studied her friend. "Evi, I've known you since we were girls, and no matter what the situation or how much you've run yourself ragged for those around you, you *always* feel there's more you could be doing."

"Well, that's because there is," Evienne stated matter-of-factly. Cecelia rolled her eyes.

"We've talked about this before. You're worth more than what you can do for other people, the queens and all of Ichorna included. You are a great example for the other Sangviere, and you've worked so hard to earn every bit of success you've had. The queens see you not just as their advisor, but as their friend. You have to be kinder to yourself."

Evienne realized she was grimacing without meaning to. Intellectually, she knew her friend was right. She would give anyone she cared about the same advice. But it just felt so much…*safer* to give people concrete reasons to keep her around. She supposed this feeling was a holdover from her marriage with Dominique, though she knew in her heart nothing she did, no value she could provide, would have made her emotionally safe in that situation.

Evienne sighed deeply, closing her eyes to let the steam from her tea roll over her face in soft waves. "I know you're right—I really do. It's just so uncomfortable to feel as confident as I seem to everyone else. I keep waiting for everyone to find out I'm secretly a fraud."

"But you're not a fraud," Cecelia laughed. "How could you think that? Do you not remember all of our years of studying together? I certainly do, though I've tried to block out Professor LeBeau's class specifically…"

Evienne joined her friend in laughter before sipping her tea. "Thank you for your confidence in me. I do not know what I'd do without your friendship, truly."

Cecelia reached over to squeeze her arm. "You will always have my friendship, Evi. I just want you to see yourself the way the people who care about you do."

"Alright, enough about me. Tell me about your week."

"*Well,*" Cecelia started with mischief lighting her eyes, "I saw Jac again."

"The nobleman from Wellsah?" Evienne exclaimed.

Cecelia nodded, her whole face lit with a smile. "He's so kind, Evi, and he said he'll be back for the celebration starting next week!"

Evienne's heart was so happy for her friend; she deserved to be courted by someone kind. Evienne had only met the Wellsah noble once, but he had struck her as genuine and his demeanor had been jovial.

"That's wonderful! I hope you get to spend some *quality time* with him," Evienne said, winking at her friend. Cecelia swatted her arm and devolved into laughter.

After the two each finished their second cup of tea, Cecelia rose from the couch, dusting pastry crumbs from her mustard yellow jacket and skirt.

"Want to come pull a few books with me?" She asked brightly. "I have a new research project I'm starting, and I need to gather my sources."

"Of course, I'd love to," Evienne answered with a smile. She cherished every moment she spent doing simple things with Cece.

The women made their way around the library, Cecelia leading with confidence, pulling books as she went. She knew every inch of this place like the back of her hand.

Their last book was hidden on a shelf in the very far corner of the library. The light from the stained glass windows didn't quite reach here, leaving the shelves in shadow. As Cecelia scanned for the book she needed, Evienne browsed the titles as well, her head tilted to the side to read the spines of the books.

The titles in this section seemed to be histories of the

various lands of Domhan na Rùin, like *Illathi: People of Illusion*, *An Agricultural History of Wellsah*, and *Daosbor and the Founding of the Dead City*...Evienne's eyes scanned the titles until one jumped out at her. The words were written down the green leather spine in faded gold leaf: *Beitar's Folklore: Tales of the Tuanadair.*

Evienne's hand reached out and her fingers grazed the cool leather. She pulled the tome out, and a clicking sound, followed by a loud thud cut sharply through the silence of the shadowy corner. Cecelia gasped and turned, and the two friends stared at each other in shock.

"What was that?" Cecelia finally asked, moving toward where Evienne stood with the book in her hand.

"No idea," Evienne said, taking a deep breath to calm her racing heart.

Cecelia took the book from Evienne and examined it, finding nothing unusual. She then turned and ducked slightly to look into the empty space the book had left on the shelf. She gasped softly and cautiously put her hand into the space. Whatever it was she had found, Evienne assumed they should probably discuss it before Cece went sticking her hand in dark corners.

Evienne tried to peer around her friend's shoulder to get a look at the spot where the book had been, but before she could see anything, a deep rumbling groan sounded from behind the shelf.

The whole thing swung inward.

Cecelia yelped in surprise as she lurched forward with the unexpected motion, catching herself the moment before she fell down the staircase that had been revealed where the shelf had been solid a second before. "It's a secret door!" Cecelia whisper-squealed.

"You didn't know about this?" Evienne whispered back, unsure of why they were whispering, but too startled not to. Cecelia shook her head, eyes wide, and turned to stare down into the gloom of the passage.

Evienne could hardly believe there was a single undocumented inch of this library. Ichorna was a scholarly nation, and this was its capital. Generations of accomplished scholars and librarians had tended this collection.

"We should probably go down there, right?" Cecelia said finally.

Evienne wasn't one to shy away from a little adventure—she was capable of protecting herself and her friend, and she had the unfortunate compulsion to know everything all the time. They were going to have to go down there or she wouldn't be able to stop thinking about it, and she knew Cece would feel the same way. So, she pricked her palm and summoned a handful of her blood fire to light their way. They descended the stairs into a small, dusty room full of floor-to-ceiling shelves.

Cecelia was immediately at a shelf, looking over all the titles.

"Oh, Evi, can you imagine! A whole room of books we didn't know about? I don't understand how this isn't documented in our records, but at least now I can catalog all of them!" Cecelia said excitedly.

Evienne hummed in agreement, taking in the thick layer of dust that covered every surface in the tiny room.

"Does it look like there's a theme? Do the books have anything in common?" Evienne asked.

"They do…it seems like they're all very old histories of Beitar and collections of their folklore," Cecelia said slowly.

"Why would a bunch of our books about Beitar be hidden away? I know they're a bit reclusive, but they are our neighbors. It's not like we shy away from talking about them," Evienne mused.

"No idea, but I intend to find out," Cecelia answered as she continued browsing through the books. After a moment, she pulled a massive tome off the shelf. It was protected by an ancient-looking velvet sleeve. *A Complete History of Ichorna* was written across the front of the book in black stamped letters.

"Another Complete History… wonderful," Evienne said sarcastically.

"Oh, Evi, stop. I know you hated history class, but it really wasn't that bad." Cecelia summoned her magic into a soft red light in her palm. The red was meant to avoid damaging fragile pages.

"Why is there more than one complete history anyway? Isn't the point that one has everything?" Evienne watched as Cecelia carefully opened the book to the title page.

"You're so literal sometimes," Cecelia said with a scoff. "Obviously, this one is much older than the one we studied, and it seems to have been lost for quite some time. Curious that it was included with all of these books on Beitar."

They both leaned in to look at the dusty page.

Published in the year 501 per the calendar of Domhan na Rùin

"Well, that's not what I expected," Cecelia said with a hint of awe. "This book isn't just old—it's five hundred years old."

Chapter Five

"There it is," Solon called from atop his horse. Orion was already staring at the great bronze mass of a city that rose out of the gently rolling fields they had been traveling through for the past few days. These fields, he knew from his studies, overflowed with golden wheat in the summer months. Now they sat vacant but neatly tended, the earth prepared for a long winter slumber.

Orion had spent so much time reading about the great cities of Domhan na Rùin, and now he was seeing one with his own eyes. Though his career had been made through his scholarship on the history of magic in Domhan na Rùin, he had had a lifelong love of architecture and cultural studies. Ichorna was an interesting nation; they had been scorned by the rest of Domhan na Rùin because of their magic's complicated moral implications. Only in the past few hundred years had they coaxed the wider world into more open trade and travel with their impressive technological advances, like the Rail Dellumine.

Orion turned as motion at the corner of his field of vision caught his eye. A bronze train slid across the open fields toward Lucinne. Knowing about the magic-powered Rail and seeing it were two entirely different things. Orion stared after it in awe. He had spent his adult life studying magic, having never actually *seen* any; it was a sight to behold and, he guessed, the first of many incredible things he would see in the next month.

They could have taken the Rail from one of the many towns they had passed on their journey, but something about the contraptions made Solon uneasy, so they had opted for horses. Orion wouldn't have minded seeing what all the fuss with the Rail was about, but he wasn't sad to have his horse with him on the trip. They did, thankfully, send their trunks ahead of them via courier. A whole month's worth of clothing took up quite a bit of space, as it turned out.

It was midday, but the sun barely pierced the overcast sky. Despite the clouds, Lucinne reflected any bit of light like a great jeweled crown. Even from this distance, tiny motes of color could be spotted. Of all the things Orion was excited to see, Lucinne's famed stained glass windows captured his imagination the most; he had a weakness for lovely things.

While Ichorna's history was a topic Orion had spent years studying, its current events were more difficult to hear about. They sent messengers to Mulhouse to document news on a regular basis, but the border town wasn't exactly at the heart of the action. Information was a slow trickle, but Orion supposed knowing something was better than knowing nothing.

Solon and Orion continued the last leg of their journey, Lucinne growing larger as they approached.

Orion wondered if they would have the chance to meet the famed High Sangviere. The stories they received of her were his favorite. She sounded fearsome—strategic and talented. It was said she was the most powerful mage Ichorna had seen in a hundred years. He knew they had been struggling with attacks from beasts called the Gevaud that had seemingly appeared from nowhere, and that the High Sangviere's leadership had helped to manage the situation.

Tales of her blood magic were told almost as legends among the Ichornians of the border towns. Orion was grateful the Gevaud attacks hadn't spread to Beitar, and he was intrigued by the woman who had so creatively managed the situation despite the lack of understanding of its causes. The blood magic of the Sangviere was considered taboo by many, but Orion had always been intrigued by it. The thought of meeting the greatest living Sangviere was incredibly exciting to him.

Regardless of who they met or how excited he was about it, Orion knew he had to stay focused on their true goal. He must do whatever he could to understand the reasons behind his people's plight.

As they approached the gates to the city, the path widened and they were no longer the only ones on the road. A small crowd had accumulated near the gate itself, and guards were speaking with people as they entered the city. It was a time of peace, but since Lucinne was the royal seat of Ichorna, the guards were likely always vigilant.

Orion and Solon nudged their horses forward when it was their turn to speak to the guard.

"Name and destination," the guard asked, not too harshly.

"I am Lord Solon Lùtair of Beitar, and my companion is Professor Orion Doehlan, also of Beitar. We are here as Queen Aldith's invited guests for the millennium celebration," Solon said in a firm voice.

"I see," the guard said, clearly surprised to see them at the gates on horseback instead of arriving on the Rail. "I will let the palace know you have arrived in the city. Please, follow the main road straight through town and you will come to the gates of the palace complex," the guard continued, gesturing for them to go ahead.

"Thank you," Solon said, already moving forward through the gates.

A light scent of spice filled the air as they made their way up the main boulevard of the city. It was just as magnificent as Orion had hoped it would be. Buildings of warm beige stone were adorned with carved naturalistic facades and touches of bronze. They had the appearance of vines, flowers, and tree trunks—every surface artistically rendered. The people of Lucinne hurried by on either side of the wide boulevard, all in jewel-toned coats, looking for all the world as if they had just stepped out of the colorful windows that adorned nearly every corner of this city.

They passed a picturesque park of evergreen trees and fountains where children played; a massive glass-domed building with a sign above the brass doors in great scrolling letters, *Centrale Lumine*; a tiny shop with colorful cakes in the window that smelled of sweet almond as they walked by.

The city was so different from Sgùrdruid that Orion hardly knew what to make of it.

Soon enough, they arrived at the entrance to the palace complex and—surprisingly—were admitted immediately without so much as a hello from the guards. Orion looked at the central building in awe; it was truly massive, and the most elegant structure he had ever seen. The reality of where he was hit him fully then, and all sorts of emotions tumbled through his heart—excitement, anxiety, determination. Above all, he felt grateful for this chance to experience the world.

All thoughts left his mind, however, as he felt a tug on his sternum. He shifted his gaze to find the most beautiful woman he had ever seen standing across the courtyard at the top of the steps to the palace. Her figure was full, all soft curves, and her dark hair was stark next to the ivory of her complexion. Her face was fixed in a polite, neutral expression, but even from this distance he could tell her eyes were sharp and intelligent. She was the most beautiful person Orion had ever seen. A rush of emotions filled his mind at the sight of her; he felt compelled to be close to her, felt as if he'd known her his whole life. He didn't have words for what he was feeling, but goosebumps covered his arms as he stared at her. He didn't know why, but this woman, whoever she was, was important to him; he belonged with her.

Chapter Six

Evienne had always found the dining hall to be one of the most breathtaking spaces in the palace. Impossibly high ceilings and tall, lean windows thirty feet high framed the room. Bronze metalwork adorned the space, outlining the windows and plating the beams arcing across the high ceilings. Warm white walls and dark wood floors gave the space a cozy, friendly feeling despite its massive scale. As in most places in the city of Lucinne, bold jewel tones danced around the room as the stained glass of the windows made their mark on the space.

Long mahogany tables arranged in two rows filled the cavernous space. The room this afternoon was bustling, but nowhere near as full as it would be for dinner. Evienne's gaze quickly found Cecelia in their usual spot by one of the many tapestries adorning the walls. This particular piece depicted Ichorna's first ruler and original Sangviere greeting the Tuanadair King of Beitar, Ichorna's northern neighbor.

Cecelia was taking another bite of a sandwich, her nose buried in a massive book. She was so absorbed that she didn't even stir as Evienne approached. Evienne sat down next to her friend and helped herself to a cup of coffee, adding a healthy pour of cool cream. Coffee wasn't lunch, but she had slept in, so it sounded good.

"What's got you so engrossed?" Evienne softly nudged her friend with her elbow.

"Well, I've started going through the books in that hidden room we found, and this was one of them. Extremely interesting."

Evienne lifted the cover from where it was resting on the table and peered at the book's title.

"*A Complete History of Beitar and its People, Vol. I,*" Evienne read aloud.

"Mhm. I know we have some of their histories in the main collection already, but this one starts much further back. It even has some of their creation folklore!" Cecelia's eyes were bright with excitement as she finally looked up. Crumbs covered the front of her black dress.

"Well tell me about it, what part are you reading about now?"

"It seems their culture is very concerned with balance, almost to the point of treating it as a religion. Back before they lost their magic, they believed their shifted forms were a necessary half of each whole person. They haven't mentioned it explicitly yet, but it seems like they even had some sort of god that they celebrated with a festival at winter solstice."

"Interesting; and we really didn't know any of that about them before?"

"I'm sure someone did at some point, but over the past

century or so, as their magic has faded, they've become a much more secular society it would seem. But you know we hardly hear a word from them, let alone see any of them, so it makes sense that we'd sort of lose touch with their customs and beliefs," Cecelia's brows creased slightly as she considered this. "It's a shame, really. I've seen the illustrations and read the reports from the last diplomatic visit there when they went to collect Léhiona; Beitar sounds like a beautiful place."

Evienne had always taken a particular interest in cultural studies. Their own culture was so focused on scientific and magical industry that the idea of something so completely different sparked her imagination now as she heard her friend describing it.

She knew that the magic of the Tuanadair had been fading over the past several hundred years. All reports said that the youngest generation didn't have a single person left who could free their beast form and shift. As a magic-wielder herself, Evienne felt a deep sadness over this loss.

Cecelia caught her wistful stare. "What are you thinking about?"

Evienne sighed. "Oh, I just think it's rather sad, don't you? That all of those people have slowly lost their connection to magic. What a tragedy."

Cecelia hummed her agreement. "I'm glad I can help us learn a bit more about their history, at least. It seems that lots of those books from the forgotten room have a similar theme. I'm sure they were just lost to time as they became less relevant. Beitar has barely had contact with us in any official capacity beyond sending consorts whenever a new king or queen takes the throne. What an odd arrangement," Cecelia mused.

Before Evienne could respond, a guard strode up to their table and cleared her throat. "High Sangviere, the Beitarans have entered the city. They will be here in a few minutes."

Evienne thanked the guard and rose. "Let the celebration begin, I suppose," she sighed as Cecelia looked up from her book.

"At least try to enjoy yourself, Evi. I'll see you soon!" Cecelia said.

Evienne set off then for the main courtyard in front of the palace complex to greet her charges for the next month with a lightness in her step she hadn't felt in ages.

She reached the main doors and strode out into the filtered light of the day. Moisture hung in the air; Evienne could feel the tiny droplets as she inhaled deeply, steadying her breath after the quick walk. The scarlet velvet gown she wore wasn't warm enough to be outside for long, but she didn't want to waste time going to fetch her cloak.

The sound of horses' hooves on the pavement soon filtered into her awareness. The lookouts had sent a messenger to say the delegation was arriving on horseback, but Evienne had expected more than the two lone horses that trotted through the gates.

A strikingly handsome man, lean and noble, sat astride a white gelding. His skin was a rich brown, his dark hair braided in many strands and gathered into a massive twist on his head. His features were sharp, his countenance reserved. Next to him, on a dappled gray mount, sat another man—willowy and graceful, with cheekbones so sharp Evienne could see them easily from where she stood at the top of the palace steps.

As they drew nearer, she was struck by his piercing, cool green eyes. They were the same shade as young grass coated in the winter's last frost, somewhere between green and teal. His hair was an inky black and fell in soft waves to his smooth, pale cheeks. He looked otherworldly.

Evienne jolted when she saw the ethereal man's mouth quirk up at one side; she had been staring at him as he and his companion came to a stop near the foot of the stairs. The pair of them made quite the imposing sight. After taking them in for a moment, she launched into action, smiling broadly as she descended the steps.

"Welcome to Lucinne, gentlemen. We are honored you made the long journey to join us for this celebration," Evienne spoke as she approached them. They gracefully dismounted their horses, handing off the reins to stable hands who hovered nearby.

"Thank you for the warm welcome; we are honored to have been included," the first man spoke, his voice gentle and polite. His features softened as he offered Evienne a close-lipped smile.

"Of course. We would never think to snub our neighbors and allies. We are grateful you've taken the time to be here. My name is Evienne Elodie D'Auclaire, High Sangviere of Ichorna," she said, extending her hand to him in greeting.

"High Sangviere, it is an honor." He took her hand and kissed it lightly before releasing it and straightening. She felt a bit flustered as he spoke again. "I am Lord Solon Lùtair, member of Beitar's Inner Court and leader of the Glenkoe province. And this is my colleague and friend, Professor Orion Doelahn, our Royal Historian and a Professor at our University."

Evienne inclined her head in a show of respect, not letting her brilliant smile falter. "It is my distinct pleasure to welcome you both to our city. Please, call me Evienne."

"Evienne," Professor Doelahn spoke for the first time. His voice was warm, open, resonant; Evienne's eyes flicked to his sea green gaze. "It's a lovely name for the deadliest woman in Ichorna," his eyes gleamed with the slightest hint of mischief.

Evienne's lips parted in surprise, her brow furrowing ever so slightly. Was this man…teasing her?

"I believe I may be at a disadvantage in our conversation, Professor," she said, turning to face him. "It seems you know of me, yet I know nothing about you." Two could play at this game.

"An injustice I will seek to resolve as quickly as I'm able," the Professor answered, his smirk making another appearance on his obnoxiously beautiful face.

Evienne laughed in earnest then, but quickly gained control of herself. She turned her attention to Lord Lùtair, surprised at her own reaction to Professor Doehlan's comment. "Lord Lùtair, Professor Doehlan, would you care for a tour of the palace now, or should I show you to your rooms?"

"Our rooms would be a wonderful place to start," Lord Solon's smile made another appearance. "We've been on the road for some time."

"I understand completely. Once you're settled and rested, I can show you around the palace. There's certainly no rush; you'll be our guests for the whole month of celebrations as far as I understand?"

Lord Lùtair nodded. "Yes, we are looking forward to our time here."

The three moved off into the labyrinth of palace hallways, and Evienne found her curiosity about their visitors growing as she let her mind replay their first encounter just now. Evienne pointed out a few of the key public spaces on their way to the guest quarters but kept her commentary to a minimum, opting instead to let her thoughts wander. At the end of a particularly long hallway, she gestured to two bronze-plated doors across from one another.

"Here we are. Please ring for the palace staff if there is anything at all that you require. They can also get word to me whenever you are ready for your tour." Evienne glanced up to find the Professor's eyes fixed on her face. She felt herself blush and quickly looked away, beginning to move back down the hall. She refused to fall all over herself; she was a grown woman, and the High Sangviere of Ichorna.

"Thank you, Evienne." Professor Doehlan's voice floated down the hall after her. She didn't turn back, but somehow she knew he was smirking after her.

A FEW hours later, a member of the palace staff came to Evienne's rooms to let her know that the Beitarans were ready for their tour. She had been full of anxious energy as she awaited word from them; she had tried to sit and read and enjoy a bit of quiet time, but it had been nearly impossible. She set out for the guest wing, only to run into Professor

Doehlan in the entry hall just inside the main door she met them at earlier in the day.

"Professor," she said in greeting as he strode up to her. She offered her hand, and he took it, brushing his lips just over her knuckles. She sucked in a breath as a shiver ran through her entire body at the contact. She had to pull herself together; this wasn't the first beautiful person she'd ever seen.

"It is a pleasure to see you again," he answered, voice smooth as honey when he released her hand.

"I was on my way to fetch you and Lord Lùtair for a tour as requested. Will he be joining us?"

"He has a bit of a headache, unfortunately, so you'll have to settle for me," he answered.

"I am sorry to hear he's unwell; I do hope he knows to alert the staff to anything he might need," Evienne said, trying to remain professional in the face of spending time alone with this man who had her stomach doing flips. It occurred to her to be suspicious that Lord Lùtair was having Professor Doehlan distract her while he poked around the palace alone, but it was still early enough in the evening that there would likely be too many people around for him to go snooping unnoticed by the staff. However improbable, she had a job to do, and she refused to be taken in.

"He does. I am sure he will make a quick recovery. Where do you recommend we begin our tour?" Professor Doehlan asked with a small smile.

"If you'll excuse me just a moment, I nearly forgot to send word to my friend in the library that I won't be able to join her for dinner this evening." Evienne returned the Professor's smile and strode to the nearest stationed guard on the other side of the entry hall. "Please alert the guard stationed in the guest wing to send word to me if Lord Lùtair of Beitar leaves his quarters," she whispered to the guard, who nodded in response. She then strode back to where Professor Doehlan waited, examining a pane of stained glass.

"My apologies again for the interruption. Let's start with the main spaces where the events will be held over the next month, then stop by the library and the gardens," Evienne said, turning to make her way toward the Throne Room.

"No need to apologize. And please, call me Orion."

She turned to look at him as they walked, and nodded her assent. "Orion, then."

Orion walked by her side as they navigated the halls of the palace. Marble floors and walls were decorated with scrolling bronze metalwork all through the building; it was opulent, but Evienne had always loved it.

"So, Evienne, tell me about yourself. Are you from Lucinne originally?" Orion asked as they walked.

"Oh, no, I came here when I was twelve. My father decided it would be good for my character to participate in a work exchange at a school here in the capital. He used to be the governor of Mulhouse; that's where I grew up," Evienne answered casually. Her situation had been unusual and she wasn't sure how Orion would react. She was the only person she knew of who had been sent away to work for their keep so young.

"I see. You grew up in the shadow of our mountains. It is very different that far north. Do you ever miss it?" He asked.

"I suppose so, yes. I miss the feeling of wild places. The city is beautiful in its own way, and it feels like home now more than anywhere else, but it is… confining at times," Evienne said, glancing over at him. She knew she was, perhaps, being too open, but she struggled to find it in herself to pull back. If anything, being open might encourage Orion to share some of his own secrets.

They continued in silence for a few minutes until they reached the throne room. Evienne told Orion about how their formal events typically went, and they moved on to the dining hall and the great hall, talking all the while about the weeks ahead.

Evienne found herself wholly distracted every time she really looked at Orion. She had been with many attractive people, but there was something about him that was so interesting; she could hardly keep her eyes off him.

"Tell me about your magic; what is it like to be the most powerful mage in Ichorna?" Orion asked as they walked toward the library.

Evienne felt a laugh escape before she could fully process what he had said, and she glanced over to find him smiling at her. A dimple, of all things, had appeared on his smooth cheek. She was in trouble.

He waited, smiling, studying her face. Finally, she remembered herself and replied, "I wouldn't say I'm the most powerful. Queen Aldith, herself, is a trained Sangviere."

"Ah, you're humble too, then, as well as incredibly accomplished," Orion said with a chuckle.

Evienne laughed again, "I am only realistic. What about

you, though? You were important enough to accompany Lord Lùtair on this trip; you must be quite well-respected yourself?" Evienne thought she should be using this time to make progress in uncovering his motives—understanding why he, specifically, was here, could be a good start.

"I just love reading, that's all," Orion said with a broad smile. "And it seems you've brought me to the right place for it." She knew he was deflecting, but she didn't want to press him.

They entered the library then, and Evienne showed Orion to the area where the catalogs were laid out alongside a map of the whole space.

As they left the library, Evienne realized she was disappointed that her time alone with Orion was coming to an end. She quickly scolded herself for such a silly feeling; she was about to spend an entire month with him.

They continued talking of things they saw as they walked—other rooms and artwork and views of the city framed by the colored glass windows. The sun had set by the time they came to the entrance of the guest wing.

"Ah, you've brought me back, I see. Tired of me already?" Orion asked with laughter in his voice.

Evienne smiled at him, "Of course not, but I am tired." She feigned a yawn.

"Oh, well, I wouldn't dream of keeping the High Sangviere from her rest," Orion answered. "You'll need it if you're going to be dealing with me for the next month," he added, mischief lighting his eyes.

"Goodnight, Orion," Evienne said, glancing up at him through her lashes.

Orion leaned down and whispered in her ear, "Goodnight, lovely, *deadly* Evienne." A soft gasp escaped her at his words—no one spoke to her like that—but by the time she had readied a retort he was already shutting his door.

Chapter Seven

Léhiona had been gazing out the massive window in her sitting room that overlooked the main courtyard when the Beitarans arrived. She stood, absently rubbing the tattooed wedding band on her finger as she watched them ride in on their horses, and her heart ached to go to them—to talk with them of home.

She knew she couldn't, though; to do so would cause her unbearable pain. She wasn't entirely sure it wouldn't kill her. When the King of her homeland put the magical gag on her before sending her to Ichorna, she hadn't understood *why*. What was he so afraid she would tell?

Some of the consorts over the years had been men and women of the royal family, but she had barely been raised at court. She had no secrets to reveal—only memories of her culture to share. But, traditions must be followed, so she was bound just like all the consorts before her. All of these years, she had tried to make the most of her situation. Sometimes, though, it was hard. This was sure to be one of those times.

Léhiona fought against the tightness in her throat as

she watched Evienne greet the two men. One she did not know, but the sight of Lord Solon sent pangs of homesickness through her heart. She had not known him well in her former life, but he had been good friends with her father. How she missed her family. She knew he would likely have seen them recently, but she simply could not ask.

She turned at the sound of steps echoing across the wood floors. She had insisted on wood instead of marble for her private space—it felt like home.

"There's my sweet sister! How are you faring?" Sylvain du Pont strode toward her, all youthful confidence and joy. She couldn't help but smile at him; Sylvain was the perfect brother-in-law, and she absolutely adored spending time with him.

"Sylvain, I am so very happy to see you. I've missed you!" She said, embracing him. "I'm glad you could spare us a few weeks. I hope we don't bore you to tears!" She added, laughing.

"With parties nearly every night? Not a chance! I wouldn't miss it," he answered with a wink. "You didn't answer my question, though. How have you been?"

Léhiona felt her smile falter as she tried to find the words to answer him without mentioning her homeland. "I… I have been well. I am just more tired lately, I think," she said slowly, trying to regain her smile to reassure him. Sylvain wasn't fooled, though. Those who didn't know him well thought him shallow and pleasure-seeking, but Léhiona knew it was all a façade. He was insightful and caring, and he had known her since she arrived in Ichorna twelve years ago.

"Tired, hm? We'll have to get you to the healers and see if they can identify what the issue is," he said with a tinge of concern.

"Sylvain, I'm sure it's nothing. I'm just run down from all of the event planning. You know how particular Aldith can be," she said, laughing.

"Oh, do I ever. I grew up with her as my older sister, remember? I'm not quite sure how I survived!" He took her hand then and gave it a squeeze. "I'll call for some tea, and you can tell me all about how things have been here."

Léhiona was grateful for his company. He had found her at just the right time—she was fairly sure her loneliness would have swallowed her whole if she stared out at her countrymen for a moment longer. She felt tired at the thought of avoiding them for an entire month, but she wasn't sure her heart could take being near them.

Chapter Eight

The next day, Evienne sent a note to Orion and Lord Lùtair inviting them to attend a lecture she would be giving at the Academie du Sangviere that afternoon. She readied herself and set off to the school, which was a part of the palace complex.

She arrived a bit early in case either of the Beitarans decided to accept her invitation. She was at the podium organizing her notes—which she hardly needed at this point—when she heard footsteps coming from the far end of the empty hall.

She looked up to find Orion making his way down the long aisle that ran the length of the hall. Mahogany tables lined the space on either side and would soon be full of students.

"High Sangviere, thank you for your invitation to join the lecture. Solon sends his regrets; he was summoned to meet with Queen Aldith," Orion said as he neared her.

"Professor, good morning. I am glad you are able to be here. Please, feel free to take a seat anywhere you like; the students should be arriving any moment." Evienne smiled at him. She had to keep things professional, but she hardly knew what to do with herself after the way he whispered in her ear the night before. What had that been about?

He smiled at her and nodded, turning to take a seat on the very end of the front row. Perfect—now she would have to look at him the whole time.

The students began filing in, their conversations filling the hall with a buzz. After everyone seemed settled, Evienne stepped up to the podium and cleared her throat.

Today's lecture was on, arguably, the most important concept a Sangviere could learn. There were many facets to blood magic, but the more morally questionable applications had caused the Sangviere—and, by extension, Ichorna—to gain a negative reputation amongst the other magical peoples of Domhan na Rùin. She began her practiced lecture, laying out the history of their blood magic methodically before arriving at her main point.

"It is critical for us to wield our magic with respect and integrity; the rules we follow as Sangviere have been put in place to help us build and maintain connections with the other nations of Domhan na Rùin. It was our irresponsible use of the Valsang in centuries past that estranged us from our neighbors," Evienne spoke confidently, trying to fix her gaze on a point at the back of the room. More aptly, trying *not* to look directly at Orion.

"Can anyone tell me why, other than maintaining our reputation, we do not practice the Valsang?"

A young mage near the back of the hall raised her hand, and Evienne called on her to answer.

"The art of the Valsang is said to corrupt the soul of the wielder and, if used often, will eventually cause the Sangviere to go mad."

"That is correct. The Valsang is never to be used. To become a Sangviere is to disown this vein of our magical heritage. The ability to control other human beings with our magic is too great a risk, to ourselves and to Ichorna's international interests."

Evienne paused to let her words sink in. Of course this wasn't the first time the students were hearing this, but as High Sangviere, she hoped her warning would carry additional weight to drive the message home.

Evienne's students listened intently as she explained that, due to the Gevaud crisis of the past decade, the Sangviere were using their Regne du Sang more regularly. It was the most effective way to combat the creatures. They would not, however, loosen any restrictions around the use of the Valsang. If a Sangviere was ever found to have used this dark magic, they would be faced with a life sentence in prison, left in complete isolation with their magic bound.

Orion raised his hand from where he sat in the front row.

"Everyone, we have an important guest with us today; Professor Doehlan is visiting from Beitar for the millennium celebration," Evienne said, and students murmured surprised exclamations in response. "Professor, please ask your question."

"Thank you, High Sangviere. I want to be sure I understand the nuance you are describing. The Regne du Sang, on its own, is not considered a dark magic when wielded with the Sangviere's own blood, correct? It is only when spells are powered by the blood of another that it becomes the Valsang?"

Evienne nodded, "Yes, that's correct, professor."

"When was the last time a Sangviere used the Valsang?" He asked—and seemed genuinely curious, so Evienne decided to give an honest answer.

"About two hundred years ago," she said, and his brows rose in surprise.

"What happened two hundred years ago?" He asked. Evienne didn't know quite what to make of his curiosity. It could be just that; he was a professor, after all. Could he be seeking information for something more nefarious? The answer to this particular question was common knowledge, though, so she supposed no real harm could come from answering.

"King Bastille du Pont sat upon Ichorna's throne at that time. He is the one who built the Centrale Lumine and expanded our Rail system. Part of bringing Ichorna back into the good graces of the other nations of Domhan na Rùin was making a good faith effort to avoid the aspects of our magic that cause our neighbors distress. He gave us technology that would be appealing to the world while making us less threatening as a magical force. Does that answer your question, professor?"

Orion nodded, considering her words.

"Are there any other questions before we conclude?" She asked, surveying the students. No one raised a hand. "Class dismissed."

She gathered her papers and made her way over to where Orion now stood waiting for her.

"What an interesting lecture; I had no idea that there was a whole facet of the Sangviere's magic that is outlawed. What a curious choice," he said as she gestured for him to lead the way. They began walking toward the doors of the lecture hall.

"Yes, well, we did what we must to be less threatening to those outside of Ichorna. Even the necromancers of Daosbor are more appealing than blood mages, it seems," Evienne said with a small laugh.

"Fascinating. Thank you again for the invitation," Orion said, stopping just outside the door of the hall. They now stood in a lovely cloister, the crisp breeze gently rustling the bushes and small trees that populated the little garden at the center.

Evienne smiled at him. "Of course, it was lovely to have you," she said lightly.

A wicked gleam lit his eyes then, and—despite her every effort not to—she was suddenly thinking of how her back had tingled when he whispered in her ear.

"When you have me, Evienne, it will be more than just lovely," he said, his rich voice barely more than a whisper. He smirked at her, his black hair falling onto his cheek. Evienne was frozen; she knew her mouth must be agape, but she couldn't manage to move. She just stared at him, taking in every detail as he studied her right back.

"Have a good afternoon," he said with a bit of laughter in his voice as he turned and strode away. Evienne stared after him and tried desperately to convince herself to forget what had just happened.

Chapter Nine

The subsequent days passed in a flurry of performative activity. Evienne and the Beitarans attended meals in the great hall, toured the city, and had tea with the queens. Lord Lùtair—who insisted Evienne should call him Solon—seemed particularly interested in Léhiona, but the Queen Consort did not return his curiosity. Evienne assumed something about the magic that silenced Léhiona would cause her distress if she tried to reminisce with the Beitarans; as a result, it seemed she preferred to keep her distance rather than test the limits of the magic that bound her.

Solon was often occupied throughout the day by various diplomatic talks with other nobles, which meant Evienne was left alone with Orion for long stretches of time. All of the conversation with him since the lecture had been pleasant, albeit shallow. No more whispered flirtations. It was enough to make her think she had imagined the whole thing.

Instead, discussions of palace architecture had featured

heavily, but always with the witty undertone of humor she was coming to expect from the Professor. She had no idea what the Beitarans' true motives for this trip could be, but at least they did not seem malicious. Despite this, she remained vigilant, trying to casually discover more about their backgrounds. She spent hours pondering all the bits of rather mundane information she managed to get from them, trying to piece together some sort of plausible deeper reason for their trip here. Unfortunately for Evienne, they truly seemed to be here to enjoy themselves and socialize with the other attendees.

The reward for her pondering was nothing more than stolen glances at Orion and his confusingly, infuriatingly beautiful face. He was tall; Evienne was of average height, and she barely reached his collarbones. His shoulders were broad, but his frame tapered elegantly at his waist. His arms and legs were toned, but not bulky. He was all lithe, graceful lines and impossible angles. Evienne couldn't keep her eyes off him.

Half of the time, she caught herself staring at him; he—embarrassingly—also caught her staring at him. It would have been entirely too humiliating but for the intense curiosity in his gaze whenever their eyes met. It was enough to make her face heat on more than one occasion.

On the evening of the official start of the celebration, the opening night ball, Evienne donned the first of many gowns she had commissioned for the month's festivities. It was a shade of purple so rich it rivaled the midnight sky. Its velvet skirt was draped to move and flow around her legs from where it began at the curve of her full waist. The bodice was corseted, with a sweetheart neckline and sleeves that draped off the side of her shoulders. The back scooped down below her shoulder blades, and she wore her hair swept up off her neck in a pile of curls atop her head. Two teardrop diamonds hung from her ears.

Evienne darkened her lips to a deep blood red, slipped her silver bladed ring onto her hand, and made her way to the throne room. It was the largest, most ornate space in Lucinne. Its glass ceiling was latticed with delicate filigree bronze work. Stained glass windows in shades of royal blue and navy were situated at intervals around the space as well. The bronze throne sat at the far end of the room on a dais with a banquet table set before it. Aldith and Léhiona were already in their places when Evienne entered through a side door.

She strode up to the dais, sinking into a deep curtsy as she approached. The room echoed with voices from all of the guests at the long tables filling the hall. She caught the sound of Cecelia's melodic laughter from somewhere nearby and smiled as she rose to address the queens.

"Your majesties, I hope you are well and enjoying the opening celebration so far?"

"We are indeed," Léhiona answered enthusiastically. This event was the culmination of years of planning for the queens. Evienne hoped they were able to enjoy the fruits of their labor over the coming weeks.

"How are your charges faring?" Aldith asked quietly, her expression remaining smooth and neutral.

"They are well, your majesty. Settling in comfortably, I believe." Evienne kept her words vague, but Aldith's appraising gaze made it clear she understood Evienne's message that there seemed to be no imminent threat.

"Wonderful. We were glad to meet them the other day for tea, but we will hope to see more of the Beitarans in the coming weeks," Aldith flicked her gaze over Evienne's shoulder, no doubt seeking out the two northerners where they sat near the far wall of the hall.

"Ah, Evienne, our very own High Sangviere!" Sylvain called to her as he made his way over to where she stood before the queens.

"Sylvain, it's so good to see you!" Evienne threw her arms around him in a hug which he happily returned. Aldith cleared her throat, and Evienne remembered herself, quickly letting go of Sylvain as she shot Aldith an apologetic look.

The prince hadn't changed much in the year since he'd seen her; she supposed he had just settled more into his adulthood. His frame was a bit less lanky, but his tan skin and dark curls were just like his sister's.

Sylvain rolled his eyes conspiratorially and whispered just for her, "Let's catch up sometime when the hawk isn't watching?" He winked at her, turning to give an elaborate flourishing bow to Aldith, and Evienne bit her lip to avoid smiling. He strode off into the crowd, and Evienne curtsied, turning to make her way to her own seat near Solon and Orion. She and the queens had decided to keep their friendship less public for the duration of the celebration—flaunting their close personal ties could raise suspicions with their Beitaran visitors—but Evienne couldn't help her excitement at seeing Sylvain. He was like a little brother to her, too.

Sliding into her seat next to the Orion, Evienne reached

for her wine glass and took a sip of the dry, spicy vintage. She could feel Orion's attention on her before he spoke.

"Are you well this evening, Evienne?"

Every time he said her name, the way the vowels rolled through his rich voice sent a chill down her spine.

"I am, thank you," she answered, a tad breathless.

"You certainly look well," he said with a devilish smile. Did this man always have a bit of dark laughter behind his words? Evienne could never quite tell if he was trying to seduce her or not. If he was, it was certainly working.

"You are absolutely shameless!" She said with a laugh. She turned her face toward him then, their gazes locking. This time Evienne didn't shy away from her body's reaction to his proximity; let him see how he affected her. She knew her cheeks had to be a vibrant pink; she could feel herself flushing.

No one had ever had this effect on her. She wondered absently if he was doing something to manipulate her, but it was unlikely since his people's magic had dwindled so significantly. And anyway, she didn't think that sort of magic had ever been part of their abilities. She only had herself to blame for all her blushing and butterflies.

"We've spent nearly a week in each other's company, and I'm embarrassed to say I still don't know what your particular area of academic interest is."

He smiled at her slowly before responding. "I study the history of magic. Both the magic of Beitar as well as other areas across Domhan na Rùin."

His answer was a bit surprising to Evienne; she didn't

know what she had expected, but it wasn't a magic historian from a nation with no magic left.

"I see. And, if it is not too presumptuous of me to ask, what is the current state of Beitar's magic?" Evienne didn't see any real harm in just asking outright. They had to know Ichornians would be curious.

"It is now extinct, I'm afraid. Save for our King's," he answered plainly.

Evienne had assumed as much, but his admission still pricked sadness to life in her heart. She let her feelings show on her face as she answered.

"I am sorry for the loss, truly. It's one no people should suffer."

"Thank you," he said quietly. "It is a point of great sorrow for our people that we are unable to shift and experience the other half of our souls. I believe many of the Tuanadair feel the lack of balance deeply."

"I can only imagine what it would be like to be cut off from my magic. I think I would feel completely disconnected from our world then. Are your people able to tell what sort of shifter they are? Is there any awareness of that part of one's soul without active magic?"

"In rare cases we can tell without any magic. Many only have a vague sense of their whole soul while they cannot access it," he replied.

Evienne was taken aback at how open he was being, considering how distant his country had been for the last centuries. She had assumed asking him about it in a crowded ballroom wouldn't get her far; she wouldn't have been surprised if they had been required to submit to a magical gag similar to Léhiona's, but it seemed their King was becoming more lax in his old age.

"Do you know what your animal is?"

Orion's brows rose at her question, but Evienne held his gaze, not backing down. She panicked internally that perhaps she had pushed him too far with such a question.

"That's a rather personal question, don't you think, Evienne?" They sat there, gazes locked, and Evienne's heart stopped. Orion's mouth pulled up ever so slightly at the corner, hinting at his amusement. He wasn't offended, then, just teasing her, as usual. Relief washed over her, and she decided to have a bit of fun.

"You can ask me a personal question in return, if you wish," Evienne answered, returning Orion's smirk. "I'm an open book."

He arched a brow at her, a dimple appearing on his cheek as he smiled. "Then tell me, High Sangviere, why it is I see your cheeks flush every time we speak?"

She felt heat creeping down her neck even now, her eyes widening a bit in surprise at his boldness. She didn't mind it; she preferred to have things out in the open. But she had never met her match in frankness, and this man was startlingly blunt.

Before Evienne could answer, the sound of music drifted through the hall—the dancing was beginning. During these grand banquets, there was no set meal time. Guests could come and go from their places as they pleased, the dishes on the table continually refreshed throughout the night.

"Would you care to dance with me?" Evienne's voice

came out more breathless than she wished, her question about Orion's Tuanadair nature conveniently forgotten.

Orion inclined his head before standing in one smooth motion. He offered her his hand, that knowing smile still warming his ethereal face.

Evienne took his hand, his skin cool and smooth under her touch. His hand was easily twice the size of her own, but held her delicately. His thumb casually ran over the back of her hand in a caress that sent a wave of tingles down her spine.

They made their way to the large open space at one end of the hall that had been reserved for dancing, the sound of the string orchestra growing more insistent with their approach. The couples parted as the first song ended, and a lush tune in three-quarter time began to play.

Orion led her to the edge of the dance floor and turned to face her, pulling her body close and resting his other hand on her waist. They stood chest to chest, and she had to tilt her head back to peer up at him.

Sylvain was on the dance floor as well, a beautiful auburn-haired man opposite him. He caught Evienne's stare and winked at her.

The music started again, and they began to move in a swirling pattern of three steps, turning as they went, moving with the other couples in a great circle. This was one of the few dance patterns that were fairly universal across Domhan na Rùin.

Evienne was painfully aware of every place where her body touched Orion's. He smelled of cardamom and sandalwood, and his sleek black hair caught the bronzy light of the room. Her fingertips dug into his midnight blue jacket; it was tailored to perfection, double-breasted, and buttoned tight around his narrow waist.

Evienne's deep purple gown flowed around her legs as they danced, their movements surprisingly natural. She was grateful he wasn't making her talk and dance at the same time; she wasn't coordinated enough for that. No, rather than talk, they only danced, and his thumb made idle strokes against her waist where he held her.

When the music ended, he kept hold of her hand and led her toward the terrace that was open to the chill night air. They made their way through the crowd and stepped out into the inky dark, finding a spot near the bronze railing.

This terrace had a beautiful view out over Lucinne. Even at night, the mage light streaming from the windows across the city was tinged with color from all of the stained glass. The bronze used so plentifully throughout the city caught the moonlight with a warm reflection, making all the buildings appear as though lit by candlelight. Evienne would never grow tired of this view.

Orion's voice pulled her from her reverie; she rarely took the time to simply admire the city she called home.

"You look at this view as if you've never seen it before," Orion observed.

She gave a halfhearted chuckle and said, "I almost never stop what I'm doing to take in this beautiful place that I love so dearly. I've lived in Ichorna my whole life, and Lucinne for nearly twenty years, and I think I'd do just about anything for my people."

"Your devotion is admirable; your people are lucky to

have you as a defender," Orion smiled at her, his words earnest.

"I try to be worthy of them, but I feel there is more I could do," Evienne sighed. "Enough about me, though. Time for you to share all of your innermost thoughts and feelings," Evienne said with her own mischievous smile.

"Well, at this moment, I find my mind consumed with a very specific topic," Orion's dimple was on display, but his gaze was heated. Evienne raised her eyebrows at him in question.

"Evienne, you appreciate bluntness, I think, so I will be straightforward with you. I am intrigued by you. I know my time in this city will be short, but I find my thoughts constantly drawn to you since my arrival, and I intend to invest my time in knowing you better."

Thoughts spun wildly through Evienne's head at Orion's words. She was supposed to be getting him off-balance, not the other way around. She wasn't cut out to spy, she realized. She craved authenticity too much to play games with people. A rather inconvenient observation given her current situation.

Evienne felt herself wanting to be closer, though she already stood quite close to him. She knew she must look surprised at his words, and she was. He was right—she did prefer bluntness—but it was a rare indulgence, especially when it came to matters of the heart. She felt all sorts of emotions as she looked at him. Excitement, longing, curiosity—all alongside the pang of fear that had kept her from letting herself really be intimate with anyone in the time since she had left Dominique.

She decided then that she would let herself have this enjoyment. She could do this without getting attached, just as she had a hundred times before. Orion wouldn't be here long; there was no risk of her losing all of the work she had done to reclaim herself. Other than perhaps being a bit unprofessional, she didn't see any harm.

"Orion," she began, placing her hand over his on the cool railing. "I do appreciate your frankness; I will endeavor to match it. I find myself drawn to you for reasons that I do not fully understand. I know your time here is limited, but I will enjoy it all the same, in more ways than one, if I understand the full extent of your proposition."

He leaned into her space then, sliding his other hand around her waist. It didn't even cross her mind to pull away.

"Well then, High Sangviere and Protector of Lucinne," his voice lowered in volume, only for the two of them. "I believe we understand each other. I would like to make good on our agreement now, if that is acceptable to you?"

Evienne peered at him through her lashes. Her breath caught at his words. She had a job to do, but she supposed getting closer to him could make him more comfortable opening up to her about his motives. If she was being honest, though, she would accept any excuse her mind could give her to be with him. She just—wanted to.

She nodded, bringing her hands to his chest. His fingers tensed on her waist, and he leaned in to brush his lips against her cheek. Evienne's breath left her in a silent pant, and she angled her head, bringing her lips to his in a gentle kiss.

Heartbeats passed before Orion deepened the kiss, his hands sliding up Evienne's back to pull her flush to his body.

He groaned softly as her lips parted for him, their tongues brushing. Evienne pulled away with a gasp, her whole body alight with desire for this man in a way she had never felt for anyone.

"Come with me." Evienne took Orion's hand and led him through the halls until they came to the library. She knew all of the librarians were attending the celebration, so it would certainly be quiet amongst the stacks. They entered the great wooden doors, and Evienne closed them behind her with a gentle thud. She silently prayed that no one would come looking for them or notice they'd gone.

They made their way to one of the hearths that was set up with a few sofas and a low table. It was one of the many reading areas in the massive palace library. This particular nook was along the back wall, far from the main entrance.

The fire that had been burning was nothing more than a pile of embers, casting a warm orange glow on the plush rug. The whole of the library was filled with windows, so the moon's light made the space bright despite the dying fire.

Orion didn't waste a moment, pulling Evienne back into his embrace. His lips found the sensitive crook of her neck and Evienne let out a little moan at the tingling she felt in her fingertips. She breathed in his warm, spicy scent and felt her pulse come to life in her core. All hesitation left her mind as she focused on simply *feeling*.

"Is this what you want?" Orion sounded breathless, his hands bracing her generous waist. His fingers were splayed, with his forefingers brushing the underside of her breasts. She looked up at him, noticing the color in his cheeks. He was just as affected by this as she was.

"Yes. Please." Evienne couldn't believe she was all but begging, but she didn't know what else to make of this pull between them. She had taken many lovers, but something about this felt new.

"Good," Orion answered, drawing his hands up her sides until he cupped her breasts fully in his hands through her dress. He bent to capture her mouth again, the kiss demanding from the start this time. She brought her hands to wrap around his neck, running them through his silky hair. He slid his hands back down her body, grabbing her rear and pulling her closer to him. She felt his hardness against her stomach and moaned again.

"May I touch you?" Orion's voice was a breathless rumble against her neck.

"Yes," Evienne moaned as he began to pull her toward one of the couches. Orion sat and guided Evienne into a position astride him. She had never shied away from being on display; in fact, she rather enjoyed it. Her skirt gathered around her waist, exposing her rounded hips and full thighs.

Orion's gaze was fixed on all of the places where her creamy soft skin was revealed. His hands slid reverently up her thighs, and he glanced up at her, his eyes full of his lust and something else she couldn't quite place. She leaned down, cupping his jaw with one hand, and whispered in his ear, "Now, touch me."

Chapter Ten

ORION WAS OVERWHELMED by his reaction to Evienne. Memories of how he felt when he first saw her had plagued him almost every moment since he arrived. That pull behind his sternum had been bizarre; he didn't know what to make of it. He thought her beautiful, of course, and her wit and intellect had drawn him in as they spent time together. But he had been attracted to people before, even had feelings for them, without this hypnotic pull on his soul. He desired to be close to her, connected to her, in every way.

His fingers skimmed her lush thighs, taking in their silky feel. He shifted his gaze and was met with a mirror of his own breathless desire in Evienne's face. All thoughts emptied from his head save one; he would bring his stunning woman pleasure as she had never known before.

She sat astride him, the apex of her thighs exposed to the cool air but obscured from view by the gathered fabric of her skirt. He slid his hands higher, reveling in the warm give of her lush hips. This woman was all roundness and curves, and he was becoming addicted to the feel of her.

He held her gaze as his hands shifted, grazing the delicate lace of her undergarments. He slipped his fingers beneath the fabric and was met with curls of downy hair that were already wet with Evienne's arousal. Her breath came in pants now, her lovely breasts rising and falling against the constraints of her corset.

An inch lower, and Orion felt the slickness of her core against his fingertips. He let out a breathy moan at the feel of it, moving his fingers around her opening. He felt her legs tense around him as he brushed over her most sensitive bundle of nerves. Orion was captivated by her every breath, her every reaction to his touch.

He rested the base of his forefinger on her most sensitive spot, applying slight pressure; his middle finger joined to make a V shape on either side of her opening, massaging where he knew those nerves spread out beneath her skin.

Evienne moaned softly and began to rock her hips, increasing his pressure. He wanted to feel her cunt pulse around his fingers; he couldn't wait any longer before he slid a finger inside her.

He worked her clit with his thumb as his finger stroked her inner wall. He added a second and Evienne's head fell back. She was tight on his hand, slick and swollen. He watched her riding him, his own release building just from staring at her. It was as if he could feel her pleasure as his own. He was overcome with the need to take her, to fill her.

He stopped himself before his thoughts became too unruly; he knew he couldn't get attached to this woman. He was indulging his attraction to her, but he was in this city for a reason and he couldn't lose sight of it. Yet every thought fled his mind when Evienne went silent, holding her breath as her inner walls clenched around his fingers.

Her breath left her in a rush, a loud moan escaping her lips as she came. He felt every pulse of her cunt on his fingers as he stroked her through her release.

He slowly withdrew, bringing his hand to his mouth as Evienne stared down at him, breathless. He licked his fingers, and the taste of her had his orgasm crashing into him without warning. He was drowning in her, the feel of her body over his, the pleasure coursing through his veins.

After a moment, his mind cleared enough to process what had just occurred. He had finished in his pants like some besotted school boy, and he found he didn't even care. He refused to be embarrassed about what Evienne did to him; she was a beautiful woman.

Evienne glanced down, noting the wet spot forming on the front of his trousers, and smiled at him when she realized what he had done. She leaned down to kiss him, tasting herself on his tongue.

His anxiety calmed further when she relaxed against him, resting her head on his shoulder. She seemed to be reveling in the power she wielded over him in this moment. In every moment, if he were to be completely honest with himself. Instinctively, his arms wrapped around her, holding her tight as though he cherished her. Orion was acting on instinct, confused by his own impulses, but too sated and content to fight them.

She was certainly worthy of desire and devotion; she was the most beautiful woman he had ever seen and seemed to be a force of nature—loyal, and bright, and passionate. But why this instant compulsion? Why did he feel suddenly as if he might die if this woman did not sleep beside him tonight?

The answer hit him with sudden and startling force, and the memory of the strange pull he had felt when he first saw her came rushing back to the front of his mind. He shouldn't get ahead of himself—it wasn't possible—but if by some miracle he was right, his whole world was about to turn on its head.

After long moments, Evienne shifted off of his lap and stood. She was flushed, her hair tousled, but she smiled at him.

"Thank you for such a lovely evening, professor," she said with a touch of laughter in her voice.

"The pleasure is all mine, High Sangviere. Will I see you tomorrow?" He asked, unable to mask the desperation that tinged his voice. He rose from the sofa and stood before her, looking down at her upturned face.

"Maybe," Evienne said, clearly holding back a laugh.

He offered his arm, and she took it. Orion couldn't bear to be parted from her just yet, so he asked, "May I walk you to your room?"

She nodded, and they made their way out of the library and through the halls of the palace.

"Will you be able to find your way back to your own room from here?" Evienne asked when they arrived at her door.

"I'm sure I'll be fine." He smiled down at her.

"Goodnight, Orion," she said over her shoulder as she slipped into her room. He watched her go, and all he could think was that after this, after tonight; he would never be the same again.

Chapter Eleven

Evienne had barely slept, her mind fixated on puzzling out what had happened between her and Orion. She had had trysts before, ones that burned as hot and started just as quickly, but those had always just been lust. What she had done with Orion last night had made her *feel* in a way that was acutely uncomfortable. She wasn't sure if she could trust herself to be that close to anyone again. Her willingness to love had ruined her the last time she let a partner in.

She enjoyed spending time with Orion—and she was obviously attracted to him—but he was only here for a month. She knew, logically, that nothing could really come of it. That's why she had jumped into it without any real hesitation last night. She found herself wanting to be open with him, despite how hard it felt. The way he had finished at just the taste of her, it had been so vulnerable. She didn't think he could have fabricated that. His interest in her, at least sexually, was genuine, and she wanted more. Normally she would balk at the idea of anything long-term, but now she found herself disappointed that it wasn't a possibility with him. That disappointment terrified her.

She was so wrapped up in her own thoughts that she slammed into someone as she rounded a corner on her way to the library for tea with Cecelia. She really had to start watching where she was going; twice in one week was bad even for her. Before she could recover, her mind was suddenly flooded with images; an old man with white hair was speaking to her. No—someone else—but she was seeing through their eyes.

"I suppose go if you must," the richly dressed old man almost grunted the words.

"I believe it is important for us to represent Beitar at this celebration; we have remained isolated too long," Solon's voice answered.

"Do as you see fit, Lord Solon. I give you my leave," the old man answered lazily.

She realized that the other man she was seeing had a crown upon his head; he must be Beitar's King. It had been surprising to her that Solon and Orion had been allowed to come at all given Beitar's policy of isolation, but she was even more confused now having seen their King's nonchalant attitude. Evienne drifted back into her own mind, only to find herself staring up into Solon's handsome face.

"Oh, Solon, I'm so sorry for my clumsiness. You must forgive me, my mind was elsewhere," Evienne said as she righted herself.

"No need to apologize. I only hope you are unhurt?" Solon asked, concern written on his face.

"Perfectly fine, if a bit embarrassed," Evienne answered with a nervous chuckle.

"Very well. May I escort you to wherever it is you are headed?"

"Oh no, I wouldn't trouble you. I am off to see my friend Cecelia, one of the librarians."

"Ah, to the library then. I wish you a pleasant visit with your friend, and I will see you later this afternoon for the garden party, yes?" Solon's smile lit up his face, ever the gentleman.

"Yes, I will see you then. Apologies again, Solon." Evienne took off walking briskly toward the library, attempting to get a handle on her thoughts.

Incidents like this had happened before, almost always by accident. She never told anyone about her mishaps. She had been tempted to tell her mentor, Hestia, a retired Sangviere, but decided it wasn't worth sharing. Her episodes were almost certainly some form of magic, but it was unheard of for an Ichornian to have anything other than the blood magic that was their natural gift. In fact, she had never heard of anyone in Domhan na Rùin having this sort of magic.

Unknown and unwieldy magic wasn't something that was accepted in Ichorna; they had worked too long and too hard to seem less threatening to the rest of the world. She was afraid that telling anyone about this ability could have serious consequences, especially since it was something she couldn't control.

Strange things had happened over the years, and the memories danced through her mind as she made her way toward the library. A vision of a moment in time when Evienne had physical contact with a person, or sometimes when she simply focused her attention on someone for too long. It had happened enough times for her to realize that these were people's memories she was seeing, moments of their lives she was stealing glimpses of. They always ended up being important somehow; it was like her magic knew she *needed* those seconds from the people around her.

The most troubling incident by far had taken place when Evienne was twenty years old. She and Cecelia had been out to one of the taverns in the city and had too much wine. They were young and unfamiliar with all of the dangers the world held for young women in a big city.

Evienne had gone to pay their bill, and Cecelia had wandered outside into the night air to wait. When Evienne stepped outside, however, she did not see her friend. She only heard Cecelia's scream from an alley nearby. Evienne rushed over, horrified at the sight of her friend pinned against the alley wall.

A man loomed over her, grinning to himself. Evienne could see evidence of his intentions outlined in his pants. Cecelia was almost unconscious as the man held her throat in his massive hand. He began to unfasten his belt, and that was enough to snap Evienne into action.

All of her Sangviere training left her mind in her rage, but she felt the zing of a different power rushing through her veins as she stared at the man. She screamed her fury as she closed her fists, and the man's grip on Cecelia faltered. Cecelia fell to the ground unconscious, and the man turned his horrified gaze to Evienne.

She watched as wrinkles appeared across his skin, his

posture hunching, his eyes clouding. He screamed, and his teeth were yellow and brittle. The unknown power continued to flow from Evienne, and the attacker disintegrated into dust on the wind as Evienne watched.

Cecelia never suspected what happened that night, but Evienne knew she had stolen every moment of that vile man's life. She had never felt guilty for what happened, only confused and overwhelmed by the power she had wielded.

Evienne was usually able to suppress thoughts of these strange occurrences, but they lingered in her mind now.

When the door to Cecelia's study came into view, she was surprised to find it shut. She knocked and called out, "Cece, it's me. I thought we could chat for a while?" No answer. It wasn't like Cecelia to be away from her study at this time of day, but she supposed her friend must be taking time away from work. Evienne hoped she was visiting with Jac.

With a sigh, Evienne turned away and decided to spend her free time buried in a good book instead. She headed for the section of the library that housed all of the folktales from across Domhan na Rùin, determined to relax for a while before the events picked back up that afternoon.

Chapter Twelve

Orion let the scent of books wash over him. He hadn't slept, his mind racing at the possibilities. He couldn't stop thinking of her, of what they had done. He had found release at the taste of her on his fingers; it had been ecstasy. None of his previous lovers ever had him falling over himself this way. He was determined to find answers. He had come here to do what he could to save his people, but he was worried now the stakes may be more personal.

He had spoken with a librarian upon arriving, asking for directions to any resources on Beitar or its history. Even a general history of magic in Domhan na Rùin could be helpful for his purposes. He had kept his inquiry general so as not to raise any suspicions; he was a Professor, after all. It was only natural he would be interested in the Ichornian royal collection.

The librarian had directed him to an aisle of the stacks that was toward the back of the library, near where he and Evienne had been the night prior. Of course the section would be near that couch. He swore he could still smell the scent of her on the air. He had been warring with thoughts of Evienne since he first saw her. He knew his suspicions about what she may be to him couldn't be confirmed without his magic. He should ignore it and stay focused—or, at the very least, let himself enjoy Evienne's company knowing that in a few weeks, he would never see her again.

He began to peruse the section the librarian had led him to. He did find a few more general works, but very little on the magic of the Tuanadair specifically. The sections about the other nations of Domhan na Rùin were more robust. He sighed in frustration; he had hoped this would be an easy place to start.

The destruction of the ancient library in Beitar was not a well known point of historical knowledge across the continent, and their King wanted to keep it that way. Apparently that, too, made them vulnerable. His people had not forgotten what was done when Ichorna's king had come to claim his royal bride two hundred years ago; the way they laid waste to Beitar's cultural heritage. This—in addition to the bizarre customs surrounding the consorts sent to Ichorna over the centuries—was why Solon and Orion were so suspicious of Ichorna.

Over the years, they had both noticed how their King stifled anyone asking questions or pushing to find the reason behind the disappearing magic. He seemed as indifferent to it as his predecessors had been. They simply ignored the problem, focusing instead on maintaining an iron grip on the people of Beitar—on keeping them secluded from the rest of the world.

None of it made sense, but people were too afraid to

seek out answers without the King's blessing. Orion and Solon had been discussing their concerns quietly for years, and the millennium celebration had presented them with the opportunity to act.

Orion pulled out a book titled *Aphana: Heart of the Sea* and began to flip through its pages. It was filled with beautiful illustrations of an underwater city and chapters detailing the ways Aphanians could wield their magic. His eyes scanned the words, but his mind still drifted.

He and Solon were here for one reason, and that was to find out if and how Ichorna had been siphoning or suppressing Beitar's magic. It had started so subtly that many hadn't noticed for years after that first Ichornian King had taken his Beitaran bride. By the time the third consort left to wed his Ichornian King, the changes to Beitar's magic were severe.

Beitar was an ancient nation of shifters—Tuanadair—with powerful magic and a deep connection to the natural world. They honored balance, and found the animal part of their souls to be a perfect compliment to their human natures.

There were many stories of what life had been like while the magic was alive amongst their people. Now, it was nothing more than folk tales, but Orion knew there was truth to them.

Stories of the Contrapensae, immortals chosen by forgotten gods who protected the world's balance, were told to Beitar's children at bedtime. They were raised dreaming of the powerful heroes, hoping that they would appear and set this imbalance in their world to right.

Orion set the book on water wielders back on the shelf and continued his search. After a moment, his eyes fell on what appeared to be a children's book—*The Tuanadair Prince.*

The book was small, and very old. Orion had heard the story before, but he still found himself opening the tiny volume. It told the story of a Tuanadair who searched far and wide through Beitar to find his Còmhanam. Though Còmhanam were said to be a soul's perfect match, they were rare. So rare, in fact, that a true mated pair only found each other about once every hundred years. The prince was determined though, and he found his match one day as he was out riding through one of the snowy valleys of Beitar.

A majestic stag, lithe and strong, had stopped to stare at the prince from across a clearing. The stag was unnaturally large, so the prince recognized it as a fellow Tuanadair. He knew the moment he saw the shifter that he belonged to them.

The pair met secretly in the woods then, running through the snow and pines in a world of their own—the stag and the prince in his shifted hare form. Despite the instant connection between them, they gave each other time to let love and devotion grow. When the time was right, the prince brought his partner back to their capital city of Sgùrdruid and introduced them to his parents, the king and queen.

The stag Tuanadair was a common-born blacksmith, though, and the king and queen did not approve of this match for their son. They turned their son's Còmhanam out of the castle, and the prince began to go mad with grief. Every night the stag found a way onto the castle grounds and waited near their love's window, hoping for their separation to end.

Weeks passed, and the pair was wasting away—the prince in his tower and the stag waiting patiently outside. When it seemed their story may end in tragedy, Aosda, the wild god of the Tuanadair, appeared to the king and queen, admonishing them for keeping a pair of his perfectly matched Còmhanam apart. Aosda himself set the prince free of his tower prison and saw the lovers reunited, and all of Beitar then rejoiced that their prince had found his soulmate—his Còmhanam.

Orion's chest felt tight as he finished reading the fairytale and closed the book. It was this particular folktale that had consumed his thoughts for the past fourteen hours or so. The irony of finding it just now in this library of all places was not lost on him.

There were details on Còmhanam bonds in some of the oldest books in Beitar's rebuilt library, but they dated to just after the first Ichornian arranged royal marriage took place. Orion had studied these writings knowing that the information in them was likely true, but irrelevant given the loss of Beitar's magic.

An instant pull, both physical and emotional, was noted as the most pronounced sign of a Còmhanam bond. It was said mated pairs would feel inexplicably comfortable around one another, and would find a seemingly impossible degree of pleasure in closeness with their Còmhanam.

There were also more… anatomical consequences of the bond, regardless of the Tuanadair's animal form. Orion didn't dwell on the long list of possibilities. It only mattered if he had access to his magic, which he—like every other Tuanadair of his generation—had never had.

He tried to put all thoughts of Còmhanam from his mind as he perused the shelves. However, he was unsuccessful after only two minutes because he *felt* her approaching.

As sure as the sun hung in the sky, Evienne d'Auclair walked briskly past the end of the aisle he was standing in. She moved in a flurry of green velvet, her skirt swishing as she strode across his field of vision. Before he could stop himself, he called out to her.

"Evienne, you seem in quite the rush. Is all well with you?"

He couldn't quite keep the hint of desperation out of his voice. He was relieved to see her after she had consumed his thoughts so wholly. He had the strange compulsion to ensure her welfare, to see that her needs were met.

"Orion," she said, her cheeks flushing to match the rosy shade of her lips. "Yes, I am well." She worried her lip and glanced away, feeling what Orion assumed was some awkwardness at seeing him after their encounter last night.

"Good, I am glad of it," he said, unable to stop himself from smiling at her.

As he looked at her, Orion realized that he had the urge to tell Evienne about the true reason for his trip to Ichorna. Could he trust her? She seemed to care deeply for others; he doubted she knew what he suspected Ichorna had been doing to the people of Beitar all of these generations. Even he didn't know the full extent of what was occurring; he knew their magic was dwindling, and that it had begun around the time of the first royal union, but he did not know how the magic was stolen or for what purpose. At this point it was purely conjecture, but would Evienne put helping others above her loyalty to Ichorna?

To truly find answers, he would need someone who had been here in Ichorna to observe, knowingly or not, what may be happening. His longing to confide in her, to trust her, further stoked his suspicions around who she may be to him, no matter how impossible it seemed. He supposed he would never know for certain.

He reigned in his feelings, opting instead to ask, "Would you like to sit with me and read for a while before the garden party this afternoon?"

Evienne's brows rose in surprise, but she quickly covered the expression with a smile.

"I'd love to. I was planning to see my friend, but it seems she is busy this morning," she answered, a wicked gleam forming in her eye as she added, "Were you planning to sit here?"

She gestured to the couch they sat on last night as he touched her; it was awash in a warm orange glow from the fire nearby. His arousal washed over him in a wave as she stood there smirking at him, waiting for his response.

"Yes, in fact. Should we call for some tea?" He answered, smiling right back at her. Orion knew he was playing a dangerous game with a dangerous woman, but he was loving every second of it.

Chapter Thirteen

Evienne knew she was flirting with Orion as she challenged him to sit with her in the very spot of their tryst the previous night, but if it was a means to talk more with him one-on-one…perhaps she could glean some valuable information. She told herself she was doing all of this just to make Orion trust her, open up to her. But a quieter voice in her mind whispered her true motivations; she couldn't look too closely at them or she would find herself poised for heartbreak.

"What brings you to the library today, Professor?"

"Well, as you may have guessed, I do love books a great deal," he answered, a dimple showing on his left cheek. Evienne cursed internally—she couldn't get enough of his dimples.

She rolled her eyes at his sarcasm. "I meant, are you working on anything in particular? Any research questions to delve into while you're here?"

"I was just reading a Beitaran folktale, actually. I heard the story told as a child, but I had never seen a written version. It was lovely," he said. She could feel the tinge of sadness in his voice.

He continued, "What sorts of stories do they tell Ichornian children at bedtime?"

Evienne was surprised at his question; she had not thought of bedtime stories in a long, long time.

"They're all sort of..." she thought back to the tales her quiet mother had told her, of noble Sangviere that vowed to use their magic for good, of brilliant inventors who made the world better with their creations, and happy farmers who made Ichorna's golden fields flourish. Thinking of her mother still gave her a pang of sadness followed swiftly by the cool nothingness of indifference that she had fostered to protect herself all these years. Her father had been the one to send her away, yes, but her mother had not raised a hand to stop him.

"They're all about how careful we have to be with our magic and how great Ichorna is, really." Evienne said thoughtfully. "Beitar chooses to be more closed off from the world, but Ichorna was scorned for so long because of our magic that our monarchs—and by extension the people—will do just about anything to be accepted."

"Believe me, Beitar's isolation is not a popular choice with its people," Orion said. Evienne nearly drew back in surprise at his admission. The only other Beitaran Evienne had ever met was bound into silence by the Beitaran king's magic; she had never heard someone speak candidly about the situation there.

"Really?" She asked, hoping Orion would go on.

He sighed and said, "Yes—and my life could be forfeit

for saying so. Our King is the only one of us to have kept his magic all these years. We don't know why; some deeper connection with it in the royal line most likely. Everyone in Beitar lives in fear of him. His father before him was no better. We are kept close and kept silent, all living under his absolute rule."

Evienne was shocked. She never would have guessed such a thing. Now she was even more curious about how Solon and Orion were here—not just for the benefit of Queen Aldith, but because she genuinely wanted to know their story.

She supposed now was as good a time as any to just ask. "How are you here, then?"

Orion stared at her for a long moment, as if he was trying to see straight into her soul. When he blinked, she felt it in slow motion—like that one second was going to shape the course of her life. His gaze reconnected with hers and he spoke. "Our king grows careless in his old age; he agreed to let us come for the frivolous reasons we put forward to him."

He hadn't really told her anything, but she could infer that the true reason for their journey, then, was not frivolous. She realized that he had decided to trust her, to some extent. Guilt ricocheted through her, and another thought quickly followed; she wanted to earn his trust, not for Aldith's benefit, but for herself. She cared that Orion trusted her, and she wanted him to trust her too, even if he shouldn't. Evienne didn't want to hurt Orion.

She knew then that she didn't actually want to know the real reason for his presence here. If she didn't know, she couldn't tell.

"Well I'm certainly glad for his odd lapse in strictness; it's been a pleasure to get to know you. And I have to say, I'm grateful to hear a more personal account of life in Beitar. All we get here are the very brief official correspondences, and they're nearly identical each year. I am very sorry for the plight of your people; the loss of magic is a tragedy on its own, but suffering under a tyrant's indifference to the situation must be very hard," Evienne said.

Orion nodded slightly before he spoke, more quietly now. "In truth, I am not sure how much longer our people can go on without their spirits breaking. Being disconnected from our animal souls so completely can cause some to waste away. There are physical consequences to being cut off from the magic of Domhan na Rùin, and I believe we are close to seeing the effects through sickness and, eventually, loss of Beitaran lives."

Evienne felt unbearable tightness in her chest. It was wrong for so many people to be without something so integral—she knew it must feel akin to suffocating. Tears stung her eyes as she thought about it, and she looked into Orion's face again. The same pain was mirrored on his features. She realized that Orion's purpose here was likely linked to the mystery of their dwindling magic as Queen Aldith had suspected. How could seeking to help their people be the great evil Aldith was worried about? She would not hinder him in finding the answers he sought; in fact, she desperately wanted to help.

When she spoke, her voice was rough with the effort of holding back her tears. "Is there truly no way to discover what has happened? What caused this horrible loss?"

Orion averted his eyes and stared into the fire for a long moment. "Time will tell, I suppose."

And with that, the spell of this quiet corner of the library lifted. A palace attendant entered the alcove holding a tray set with two delicate tea cups and a pot of floral tea. Evienne collected herself, adjusting her position on the sofa and blinking away the tears that had threatened to fall. The attendant set the tray on a small table and smiled briefly at Evienne before leaving again.

Orion took the pot of tea and poured each of them a cup. The dark, wet leaves gathered in the dainty silver strainers on the cup as he poured. The scent of jasmine calmed Evienne's heart, and she smiled at Orion. She hoped her gratitude for his openness showed on her face as he looked back at her. His startling green eyes crinkled at the corners.

They were silent then, both turning their attention to their respective books. Evienne stared at the page, but her mind churned and she did not comprehend a single word she read.

Chapter Fourteen

Léhiona surveyed the garden, her exhaustion a palpable thing pulling her down. She had been overseeing the preparations for the garden party all afternoon, and now she wasn't sure she would even feel well enough to attend.

She went over to the table where a massive glass bowl of lemonade now sat and used the ladle to fill a cup for herself. Tiny violets and other edible flowers floated on the surface, and she stared and stared at the way they moved around the bowl as she took a sip from her cup. The sour tang of the lemons and the sweet kiss of sugar had her closing her eyes in pleasure.

"Léhiona, I thought I might find you here," Sylvain's voice cut through her fog of exhaustion and she started.

"Sylvain, you startled me!" She said, setting her glass down next to her on the table.

He smiled at her and ladled himself a cup of lemonade, sidling up to her where she still rested a hip against the table.

"Have you been to see the healers yet?" He asked, cutting straight to his point—in a kind way. Léhiona looked at him sidelong.

"No, I've been busy! And I'm sure it's nothing."

"Well, better to be *sure* sure. Can I escort you there now?" He asked, offering an arm.

"Don't be silly, I can't go now! The garden party will be starting soon, and what kind of hostess would I be if I'm not here?" She said, a bit indignant. Though, her head did feel rather light.

He gave her a skeptical look, as if he could hear her thoughts.

"Please, sister, just humor me. We'll be back before anyone notices you're gone," he offered his arm again.

Léhiona sighed her resignation and took the arm he offered. They made their way through the gardens toward the steps that led up to the palace. As they approached the steps, she noticed black edging her vision. "Sylvain, I…" she began, pausing their progress.

Then everything went dark.

Chapter Fifteen

After a quiet cup of tea and a lot of not-reading, Evienne and Orion parted ways to prepare for that afternoon's official event—a garden party.

One would think the late autumn weather would have saved them from any outdoor events, but unfortunately Ichorna was just temperate enough to make it possible. Though, instead of airy linen dresses and sun hats, everyone would likely be in lush wool coats.

Evienne chose to wear her blood red uniform to the event. It was unlike her, but for some reason, it felt right for the day. She slipped on the black leggings and long-sleeved black top before buckling the knee-high boots into place. She then put on her red coat, fastened the buttons, and added the silver gladiolus blossom pin that denoted her rank as High Sangviere to the lapel of her jacket.

As soon as she descended the palace steps into the garden, Evienne could feel the eyes of others on her. It made her feel powerful for once, instead of insecure.

She found Orion's sea green eyes in the crowd. They were locked on her, and even from where she stood above him on the stairs, she could see his jaw flex as he took her in. If he kept this up, she would have quite the ego by the time this party was over.

She got to the bottom of the stairs and caught sight of Cecelia talking animatedly with a tall, pleasant-looking man with light brown curls—Jac. Solon stood with them, conversing easily. It appeared he had made some friends. She made her way over to them, grabbing a goblet of wine from a server as she passed.

"Well hello, *High Sangviere*, you certainly know how to make an entrance!" Cecelia laughed as she hugged Evienne in greeting. "You remember Lord Jac from Wellsah?"

"I do indeed! It is very good to see you again, Jac," Evienne smiled at the man as he inclined his head to her. He smiled broadly, his countenance open and warm.

"It is wonderful to see you again, Evienne. I hope you have been able to relax and enjoy the festivities a bit?"

"Oh yes, you know Cecelia wouldn't let me get away with working this *whole* time," Evienne laughed. "And I see you've met Lord Solon! You've found the best people at the party, Solon; you have excellent taste."

She noticed Jac's gaze shift to a point over her shoulder, and she turned to see what had caught his attention, still smiling. Orion was approaching, only five feet or so behind her when she met his eyes. He looked at her as he closed the distance and smiled as he came to a stop at her side. He inclined his head to Cecelia and Jac as he spoke.

"Hello there. I am Professor Orion Doehlan. Evienne, would you mind introducing me to your friends?"

Orion's face was relaxed, a friendly smile gracing his plush lips. Evienne was so wrapped up in staring at him that she waited a moment too long before responding.

"Yes, of course, Professor. This is my dear friend Cecelia Chandelle, the Head Librarian here in Ichorna. And this is Lord Jac Yarwood of Wellsah," Evienne gestured to her friends with a smile. Cecelia caught her eye with her brows raised, and Evienne gave her a small wink.

"It's wonderful to meet you, Professor. Have you been enjoying your time here thus far?" Jac asked.

"I certainly have! It is rare that a Beitaran is given the opportunity to travel, as I'm sure you know, so I am attempting to make the most of my time here," Orion answered, then took a sip of his wine.

"We are very lucky indeed. I've been particularly enjoying the variety and quality of pastries available here," Solon added.

Evienne saw a flash of blonde hair in her peripheral vision just as she noted Cecelia's eyes widening in horror. Before anyone else could speak, none other than Dominique Malinois cleared her throat as she stepped up to join their group. She dropped into a curtsey next to Orion.

"Lady Malinois, a pleasure to see you again," Jac said. Cecelia grimaced and gave him a look, which he noted, and seemed confused.

"You as well, Lord Yarwood. And I believe these are our Beitaran guests—my name is Dominique Malinois. You are?" She extended her hand toward Orion, expecting him to kiss it, but instead, he bowed slightly at the waist. "I am Professor Orion Doelan; the pleasure is mine. And this is Lord Solon Lùtair of the Glenkoe province."

Evienne watched the whole exchange with her breath held. She was glad Orion hadn't taken the hand Dominique offered, for whatever ridiculous reason. She wasn't sure what she would have done if he had, but she felt incredibly on edge. Dominique seemed to take genuine pleasure in humiliating Evienne by the end of their relationship, and that hadn't changed in the years since their divorce. Her opportunities to be vicious had simply dwindled.

"So I heard," Dominique said with a laugh. Her eyes glinted with joyful malice as she continued, "A little bird told me that you and our very own pretty High Sangviere were seen quitting the library last night in a bit of a... disheveled state." Evienne couldn't believe what she was hearing; Cecelia's mouth was hanging open. Jac's brows were at his hairline. Solon scowled. Evienne couldn't see Orion's face, but she was prepared to melt straight into the ground and live out her life as a worm if it meant this interaction could end.

Before anyone could respond, Dominique continued speaking with a laugh. "Well, I hope she's improved since our divorce at least. You should experience the *best* Ichorna has to offer while you're here after all, Professor." She finished with a vicious smile. "Enjoy the party," she added, turning away with another laugh.

Evienne thought she might simply perish. She knew

Dominique was petty and horrible, but this was truly low even for her. She suddenly felt too close to everyone.

"Excuse me," she said with an attempt at a smile. She turned quickly and fled into the vast arboretum that surrounded the gardens proper.

Chapter Sixteen

Orion watched as Evienne disappeared into the crowd milling around the garden. This snake of a woman—her former wife, apparently—had clearly shaken her. Orion struggled to contain his anger over how she had treated Evienne. He turned to look at Cecelia, who had a deep scowl on her face.

"What a horrible woman," she hissed.

"I was not expecting such rudeness from someone of her standing; a surprise indeed," Jac mused.

"Is she always that awful?" Solon asked Cecelia.

"Unfortunately, yes," she answered with a sigh.

"Excuse me," Orion said, bowing his head to the group before striding after Evienne. He knew he couldn't just let her go; she had clearly been upset. He found himself wanting to comfort her, to ensure she was alright.

He followed the path she had taken into the vast wooded area outside the manicured, eerily perfect lawn that hosted the party. This part of the garden was natural and full of seemingly untamed life.

He found her on one of the forested paths, surrounded by hundred year old trees and mossy ground. Red and yellow leaves caught the fading rays of the sun, and the sound of songbirds floated on the air.

"Evienne, are you alright?" He asked as he approached. She was flushed and breathing faster than normal.

"Yes, thank you. I am sorry you had to see that."

"Why would you apologize for the rudeness of another? You did nothing wrong."

She closed her eyes and took a deep, steadying breath.

"That is not exactly how I imagined you learning about my past," Evienne said with a nervous laugh. "I honestly didn't expect it to come up at all, and I don't know why it is bothering me so much that you know now. It's not as if whatever is between us can last beyond this month."

Evienne's words sent a jolt of sadness through Orion, but he ignored the feeling for now. He already knew he wanted more with her, but now wasn't the time to discuss it.

"She had no right to speak to you that way, but please do not be embarrassed on my account. You don't owe me any answers, but I am here to listen if you need me."

Evienne nodded and looked at him then, shame written across her features though she was clearly trying to stifle it—it broke his heart.

"Dominique and I separated three years ago. Our relationship was one of the darkest times of my life."

"Thank you for sharing with me, Evienne. Would you like to walk?"

Orion offered her an arm. He wasn't all that surprised that she had been married before; she was an incredible woman who had lived a full life. He was glad, selfishly, that it hadn't been the right fit for her; that they had a chance now.

Evienne accepted his offered arm, and they started down the lovely forested path in the late afternoon light. As they walked in silence, the urge to tell Evienne everything about the true reason for his trip to Ichorna returned in full force. Her honesty had him wanting to confide in her even more. Every moment he spent with her made him feel more sure that she would prioritize what was right over her loyalty to Ichorna. He was sure her curiosity, at the very least, would have her eager to help him find answers.

Now that he was here, he realized that to truly find answers, he would need someone who had been here in Ichorna to observe—knowingly or not—what may be happening. He and Solon had discussed the possibility of finding someone on the inside to help them in their search; perhaps Evienne was the right one for the job. His longing to be open with her, to trust her, further stoked his suspicions around who she may be to him, no matter how impossible it seemed. He would never know without his magic though, and he felt the ache of sadness at the thought.

He suddenly found he had made his decision. Caution and withdrawal had not gotten his people any closer to restoring their magic. He had an opportunity here to make things right, and he would trust his intuition.

"Evienne, there is something I'd like to share with you, if you are willing to hear it," he began, pausing their stroll. "Do you believe we are quite alone here?"

Evienne cast her gaze around the forest, listening. In the next breath, she pressed the tip of the bladed ring she wore to her palm, and the cold, salty smell of her magic filled his senses.

"We are quite alone, but just in case, I've just shielded us. I am happy to hear whatever it is you have to discuss." She assessed him openly, her curiosity apparent on her face.

"You must know that there is a reason Solon and I have come to Ichorna that runs deeper than attending the celebration," he began. She blinked and nodded her understanding, tilting her head slightly to the side in an invitation to continue.

"I would like to share our purpose with you in confidence. I have not known you long, Evienne, but it is apparent to me that you possess a noble heart, and a kind spirit. You have a love for your people that is admirable, and I would like to believe your empathy extends to all the peoples of Domhan na Rùin." He paused, waiting for her response.

"I am flattered by your assessment of my character; I should hope your trust in my integrity is not misplaced." Her eyes softened as she spoke, and she stepped toward him slightly.

"Solon and I are here to find what answers we can about the disappearance of the Tuanadair's magic. I shared with you that it has now fully gone. We can trace its slow draining to the first royal union between Ichorna's King Bastille and his consort, a Beitaran noblewoman named Alina, two hundred years ago. We do not know how the siphoning continues to take place, or for what purpose, but we believe it has been Ichorna's doing. The timing cannot be only coincidence. I am here to research and make some sense of our plight if I can."

He held her gaze, hoping she could see the truth of his soul—that his intentions were noble, that he sought to help his own people just as she served hers each day. Evienne's mouth opened slightly in shock; she was unable to keep her surprise from her features. She blinked slowly, clearly processing all he had just told her. Orion second-guessed himself for a moment, but mostly he felt relieved. He wanted desperately to find her an ally, to be closer with her.

"If what you say is true, Ichorna has committed, and continues to commit, a grave injustice against your people, Orion. As difficult as this is to hear, and as impossible as I hope it to be, I cannot dismiss what you've told me. I just hope it is some kind of misunderstanding." She raised her hands to press against her temples, her sadness, shock, and worry clouding the air between them.

"I understand this is a heavy accusation to level, and I hope it is not true; but you understand I must search for answers. My people deserve the truth of what's been done to them," he said, his tone soft. Orion knew this was a difficult thing to ask her to hear out.

Evienne turned her delicate round face to meet his gaze with her honey-colored eyes. "I will think on it."

Orion nodded. He wished her answer had been an immediate yes, but he respected what a significant decision it would be for her. Her thoughtfulness gave him hope, but his anxiety at having to trust her was rising. Somewhere in the back of his mind, he knew he had nothing to fear from her; that did not, however, make the rest of his racing thoughts any calmer. He supposed he would have to wait and see if she chose her duty or the truth.

Chapter Seventeen

Léhiona awoke to the scent of cloves—she was in her own bed, with a warm hand wrapped around her own. She opened her eyes to see Aldith's worried features hovering over her. She took a deep breath.

"What happened?" She rasped.

"You fainted, dearest," Aldith answered gently, stroking Léhiona's hand with her thumb.

"Oh, I'm so sorry; I think I'm feeling better though, we really should get to the party."

"No, no, you're going to rest. Besides, the garden party ended an hour ago. It was lovely, and you were missed, but everything went well. I'll call for some tea," Aldith said, patting her hand as she shifted off the side of the bed where she'd been sitting.

"I'm so glad Sylvain was with me, Aldith. I don't know what would have happened without him," she said, moving slowly to a sitting position.

"Yes, it was very lucky he was there with you."

"He wants me to go see the healers about my exhaustion. I suppose this proves his point," Léhiona said begrudgingly.

"If it will make you feel better, you should speak with them—though I'm sure you're just tired from all the celebration preparations. You've been running yourself ragged to get everything planned," Aldith said from the other side of the room.

"That's what I told Sylvain! I'm sure you're right," she answered.

Aldith returned with a tray that one of the palace staff had brought; a pot of tea and a bowl of clear broth. Both wafted steamy tendrils into the air. She sat the tray on the nightstand, and Léhiona found herself feeling grateful that her wife was her one comfort in this impossible situation that was her life. She had been so frightened when her father had told her of the arranged marriage when she was a girl, but being married to Aldith had been better than she ever could have hoped.

Back in Beitar, her family had been of noble blood, but her marriage elevated their status with the king. She knew bearing this burden had meant a better life for her family. It was difficult, but Aldith's love, and the family she made for herself here, made it bearable.

Léhiona sipped the broth while Aldith sat with her and had a cup of tea. When she finished and set the bowl aside, Aldith leaned over her and kissed her, cupping her cheek gently with one hand.

"You should get some sleep, dearest. We have a long few weeks ahead of us," Aldith said with a small smile.

"Promise you'll come to bed soon, too?"

"I promise," Aldith said and kissed Léhiona's hand before departing, leaving her alone with her thoughts.

Chapter Eighteen

Evienne spent the next day drifting through the motions of her life, the seconds flitting by while her mind was a tempest of worry and questions.

Aldith had suspected an ulterior motive for the Beitarans' visit, but she was certain she never could have guessed this would be it. Surely there was some other reason the magic had disappeared; the connection to Ichorna must be purely coincidence, right?

But Aldith's suspicion of the Beitaran's motives left an uneasy feeling in Evienne's stomach. If Ichorna had nothing to hide, why be so suspicious of a people who had been their peaceful neighbors for a thousand years? She had thought it odd that Aldith was so harsh about the possibility of the Beitarans seeking aid.

Evienne's intuition rarely led her astray, and for some reason it was now urging her to hold her tongue to the queens about Orion's confession. Surely nothing would come of it, and she could report it to them in a few days when his suspicions proved to be unfounded. More than that, the thought of betraying Orion's confidence made her feel physically ill.

Orion and Solon were tied up for the afternoon at some sort of diplomatic luncheon, so Evienne took the opportunity to head out into the city for a walk. She rarely had time to just stroll these days, so it was a welcome reprieve.

She left the palace through the side entrance, an unassuming door for deliveries that was located on the lower level near the kitchens. Evienne crossed a small courtyard and nodded to the guards stationed at the gate as she moved into the city.

It opened to a tiny, winding alley, less crowded than the main thoroughfare that led to the front gate. Evienne preferred to slip out this way when she could; it was quieter. She enjoyed the forgotten corners of the city—they gave her time and space to think.

She meandered through the maze of streets, taking moments here and there to admire the vignettes the city offered her. The afternoon sun sent a pinprick of light bouncing off a deep violet window; a tangle of crisp dried leaves, loose and caught swirling in the breeze, scraping against the pavement; the sweet smell of fresh, warm bread on the air.

Soon, her winding path brought her to a busier street, and she looked up into the open blue sky as the buildings parted to make space above her. Her gaze landed on the massive glass dome of the Centrale Lumine. It truly was a marvel—both the architecture and the energy produced within.

Ichorna was now known across Domhan na Rùin for

their technological advances, but what made their energy source so incredible was that it only required a few mages at a time to channel their magic into the system. The lights that kept Ichorna bright and the Rail system that kept them connected were both extremely efficient in their use of magical energy.

The Centrale Lumine was so large because of all the energy storage it housed. There was often a surplus. The facility was created primarily to store any overflow to be used in the case of emergency.

Evienne sighed and turned away from the Centrale Lumine, heading instead for her favorite tea shop in the city. After walking a few blocks, she pushed open the large wooden door of the shop and the tangy, herbal scent that greeted her made her close her eyes in pleasure. She stepped in and began to make her way toward a table, but a familiar voice called her name.

"Evienne, hello!" Lou called from a small table tucked behind the door, right by the window.

"Oh, Lou, what a lovely surprise! What are you doing here?"

"Had the day off, so I thought I'd stop by to get the best cup of tea in town," Lou answered with a smile. They gestured for Evienne to take the seat opposite them.

Evienne returned their smile and took a seat. "So how are things, Lou? Did everything go alright after I left Cambrie?"

"Oh of course, we had everything under control! You worry too much, you know?" Lou said with a laugh.

Evienne did know; she wished she could stop worrying,

actually. She laughed along as she waved over the waiter and ordered a pot of tea.

"Other than that, things have been… alright, I suppose. Something odd happened the other day," Lou said, concern creasing their brow. They continued, "I had a few of my mages pulled from my cohort this week, but no one will tell me why or where they've been reallocated."

Evienne felt herself frowning. "Who told you, though? Who gave the order?"

Lou rolled their eyes. "Dominique did; she came to tell me herself and then refused to answer any of my questions. Typical."

Lou knew the history between Evienne and Dominique, and they were the type of loyal friend that could hold a grudge on your behalf forever if needed. Evienne really liked them.

A flash of anger surged through Evienne at Lou's words. "What gives her the right? She's not in charge of assignments."

"Oh I know it—I planned to come talk to you tomorrow when I'm back on duty. I thought you handled all Sangviere assignments."

"I do! I do handle them," Evienne said, her indignation flaring. "I'll figure it out, Lou; thank you for telling me."

"Thanks, I appreciate it. I just can't imagine what Dominique is slinking around doing that she needs more mages," Lou said with a sigh.

"No idea, but I certainly intend to find out."

Chapter Nineteen

Evienne's anger had settled into a simmer by the time she returned to the palace to prepare for the evening's events. Dominique's meddling was a problem for tomorrow, so she tried to put it from her mind. Her thoughts drifted instead to that night in the library—when she had felt Orion's fingers pressing into her thighs. He had found his release at the taste of her on his fingers. She felt her core begin to throb at the memory of it; she had never felt more desired than in that moment, and she wanted more.

Evienne tried to get a handle on her thoughts as she stepped through the front doors of the Royal Concert Hall that was situated just outside the palace complex. Tonight's event was a performance of a symphonic work that had been composed in honor of the millennium celebration.

Evienne's black silk gown trailed slightly behind her. The skirt and bodice hugged all of her curves, leaving almost nothing to the imagination. The neckline was daringly low, and an emerald necklace dangled just above her cleavage. Her hair was pinned at the sides but fell in soft waves down her back. She knew she looked devastating; she had dressed for seduction. She intended to have a repeat of their night in the library.

As she strode through the lobby, a familiar lanky figure entered her field of vision.

"Sylvain!" She called out to the prince, who was currently talking animatedly with a tall brunette woman. He turned and saw her, waving her over with a grin.

"Evienne, hello! May I introduce Lady Cora Galanis, one of our esteemed visitors from Aphana." Sylvain gestured to the striking woman and Evienne bowed her head in greeting.

"Lady Galanis, lovely to meet you," Evienne greeted her with a smile.

"You as well, High Sangviere. I am looking forward to the mage tournament; will you be participating? Your skills are a bit of a legend in Aphana," Lady Galanis said. Her voice was open and rich, and her striking pale blue eyes were like nothing Evienne had ever seen.

"Oh, no I won't be participating personally, but you can expect a great show from many of my students at the Academie!" Evienne answered with a smile toward the Aphanian.

"I can't wait, I'm sure that alone will be well worth the long trip here," she said. "If you'll excuse me, I should rejoin my father so we can find our seats." The woman bowed, giving Sylvain a sidelong glance and a faint smile before she glided away.

Evienne raised her brows at the prince, who laughed nervously and blushed. She couldn't believe he was so flustered. They may yet see him find a partner to settle down with—or to travel the world with. Who could say?

"She's lovely," Evienne said, elbowing Sylvain a bit. He rolled his eyes, blush deepening, and changed the subject.

"Have you spoken privately with Léhiona lately?"

"I haven't, she's been so busy planning everything; why do you ask?" Evienne felt a pang of worry at the prince's question.

"She said she's been feeling more tired than usual, and yesterday she fainted before the garden party."

"She fainted?!" Evienne whisper-yelled.

"Yes. She's alright, but I wondered if she had spoken to you about it. I'm worried about her, Evi," Sylvain said. "If you talk with her, please try to convince her to go see the healers. Maybe she will listen if more of her loved ones are telling her."

"Of course, yes, I'll try to talk with her. Thank you for telling me," Evienne met his gaze just as the lights in the lobby flashed twice—their sign to take their seats.

"See you soon, and enjoy the concert," Sylvain said with a small wave as Evienne turned to climb the massive spiral staircase on one side of the lobby.

She made her way to one of the boxes that hung above the main seating area; it had been reserved for Solon and Orion as honored guests, but Orion had invited her to join them before they had parted this afternoon.

She entered the ornate, private box and smiled warmly at Solon as he stood to welcome her. He took her hand and pressed a light kiss to her knuckles.

"Good evening, Solon. Thank you for including me, in more ways than one." She let Solon guide her to a seat.

"Of course, we are more than glad of your company whenever you decide to join us," Solon answered, giving her a knowing smile.

Evienne found herself viewing Solon with new eyes now that she knew what he was risking for his people. She smiled back at him, her head tilted to hold his gaze. She hadn't decided to help them, though her heart begged her to. She empathized with their situation regardless. Just as Solon settled in his seat at the very front of the box, Orion parted the curtained entrance to the space and froze as he caught sight of Evienne.

She locked eyes with him and couldn't help but let her lips twist into the slightest smirk. He had kept her off balance since that first night he whispered in her ear; it was high time she returned the favor. Orion seemed to remember himself and moved to take the seat next to her just as the lights dimmed. The musicians made their way onto the stage.

Tuning notes rang out across the hall as Orion leaned toward her, whispering, "You are breathtaking."

She felt his words racing through her blood, her pulse kicking up at his closeness. She angled her head slightly, brushing her cheek across his lips. At the same time, she slid her hand onto his thigh and dug her fingers slightly into his lean muscle. The way the light from the stage cast shadows across their bodies revealed the effect she was having on him.

"I'm suddenly feeling *quite* unwell, Professor," Evienne

whispered against his ear. "I think I should be getting back. Do give my apologies to Solon at intermission." She leaned back just enough to watch Orion's face as she slid her hand further up his leg. She heard him draw in a sharp breath.

"I happen to be feeling rather under the weather as well; perhaps I will follow your sage example and rest this evening," he whispered, holding her gaze with his own heated stare.

Evienne smiled at him then, rising to leave. She knew he would follow her and seek her out back at the palace, but she turned at the curtain anyway and gave him a wink just to be sure.

EVIENNE sat in one of the plush chairs by the fireplace in her chambers, a glass of wine clasped in her fingers. She knew he would be here any moment; her fingers tingled in anticipation.

A soft knock sounded at the door, and Evienne rose, setting her glass on an end table. She pulled the door open a few inches and found Orion's perfectly cut jawline and piercing eyes on the other side. His lust hit her in a wave as she opened her door to him, and he entered the room. She closed the door behind him, and he grabbed her waist, pulling her to him.

The next moment his mouth was on hers, a moan escaping him. She ran her hands along his chest, pushing his black jacket off his shoulders. He broke their kiss to press his lips to her neck, moving up to her ear and gently biting.

She made a needy, whimpering sound before she began

undoing his black silk cravat. She let it float to the floor as she quickly began to unbutton his crisp white shirt. His cologne washed over her, the scents of cardamom and sandalwood dancing across her senses, and she felt every nerve ending in her body zing to life.

They were desperate, undressing each other from their finery, letting each item of clothing fall until she stood before him in nothing but her black lace undergarments and her emerald necklace.

"You're perfect," Orion whispered as he reverently ran his fingers down her neck, brushing over her breast, and continuing on to caress the gently curving planes of her abdomen. He hooked his finger into the band of her black lace panties and pulled them down over her full hips, letting them drop to the floor on top of her discarded gown.

Orion trailed his hand over her hip before sliding it to her throbbing center. He held her gaze as he slid his fingers through her wetness, and leaned down to catch her moan with his mouth as he kissed her again. He deftly released the clasp of her bra as he stroked her.

He wore only his tailored pants still, and Evienne found enough clarity in the haze of her pleasure to reach for the buttons around his waist. He let her unfasten them, and as they fell to the ground, she caught sight of him fully hard for her.

She groaned, pushing against Orion's chest gently with her palm. She guided him back toward her bed before giving him one last nudge to lay back. She stood between his legs as they draped over the end of the bed and just looked at him. He was magnificent; all sharp lines and clean angles. He was slender but corded with muscle, graceful and strong.

She let her hand drift to his erection. She could barely wrap her fingers all the way around him as she began to slowly stroke him. She watched the muscles of his abdomen tensing in response to her movements. He seemed just as affected by her touch as she was by his.

Standing there, with this beautiful man at her mercy, Evienne suddenly felt the overwhelming need to have him inside her.

She climbed onto the bed, kneeling astride him. "Is this what you want?" She asked him.

"I am desperate to be connected with you, love, please, let me feel you," Orion answered in a rush.

Evienne took him in her hand and positioned him at her entrance, not taking time to process his words other than "please". She was so wet, but she still had to rock her hips several times to work the head of his cock into her because of his size.

Orion stared at her as she worked to take him, his brow creased, soft moans escaping him with each movement she made.

Slowly, she sank further and further down his length, until he was finally fully seated inside her. The feeling was like nothing she had ever experienced; she could feel her orgasm at the edge of her mind just from taking all of him.

She waited a moment, adjusting, and then began to slowly circle her hips, keeping him deep inside her. She continued this torment and held her breath, letting the sound of Orion's soft moans settle into her mind. She kept going until she could barely stand it, when Orion put two of his fingers against her clitoris. The movement of her hips against his fingers was too much, and she came undone, her orgasm tearing through her. Her toes tingled as her cunt squeezed impossibly tighter around Orion's thick cock.

"Fuck," Orion whispered, panting, as he grabbed her hips and rolled them, staying deep inside her. "Should I pull out?" He asked, breathless.

"No, I use protection," she answered quickly.

He began moving then, rutting into her with short, deep thrusts that stroked her in exactly the right spot. He was going to make her finish again.

"Evienne, you feel so good; you're taking me so well."

"Orion, I'm going to come again," Evienne moaned.

Orion's thrusts became less even, and Evienne's pleasure crested. She pulsed around him, and the fit of his cock inside her somehow became even more intense. Just as Evienne noticed the tightness of his fit inside her increasing, Orion buried himself fully inside her and groaned as he came.

The sensation of his release was overwhelming; he was impossibly tight inside her, and she could feel the heat of his seed filling her. They were both breathless, staring at each other in the afterglow of their orgasms, when Orion moved to pull out—and a look of panic crossed his face.

"What is it, is something wrong?" Evienne asked, a pulse of worry rushing through her addled brain as she attempted to lean up on her elbows to peer at the place their bodies were still joined.

"No, no, I uh…" Orion eased himself down over her,

kissing her neck and smoothing a hand over her hair. His touch was gentle, but Evienne was confused.

"I've knotted you."

"You've *what*?!" Evienne couldn't keep the surprise from her voice. She wiggled her body, attempting to pull away from him, only to be met with resistance and another wave of pleasure that took her breath away.

"It's alright, just stay still. I'm so sorry, Evienne, I would have warned you if I thought this was a possibility," Orion said, gently rolling them onto their sides, every inch of movement sending shockwaves of sensation through Evienne's body. Orion moaned, and she felt more of his seed spilling into her.

"Please explain," she panted, now looking into his face fully. She knew she must look as horrified as she was feeling.

"Evienne, I—" Orion began, clearly lost for words. She watched him for a moment before she reached up to brush his hair away from his sweat-damp face. Her own worry was reflected in his features.

"This can only happen between Còmhanam."

Chapter Twenty

"Between *what?*" Evienne tried desperately to keep the panic from her voice, but she knew she must be failing miserably. They still lay side-by-side, locked together.

His face was mere inches from hers, and he wore an expression of worry tinged with awe. "Còmhanam are a topic of many of our folktales; I had no idea that the bond could be real, let alone without my magic. They were said to be so rare, only once a century did a pair of Tuanadair find their soulmate. I believed it was a myth perpetuated by disillusioned romantics, I didn't know…" Orion let his hand drift to cup her face as he spoke, his expression relaxing.

Evienne wished she could relax, but his words refused to fully process in her mind. "I'm so sorry, but what does any of that have to do with you being *stuck inside me* right now? It seems debating if it's real or not may not be worth our time at this point."

"The… anatomical differences we are currently experiencing are one of the main tells. Some Tuanadair have a knot that appears only when mating with their Còmhanam;

others, who have vaginal anatomy, apparently have an internal version that forms to achieve the same latching effect. The knot, in my case, has swollen so that we cannot separate—it is believed to function to increase the likelihood of conception." The worry was back on Orion's face as he explained.

Despite her slight panic, hearing him talk about it as it was happening sent a zing of pleasure down Evienne's spine. "Alright, I am following what you are saying about what is happening…physically. I still need you to explain, *in detail*, what you mean by Còmhanam," Evienne said, trying to remain calm.

"A Còmhanam bond is formed when the two parts of the same soul find each other. It was said that Còmhanam would develop a sense of the other's emotions, and feel them as their own in heightened moments. A fierce protectiveness and loyalty were also said to be hallmarks of a Còmhanam bond. It's not a full bond until I…mark you."

"And you think I am your Còmhanam? And I'm sorry, what do you mean *mark* me?" Evienne stared at Orion and saw a blend of concern and wonder in his face, but her questions felt quite urgent. She waited, searching his face, before he finally spoke.

"I've been drawn to you since the moment I set eyes on you, and the pull has only increased as I've learned more about you. Obviously, the attraction was there from the start, but I haven't been able to stop thinking about you, wanting to know everything about you. I've never been so undone by someone. And the knotting is…something that I didn't even know was really possible. I don't have my magic, so by all rights it *shouldn't* be possible. Còmhanam bonds go silent when no magic is present. But yes, Evienne, I can't deny that I find myself believing the impossible. There are signs I cannot explain away, but more than that, my soul whispers to me that I have found my home with you. At this revelation, I feel peace and joy, and I cannot dismiss that."

Tears stung Evienne's eyes at Orion's earnest confession. How could this be real? Not a week ago, she was wondering if she would be always alone, left with the scars of her broken marriage and a penchant for single night flings.

"As for the marking," Orion began, "it's a bite—a claiming. From what I understand, a marking means the pair accepts the Còmhanam bond, and all of the feelings and sensations that go along with being bonded become more intense. It is much harder to walk away from a Còmhanam once marked."

Before she had a chance to respond to him, she felt the pressure lessening where they were still joined. He gently slid himself out of her, and she closed her legs, his release coating her inner thighs. Somehow, she already ached to feel him inside her again.

"Orion, I understand that this is very real for you, and I can't deny that I have felt the pull toward you that you described," Evienne began. "I just need a bit of time to sort out my feelings about everything you've shared with me. It seems we're dealing with something that's been unheard of for centuries. Will you give me a bit of time? Between this and the suspicions you shared with me about the Tuanadair magic, you seem intent on turning my world upside down."

She placed her hand against his heart and stared into his sea green eyes.

He smiled softly at her, taking her hand in his where it rested against his chest. "Of course, please take the time you need. We can figure out what this means together, and regardless of what happens, I am grateful to have shared this night with you, Evienne."

She returned his smile and nodded. "I am, too."

EVIENNE drifted into consciousness feeling safe and warm. Her unsettling dreams hadn't plagued her sleep, and she felt rested. Minutes drifted by as she soaked in the feeling, gradually becoming aware of her body and her surroundings.

She inhaled sharply when she realized her legs were tangled with someone else's. She hadn't slept through the night with anyone since she left Dominique. Suddenly, she remembered where she was, and her eyes shot to Orion's face, peaceful with sleep in the soft light of dawn.

Evienne relaxed, memories of the night before rushing back. Orion had pulled her close, and she had let him. She wasn't sure what had come over her; she hadn't let anyone care for her like this for a long time. She felt she could trust Orion, though. It startled her, but she realized she felt she could be vulnerable in front of him too, and he wouldn't see it as a weakness.

Despite the calm she had awoken with, all of the information that had been thrust upon her the night before rushed back into her mind, and Evienne's anxiety rose. She began to slowly, carefully extract herself from her bed where Orion peacefully rested. She managed to free herself and dress quietly enough to avoid disturbing him.

She washed and dressed, barely remembering to slip on her bladed ring before rushing out the door. There was one person she needed to speak with about all of this; someone who she trusted, but that would also set her straight if they thought Evienne was in over her head.

Hestia had been one of Evienne's first tutors when she began her studies as a Sangviere. She appeared to be in her sixties but suspiciously hadn't aged a day since Evienne first met her fifteen years prior.

Hestia was no-nonsense, possessed a dry sense of humor, and fiercely loyal to anyone she deemed to be a part of her family. Evienne counted herself lucky to be one of Hestia's adopted children.

Hestia had challenged Evienne not to rely too heavily on her natural talent, pushing her instead to learn how to study diligently to move herself forward. If not for Hestia's guidance and unwavering emotional support, Evienne would not be the High Sangviere of Ichorna, she was certain of it.

Evienne knew that Hestia would never betray her confidence, so she felt safe sharing the Beitaran's true motives for being in Ichorna. Beyond that, she knew Hestia would help her make sense of this Còmhanam business. It wasn't so much that Evienne didn't believe Orion; it was just that she didn't see how it could really be possible or, frankly, what to do about it if it was.

As she walked out of the palace into the quiet streets

of the city, Evienne searched her heart. How did she feel at the thought of having one fated for her? A person that was supposedly a perfect match for her damaged soul? She found that the idea, while jarring, was not wholly unwelcome. She had never been as comfortable with someone as she felt with Orion; that feeling of freedom had to mean something, right?

The sun was warming the sky to a gentle orange by the time she arrived at the sandstone facade of the townhouse Hestia called home. Since the older woman had retired from teaching at the Academie du Sangviere, she had moved out of her old quarters in the palace complex and now called this fashionable spot home. The street was one of the prettiest in Lucinne; a wide boulevard with ancient trees and a generous pedestrian walkway made it feel more like a park than a street.

Evienne heard the quiet whoosh of the Rail Dellumine as it glided by on its track a few blocks away. She stepped up to Hesitia's door and lifted the heavy brass knocker. After a few breaths of silence, Evienne heard someone fiddling with the latch.

The door opened a few inches and Hestia's dark brown eyes peered out. Her brows rose in surprise at the sight of Evienne outside her door so early in the morning, but after a moment, her lips pulled into a smile.

"Oh, it's you! I was certainly not expecting to see anyone here at this hour." Hestia opened the door the rest of the way and gestured for Evienne to enter. Evienne stepped across the threshold and stood before the woman who had been her mentor for the past decade.

She was sure Hestia could read each one of her emotions on her face, but she would make Evienne explain nonetheless. In the absence of any parental influence during Evienne's adolescence, it had been Hestia that taught her some of life's most useful skills, such as the value of communicating clearly about one's feelings.

"I'm sorry for the intrusion, but I didn't know where else to go." Evienne took a deep breath and met her mentor's steady gaze. Hestia extended a warm brown hand, and Evienne readily took it in her own. She was promptly pulled into a hug, something she hadn't even realized she'd needed. Tears filled Evienne's eyes, but she took a deep breath and returned Hestia's hug, attempting to gather her thoughts to explain what had happened.

"Hestia, what do you know of the Tuanadair's magic?"

"That's a big question, Dove; can you give me some context?" Hestia asked as she led Evienne to her cozy living room. A fire crackled softly in the hearth, and the dark wood paneling and mismatched textiles of the familiar room drained some of the tension out of Evienne's shoulders.

"I'm not sure where to start, Hestia. Things seem to have spiraled rather out of my control," Evienne said quietly as she slipped off her shoes and curled up on one of the sofas.

"Does it have anything to do with your special assignment for the celebration? The delegation from Beitar?" Hestia gave Evienne a knowing look.

"Yes. The Professor, Orion, told me of their true purpose here. He suspects Ichorna has something to do with the waning of Beitar's magic, and he's here to seek answers in our library or wherever else the trail may lead. He's asked for my help in seeking those answers."

"And you are unsure of sharing this information with Queen Aldith as she ordered," Hestia says slowly, immediately putting the pieces together as Evienne assumed she would.

"Yes," Evienne nodded.

"You suspect his theory may not be wholly unfounded," Hestia added.

"I have questions that I fear will go unanswered if I immediately take this information to Aldith, yes. And…I find I do not want to tell her for other, more personal reasons as well." Evienne held her mentor's knowing gaze. "If we have played a role in Beitar's decline and we do not realize it, that is one thing; but I cannot imagine the implications if what he suspects is true *and* someone here knows what we are doing." Evienne closed her eyes and ran her hands through her already tousled hair.

"That is quite a choice to make." Hestia nodded and leaned back in her armchair. "I suppose, then, you must consider what your values are. Is your loyalty to Queen Aldith greater than your hunger for the truth?"

Hestia paused as Evienne sighed and stared into the fire. She had expected Hestia to take this information in stride to a certain degree, but this total lack of surprise was a bit unexpected. Hestia had always seemed to just *know* things, though.

"That isn't all that sits upon your heart, is it Dove?"

"No." Evienne smiled slightly at her mentor's ability to

read her so easily. "Orion and I…" She felt a blush creeping up her neck. "Well, we've become quite close—physically—since he arrived." Evienne took a deep breath. "Last night something happened between us that Orion said he has only heard of in Beitar's folklore—something that requires Tuanadair magic that hasn't been seen in decades. Because of what happened, he believes we are something called Còmhanam—some type of soulmates." Evienne started massaging her temples.

"I see…and this was surprising because he assumed he was without his magic?" Hestia asked, her head tilted to the side in thought.

"Well, yes, he *is* without his magic. All of Beitar has now completely lost their connection to their magic except their King. No one of his generation has ever even shifted." Evienne suddenly wondered at the implications of her mentor's question. "Do…*you* think he has his magic?"

"I think, logically, if he believes there is a chance the Tuanadair's magic is being suppressed by Ichorna; is there not also a possibility that it would become un-suppressed once he was outside Beitar's borders?" Hestia's brown eyes now felt piercing somehow as she looked at Evienne.

"I suppose…I suppose that could be possible." Evienne's mind was spinning. "It may well be the only rational explanation to what happened between us last night. But Còmhanam, Hestia? Is that a real thing?"

"I have heard the tales. I suspect there is truth to them, as there almost always is with folklore." Hestia's lip quirked up at the side. "Dove, if I have taught you anything, I hope it is the importance of curiosity and a love of the truth. Ask the questions others have yet to ask, pull on loose threads, seek out answers. Questions beget answers, and answers bring clarity. Clarity fosters balance." Hestia reached out to take Evienne's hand in hers. "Balance is what makes our magic powerful and keeps our world as it is meant to be."

"I have not forgotten your lessons, dear teacher." Evienne smiled at the older woman. "I just needed to hear from someone I trust that following this path—that many will call treason—is not lunacy."

"No, clever one, I do not believe so. Treacherous, certainly; especially if any of your suspicions prove true. But I do not think it is unwise to pursue this course in the service of balance. Blind loyalty is something to be avoided," Hestia said.

"And you think I am his Còmhanam? I don't even fully understand what all that could mean," Evienne said, her voice weary.

"I think it is possible. I am not sure what this man has to gain from lying to the most dangerous woman in what he believes may be an enemy court. Explore the logical possibilities and keep an open mind, Dove." Hestia patted Evienne's hand in a familiar gesture. "Now, let's eat something. It's too early to stage a coup, so let's start with some pastries, yes?"

BACK at the palace, Evienne found Cecelia in her study, carefully wielding her physical magic to repair a page of an ancient tome. Evienne had come straight from Hestia's townhouse and felt more settled now, but she needed to talk to her best friend.

"Evi, good morning!" Cecelia brightened as she looked up from her book. "It's not our usual day, what a treat!"

Evienne smiled and plopped down on the couch.

"Cece, we need to talk. I…" She paused, not quite knowing where to start. She didn't want to tell Cecelia everything Orion had shared with her without his permission. She decided to stick to the mate part.

"Have you read anything about the Tuanadair's mate bonds?" She asked, glancing up at Cecelia.

"The Còmhanam bond? Sure, I've seen it in a few of their folk tales."

"It's real," Evienne said plainly.

Cecelia stared at her with her mouth hanging open.

"It's real, and I know because I have one, apparently."

"You can't be serious. Evi, it's too early in the morning for you to joke with me like that," Cecelia said with a slight frown.

"No, I'm being entirely serious, and I don't really know what to think about it," Evienne answered. She wanted to feel excited, but she was still scared as well. Cecelia made her way over to the couch and sat down next to Evienne, her expression now more shocked than anything else.

"How…how did you come by this information?" Cecelia asked carefully.

"There are some *anatomical* differences that we, uh, stumbled upon. It's Orion if you hadn't already put that together," Evienne added.

"Well, obviously, you two seem…close," Cecelia said,

suppressing her laughter. "He seems really kind, Evi. Does spending time with him make you happy?"

Evienne paused a moment to consider. "Yes. Yes, it does make me happy to spend time with him. I think I'm starting to have feelings for him."

Cecelia took Evienne's hand in hers and gave her a small smile. After a long moment, Evienne looked into her friend's face.

"What do you think I should do?"

"Do? What do you mean 'do'? Just *be*! Just feel what you feel and see where it leads. Don't be afraid, Evi. You seem happy, and he seems kind, and those are the most important things. I know it's overwhelming, and who knows if the bond thing is even real, but what you're feeling for Orion is! I think you should do what *feels* right."

"But he's going to leave in a few weeks, and I'll probably never see him again," Evienne said, surprised at the emotion now clogging her throat.

"He may, and it might hurt you. Or he might stay, or take you with him, or any number of possibilities, no matter how unlikely. You cannot control the future, but you can miss out on the present. I think you ought to keep an open mind."

Chapter Twenty-One

Orion awoke alone in Evienne's bed, the smell of her surrounding him as he lay tangled in the soft sheets. He let consciousness settle over him; he savored his sense of peace as he slowly took in his surroundings. Every inch of this room felt like her.

As memories of the previous night trickled into his mind, he smiled; his Còmhanam was magnificent. He had planned to tell her what he suspected once they had a chance to get to know each other better; he had certainly *not* planned to just knot her immediately. That could have been an absolute disaster, but she seemed to have taken it as well as possible…the knot and the news.

She wasn't here, though, and worry took root in his mind at her absence. Perhaps she had just pretended to be alright with it until she could get away from him. He didn't think she was the sort to do that, but he supposed he didn't really know her all that well yet. He knew enough, though, to know he'd turn his whole life upside down to be with her.

Evienne was a masterpiece—open and bright and kind,

but ruthless and strategic when she needed to be. He had never met anyone like her.

Orion dressed quickly and made his way back to his own room to freshen up. Waiting around wouldn't do any good, and he needed to talk with Solon. Not only had he made their mission extremely vulnerable by sharing their true purpose with Evienne, he had gone and mated the High Sangviere of Ichorna. That had not been part of the plan.

He knocked on Solon's door a short time later, and Solon answered immediately.

"Orion, where in the world did you go last night? I tried to check on you when I got back from the concert, but you weren't in your room," he said, an edge of irritation in his voice.

"Well, I was..." Orion began but thought better of spilling his secrets here in the hallway. "Let's take a walk and I'll tell you."

The two stayed quiet as they made their way out the gate of the palace and onto the main boulevard that ran through the heart of Lucinne. Once they were off palace grounds, Orion felt more sure they weren't being spied on, so he began.

"I was with my Còmhanam," he said plainly. "Evienne is my Còmhanam."

Solon showed no signs of shock other than a slight widening of his eyes. Orion remained silent and gave Solon a moment to process.

"Is this simply a hunch, or do you have a concrete reason to believe this?" Solon asked, his voice hushed and even.

"I have a very real reason to believe it. The uh...stories

are true," Orion said, running a hand through his hair as embarrassment colored his cheeks. Solon did surprise Orion then, as a booming laugh escaped him. Orion had not heard his friend laugh like that in years.

"The stories are true? Incredible! I am sorry for laughing, I am simply trying to imagine what it was like to accidentally come across that particular aspect of the Còmhanam bond. I can't believe such a thing could happen without our magic, but who are we to question the workings of Aosda? I believe congratulations are in order. How did she…take the news?" Solon asked, a broad smile now adorning his handsome face.

"She seemed alright, but I am worried about her. It's a lot of new information to come to terms with. It isn't how I would have chosen to tell her, I will say that."

"I should think not!" Solon said, another laugh rolling from him.

"Solon, there's something else I should tell you," Orion said, glancing anxiously at Solon, who waited silently for Orion to continue.

"I told her of our true purpose here and asked for her help." Orion was confident in his decision, but he was unsure of how Solon would react. They had discussed the possibility of asking someone on the inside for help, but they hadn't agreed it should be Evienne. Solon was silent for a long moment before he nodded his head.

"I think this was a wise choice. I wish you had talked with me, obviously, but the High Sangviere gives me the impression of a woman of integrity. She does not appear to be blindly loyal to Aldith, and if she really is by some miracle your Còmhanam, then she is certainly a woman of honor to be your match. Did she agree to help us?"

"Not yet—she asked for a bit of time to consider it. I believe that's only fair given we are asking her to commit treason."

Solon hummed in agreement. "Well, you've certainly made this trip exciting, Orion. I shouldn't have expected anything less."

Chapter Twenty-Two

THE DOORS TO the Grand Hall of the palace stood open, bronzy light spilling out as the sounds of the small string orchestra reached Evienne's ears. The moment rested against her skin, hovering, suspended; this tiny fraction of her life that would never come again.

Her lungs expanded with her next breath, time spiraling forward as she slowly became aware of the soft bristling feeling of the blood red velvet of her gown against her fingertips.

She strode forward, the long slit in her skirt revealing the ivory curves of her leg. This dress was her favorite; a slight train to her skirt, a wrapped bodice, and sleeves that gracefully sat off her shoulders. Her long dark hair, smoothed into graceful waves, fell down her back in a silky sheet.

She felt at her most powerful in this moment; she had decided to examine the new possibilities, to find answers to her questions, and—most importantly—to trust her intuition about her path forward. This morning, she had been off-balance and unsure, but she knew what her values were.

Her purpose now was to bring her life, and possibly the Tuanadair's magic, back into balance.

Evienne crossed the threshold into the grand hall, her head held high, and found Orion's eyes already locked on her. She suppressed a smile as she held his gaze from across the hall. She winked at him before turning to seek out her first target for the evening. Just before she turned away, she saw his expression of awe—and a bit of shock—turn to one of heat and hunger.

Evienne found Solon leaning against the wall near one of the floor-to-ceiling stained glass windows. She took the space next to him, digging her ring into her palm ever-so-lightly, just enough for a tiny drop of blood to gather. She summoned the barest hint of a shield; just enough to block their voices from those around them but not enough to be visible, as blood-made shields usually were. The next moment, the sounds of the hall had fallen silent. Evienne kept her gaze out toward the crowd as she said, "No one will be able to hear us now."

Solon nodded, but also kept his gaze out toward the hall. He instinctively picked up on the need for discretion. Good; she was about to make herself incredibly vulnerable to this man she hardly knew.

"I assume you know Orion told me of your true purpose here in Ichorna," Evienne began. "He asked for my help in uncovering whatever truth there is to find, either in our library or out in our city." Evienne saw Solon tense slightly out of the corner of her eye as he waited for her to continue.

"I want to help. But you have to understand that from this very moment on, if anyone here were to discover not only that I am helping you, but that I have withheld information from our queens, I would be considered a traitor to Ichorna. Our lives would be in grave danger. Aldith does not often have cause to be cruel, but she will not hesitate to remove us as a threat if she learns what we suspect." Evienne kept her voice even. Solon needed to understand the risk his friend was taking.

"I understand," Solon breathed, his deep voice barely a rumble. "I am grateful to have found you in possession of the integrity and courage you are known for. People know of your prowess as a Sangviere, certainly, but it is your true heart that sets you apart. We are lucky indeed to call you an ally." His voice solemn.

"Yes, well, thank you for your kind words, Solon," Evienne answered, a bit flustered at the high praise.

"Queen Aldith knew there must be some deeper reason for your visit. Other than Queen Léhiona, we've barely seen a Beitaran for the past decade," Evienne continued, relaxing into honesty with the normally formal Beitaran lord.

"Yes, Léhiona is certainly an anomaly. I knew her as a girl, you know. She was friends with my daughter. She seems… happy enough, but I am sad to see her here, so isolated from her people," Solon admitted, his voice tinged with regret.

"I am glad of your help, Evienne." Solon's gaze finally shifted to meet Evienne's.

"Someone very wise taught me the importance of balance, and the path to balance is through truth. While I love my homeland, I hope I am not so shallow as to be blind to the possibility of wrongdoing. It is possible to hold love for a place alongside skepticism. Orion has given me enough questions that I cannot simply stand by without answers. We will find the truth together and decide how to move forward." Evienne shifted from her place on the wall, dropping the sound shield with a flick of her wrist.

Solon smiled at Evienne before she strode away, slipping into the crowd.

Evienne could feel Orion's attention on her before she spotted him. As she approached the doors that stood open to the cold night air of the veranda, he appeared with a wine glass in each hand. He met her as she walked toward him, extending a glass to her.

"Evienne." Orion's voice was a sensual purr that had an instant effect on her. Her name on his lips was a greeting, an understanding, and a promise, all at once.

"Hello, Orion. Walk with me?" Evienne flashed a look at him through her lashes as she took the wine glass he offered. She didn't wait for him to agree before she headed out onto the veranda; she knew he would follow.

She pricked her palm again, settling the sound barrier into place around them as they walked slowly down the length of the veranda. The night was particularly cool, so they found themselves alone despite the crowded hall.

"I assume you've made a decision then?" Orion asked.

"I have, yes." Evienne glanced at him to read his expression. He looked… worried. Did he really doubt her? She hadn't said yes immediately, but it wasn't because she didn't want to help. She just needed space to decide to risk everything she had worked for.

"Orion, you cannot think that I would be so blindly loyal as to ignore the questions you've shared with me. I love

Ichorna and its people, certainly, but I value the truth more. I only needed time to be sure I was ready to commit treason. I am, as it turns out, so of course I will help in whatever way I'm able." Evienne stopped and turned to face him.

"I did not doubt your integrity, but it is a great thing to ask someone to willingly become a traitor to the nation they have loyally served. I am not ignorant to the weight this carries." He reached out to grasp her hand then, drawing her closer to him.

"While I am eternally grateful that you've decided to help us find the truth of our magic, it is your thoughts on our other matter that I have worried over the most." Orion's thumb stroked over the top of Evienne's hand as he spoke. She lifted her gaze to his, studying his features bathed in the moonlight.

"Orion, I don't know what to make of what is between us, but I do not believe it is nothing. Who am I to dismiss something so rare and revered among your people? I don't know what the truth is, but I am willing to seek it out alongside you." She held his gaze as she spoke, and she saw relief and hope and something deeper shining through his eyes.

Orion set his glass on the wide railing and let his other hand drift up to her waist. The warmth of his hands seeped into the velvet of her gown. "Evienne, I…" Orion trailed off, raising his hand to cup her cheek lightly. "I am grateful for your openness and your trust; I will endeavor to be worthy of both. I must tell you, Evienne—in answer to your honesty—I have never felt anything like what I feel when I am near you. For the first time in my life, it's as if I can feel my magic coursing through me, and the draw I feel to you grows stronger each time I'm near you. Last night..." he closed his eyes for a moment, and his fingers tensed on her waist. Evienne was aware of every place he touched her, but she waited to hear what he would say.

"Last night, I experienced something with you that I thought was little more than a fairytale. For me, there will be no other but you, Evienne Elodie D'Auclaire," he said, barely more than a whisper on the cold autumn wind.

Evienne's breath caught at his admission; no other but her? Did he mean forever? Before she could respond, he continued, "I do not expect the same surety from you, Evienne. I simply hope to have the chance to earn your love in time. I do not want you to feel as though you have no choice—I only wish you to know that mine is made."

"Orion." His name sounded breathless on her lips. She trailed her hand up his chest, her fingers grazing the warm skin of his neck before coming to rest on his jaw.

"I think I would like you to kiss me now," she said, leaning into his warmth.

"Anything for you, love," he whispered, lowering his lips to hers.

Chapter Twenty-Three

Evienne pricked her palm and extended her hand to unlock the door to her rooms. Orion watched her intently, clearly studying how she wielded this seemingly simple magic. She smirked at him and pushed her door open. He followed her inside, glancing over his shoulder to ensure no one saw them.

They had slipped away from the ball after making a bit of an appearance, dancing twice and splitting up to chat separately with various members of the court. The entire time they spent apart, Evienne could sense where Orion was in the hall. Maybe this idea of Còmhanam wasn't completely unfounded.

Evienne strode over to her vanity and began to remove her jewelry. Orion stayed just inside the door, watching her with desire coming off him in waves.

"I'll never understand how you manage having to cut yourself every time you use your magic," Orion said, watching her intently.

"You get used to it after so many years of practice. Besides, we're taught to end every casting with a healing spell, so the cuts close before I ever really notice them," Evienne caught his stare in her mirror and turned to face him. "Will you help me with the laces?"

Orion prowled across the room to stand behind her. She could feel the heat of his body against her bare upper back as the tips of his fingers brushed lightly over her exposed shoulders. She heard him inhale sharply as she leaned back into his touch.

Orion's fingers found the laces at the back of her dress and began to slowly loosen them. Evienne reveled in his closeness, in the quiet intimacy of this moment. She found herself wondering what it would be like to end every evening like this.

As she felt the dress fully loosen she let it fall to the ground before stepping out of it. She stood before him in nothing but her black lace panties; the dress had a built-in corset, so no other support had been needed. Orion's gaze traveled the full length of her before coming to rest on her face.

"Evienne, you are the most beautiful person I've ever seen." He was breathless. Before she could answer, his hands were cupping her face, his lips pressing to hers in a passionate but reverent kiss. She opened to him, his tongue sweeping in to claim her, and her body ignited with desire for him.

Her hands found the buttons of his pants as he shrugged out of his immaculate jacket and beautiful linen shirt. Soon, they were both bare before each other, a tangle of limbs falling onto the plush rug before Evienne's fireplace.

The heat of the fire pressed against Evienne's heated skin

while Orion's cool fingers grazed the underside of her breast. She gasped at the gentleness of the contact and wrapped her arms around his neck to pull him into a kiss. They explored each other with languid, hungry touches and tastes, when Evienne decided she didn't want to wait any longer.

"Orion, please," Evienne begged in a breathy moan.

"Tell me what you want, love," Orion whispered in her ear as his fingers worked her most sensitive bundle of nerves. She writhed against the friction he created, his touch driving her closer to release. She let out another moan as he slipped two fingers inside her, the pleasant stretch leaving her wanting more.

"I want you to fill me," she panted, grinding her hips against him, his fingers buried deep inside her.

"I won't make you ask twice," Orion answered, just as breathless. His need for her was a palpable thing; Evienne felt it in her soul.

Orion sat back on his knees, pulling Evienne into a sitting position astride him. She braced her arms on his shoulders, kneeling so she was hovering just above his hard length. Orion placed his hands on her hips and guided her down onto him, inch by inch, letting her adjust to the stretch. He stared into her eyes, and Evienne watched him savor every expression on her face as she took him.

When he was seated to the hilt inside her, Evienne's head fell back on a moan. Orion groaned and wrapped his arms around her to support her, shifting so that her legs wrapped around his hips. Evienne cried out at the deepening of the sensation at this angle; she felt impossibly full of him, so connected that every thought began and ended with him.

Evienne took a deep breath, feeling this moment burrowing into her very soul. These seconds, minutes, hours, spent with him; she knew these moments would linger in her mind as some of her most cherished memories.

Just as she adjusted to the feel of him so deep inside her, Orion lifted her hips gently and began a slow rocking motion that had her clenching around him. She gasped, feeling every glorious inch as he ground slowly inside her. She looked up at him, his gaze already upon her face, and they stared at each other in awe at all they were feeling together.

Evienne took over the rocking motion, gradually increasing the speed until she could feel her release about to crest. Orion slipped his hand into her hair at the back of her head, tilting her face up to him, and kissed her deeply. Before Evienne realized what was happening, she was seeing... herself?

She stood on the steps at the main entrance to the palace, hair flowing in the autumn breeze, with a pleasant expression on her face. Evienne realized Orion was looking at her from where he sat mounted on his horse, moving toward the palace.

"Breathtaking." Orion's voice filtered through Evienne's mind. She must be seeing his memory of the day they met.

Evienne felt, or rather Orion must have felt, a jolting intuitive pull as he neared her in the courtyard that day. *"I must be near her,"* the thought, overwhelming in certainty, came unbidden. She felt his shock, denial, surprise, confusion—all in a swirling torrent. In the next heartbeat, she was back in her own mind, Orion still deep inside her. No more than a second had passed from when her vision began.

She blinked as Orion's lips left hers, and she looked up into his perfect face and smiled. He smiled back and leaned in to whisper in her ear, "I want to feel you coming on my cock, my love; can you do that for me?"

He reached between their bodies and began to knead her clit in a firm, rolling motion, and she cried out, pleasure flaring through her. He kept stroking until her orgasm crashed over her. His cock was buried so deep, and he had stilled inside her, so they both felt every pulse of her release. Orion tensed, moaning her name as he followed her to completion.

Evienne felt the pressure inside her increasing, just as it had before, but she knew now what was happening. She had never considered the possibility, but now that she was faced with it, the fact that Orion's magic had woken in response to her, his Tuanadair nature taking over to lock himself inside her, she found it incredibly erotic and deeply meaningful.

His knot expanded fully, sealing their bodies together. Evienne's nails pressed into the expanse of Orion's back as she fought to catch her breath. He caught her chin in his fingers, tilting her face to him, and the corner of his mouth pulled up as he stared at her. She shifted slightly to lean her head against his shoulder, and the small movement made Orion moan. She felt him fill her again, and her own release found her once more at the sensation.

Orion gently turned them and laid them on their sides, facing each other with their legs still entangled. He brushed

Evienne's sweat-damp hair from her brow, observing her with what appeared to be reverence. She smiled at him then, and took his hand in hers, squeezing gently.

"Orion, I believe there are two things we should discuss," she said, her voice barely more than a whisper.

"What's on your mind, love?" He answered, holding her close to him as he remained locked in place inside her.

"First, I think I should tell you something about my magic that I've never told anyone..." she trailed off, feeling overwhelmed at how vulnerable she was about to make herself to him. She had to tell him though, after she had invaded his privacy just now. "I can do more than blood magic, and I don't know how or why," she said with a small sigh.

Orion's brow furrowed slightly as he listened intently, not rushing her but leaving space for her to continue when she was ready. After a moment, she went on, "Sometimes, when I touch people, it feels like I'm thrown into their memories. I never control what I see it's always a shock when it happens, but no time passes no matter how long the memory is that I see."

She searched Orion's face for any fear or disgust and found only gentle curiosity, and maybe a bit of concern. So she went on, "It...well it happened just now. With you," she said with a bit of a wince. She didn't take lightly what an invasion it was to see someone's memories without permission.

"Oh really?" Orion looked more interested than upset. "What did you see?"

"You aren't angry?" Evienne said, uncertainty lacing her words.

"No, love. All my secrets are yours to take should you wish it." Orion smiled as he spoke, and pressed a kiss to her brow. She shifted as she felt the pressure in her core decreasing, a gasp escaping her lips as Orion withdrew.

"I saw the first moment you saw me when you arrived in Ichorna," she breathed, looking anywhere but into Orion's eyes. "I heard your thoughts."

Orion pulled her closer so their bodies were fully wrapped in each other. "I am glad you saw; now you can be sure of me when I tell you there was a pull for me from the very second I beheld you."

Evienne had felt the fire between them, had been intrigued by Orion since she met him, but she had not expected him—or anyone for that matter—to say such things to her. She planned to keep an open mind, but Orion had her falling for him faster than she thought possible.

"Like I said, I don't understand this part of my magic. I've never had to use blood to power the spell, not that there even is one really…it just happens when I'm least expecting it."

"Well, love, it sounds like you have some studying to do to see if anyone has recorded similar magical abilities here in Ichorna," Orion said with a smirk.

"Yes, I suppose that's a good place to start. Like I said, I've never told anyone, and I've honestly been a bit afraid of what I would find if I looked into it," Evienne admitted.

"What was the other thing you wanted to discuss? You said two things," Orion asked as he stood to collect a towel from the bathing room.

Evienne sat up and took a deep breath. She took the towel he offered when he returned and looked up at him.

"I think you should try to shift."

Chapter Twenty-Four

THE NEXT MORNING, Evienne and Orion rose with the dawn, taking their horses to ride out of the city limits. Evienne went riding often, so their departure wasn't suspicious in the least. Autumn had slipped away into winter in earnest, and the morning breeze carried a cruel bite.

They rode in silence, anticipation and anxiety hanging in the air as the countryside passed them by. Ichorna's land was a mixture of rolling fields, grasslands, and wild, mostly untamed forests. The fields were what made Ichorna prosperous; Lucinne sat at the center of the heartland, the jewel in a crown of golden wheat.

Evienne had decided that her plans to find out what nonsense Dominique had been up to could wait; this was important, and they had a morning free from any official agenda. She would find Dominique another time. She knew she was likely just making excuses to avoid the confrontation, but she was enjoying her time with Orion too much to feel truly guilty.

Their destination was the Assombrie Forest, the closest stretch of woodland to Lucinne. Its ancient oaks and romantic drooping pines cast deep shadows across the dirt path as they entered the shelter of the woods. The cold air carried the scent of evergreen and soft, loamy earth.

This place had always felt separate from time as Evienne understood it. She hadn't come here often, too unsettled by the sentience of the trees and the feeling of eternity that suffocated her here. The forest was desperately ancient and heartbreakingly new all at once, and her soul never quite knew what to make of it. She had thought once that it unnerved her because being here felt like looking in a mirror; her spirit eternal and also just beginning.

They reached a small clearing in the trees. Even the chill fog seemed to recoil from this circle of mossy ground. Tiny, tightly-furled ferns braved the assessing gaze of the gray sky above, while the trees found comfort huddling near their neighbors.

Evienne slowed her horse, and Orion did the same as he took in the clearing. A look of reverence and apprehension adorned his perfect features. The sight of him here in this ancient, wild place nearly took Evienne's breath away. She knew it had been right to bring him here; he looked like he belonged to this place.

"I think this will do," Evienne said as she slid off her horse. Orion nodded, his lips tightening into a line. Evienne knew this was a difficult thing for her to ask of him, trying to shift after a lifetime of grief over the Tuanadair's failing magic. Hope was more cruel than apathy.

Evienne ventured, "Do you know how?"

Orion's face fell slightly at the question. "In theory, but obviously, it is likely to be quite different in practice."

Evienne nodded. "Can I do anything to help?"

Orion shook his head, took a deep breath, and stepped to the center of the clearing.

THE cold mists clung to Orion's hands and face in invisible droplets. This forest was alive in a way he had never encountered before, but it called to something in his soul. It felt at once like embracing an old friend and the breath taken before leaping off a cliff. The air was rife with ancient magic.

Orion filled his lungs with the forest air, closed his eyes, and sent his attention toward the place he knew his inherent magic was meant to reside. The books he had spent his whole life studying described the sensation as strongest just behind one's sternum.

He focused on the feeling of the mist and the second, more primal voice in his soul that had long been silent.

The sensation slammed into him suddenly, like he had jumped into icy water. It stole his breath, and he couldn't open his eyes. One breath the icy pain was there, and the next, only the sensation of raw, uncut power.

Orion kept his eyes shut, overwhelmed by his senses. He heard and smelled things he never had before. The iron tang of blood was on the air; the howls of the wolves celebrating their successful hunt in the distance echoed through the trees. He heard Evienne's pulse from across the clearing—it raced.

He opened his eyes at last, panic cutting through his shock. If Evienne was frightened, something must be wrong. He could keep trying to shift after they dealt with whatever threat caused her fear.

His eyes immediately found hers, but it was awe, not fear, that graced her lovely face. He moved toward her, confused, and she drew back slightly. From him, he realized. He extended his hand toward her, intending to offer comfort, but found instead a great white paw.

Orion stumbled back in shock, the movement causing him to trip over his *four* paws. He again extended one into his line of sight and tried to take it in.

He had massive, fluffy white paws dappled with soft gray spots. He whipped his head to look behind him and found a massive, powerful feline body and a thick white tail.

"You're a snow leopard!" Evienne exclaimed from where she stood, her shock melting into excitement.

"I'm a snow leopard," Orion repeated, and Evienne's eyes grew wide again.

"You just said that in my head."

Orion knew about this part of Tuanadair magic from his research, but experiencing it for the first time, with his Còmhanam no less, made his throat tighten with emotion.

"I have no words to tell you how grateful I am," Orion said, moving toward his mate. *"How did you know this would work?"* He asked, rubbing against her with a purr rumbling in his massive chest. He stood nearly up to her shoulder, larger than any regular snow leopard would be.

"I didn't know, I just suspected," she answered, carefully

placing her hand on his head, her fingers sinking into his thick fur.

"After the Còmhanam magic surfaced for you here, I suspected that perhaps all of your magic had found you after being away from Beitar for a while," Evienne continued.

"As happy as I am to have my magic, this doesn't bode well for my suspicions about what is happening to the Tuanadair," Orion mused, savoring the feeling of Evienne's closeness.

"It certainly doesn't," Evienne answered, clearly deep in thought, already parsing through the possibilities. "But I think this mystery can wait an hour while you enjoy your magic, hm?" She looked down at him with a small smile, her eyes shining with joy. It took his breath away when she looked at him like that.

"I suppose you're right," Orion purred. Evienne was already turning to mount her horse, Belle. The brave beast had stayed with them, somehow sensing that Orion didn't mean any harm. Maisie, Orion's faithful mare, was tied to a branch nearby. She also seemed to be taking his transformation in stride.

"Then let's run," she said, smiling fully now. Orion didn't hesitate; he launched himself into the forest, savoring the intuitive way this body moved. So graceful and full of power.

A snow leopard. What a majestic beast to share his soul with. Strong and brave and independent creatures, and native to Beitar's highest peaks. This form, his magic, felt so natural, and his heart was filled with joy and determination that all Tuanadair should know this freedom. He would have to tell Solon as soon as they went back to the palace. Perhaps they could bring him out here to shift too.

But for now, Orion ran, his magic coursing through his veins, his mate at his side, and he felt more hopeful than he ever had.

Chapter Twenty-Five

Later that afternoon, Evienne found herself seated at a small table in Léhiona's private rooms. Cecelia sat to her left, Léhiona on her right, and Sylvain directly across from her.

Evienne loved Queen Léhiona's sitting room; it was so full of joyful colors and delicate touches. Vibrant pinks and purples danced across nearly every surface, and dainty floral patterns collided around the room.

Her focus drifted to her friends, and she noticed Léhiona's hand shaking as she poured the tea.

"Oh, let me help you with that!" Cecelia offered, only for Léhiona to wave her away gently, laughing.

"I don't need help, silly. I'm just a little tired! All of this celebrating has me ready for a vacation," Léhiona said lightly. Evienne usually believed her friend, but the purple smudged under Léhiona's eyes told a different story.

"Do you think perhaps a visit to the healers could be helpful? Didn't they see you after your episode at the garden party? I am sure they could give you some sort of insight into why you're feeling this way." Evienne offered carefully, glancing at Sylvain.

"I suppose I could go. Sylvain has been telling me the same thing," Léhiona said, her brow slightly furrowed.

"So will Aldith be joining us then? It's been ages since we were all together," Cecelia asked, taking a bite of a dainty sandwich. Evienne had hoped Aldith would be there as well so she could—very casually and not at all in an angry way—ask about why Dominique had been meddling in the Sangviere assignments. Despite all that had happened the past few days, it still bothered her that Dominique had the nerve to interfere like that. She just hadn't had a moment to figure out why.

Léhiona's face fell before she answered softly, "Ah, no, she won't be able to join us today, sadly. Duty calls."

Cecelia harrumphed a bit, unsatisfied with this answer, and Sylvain didn't look surprised. Evienne nudged Cecelia with her knee beneath the table in a sign to leave Léhiona alone; they knew Aldith's obsession with work was a point of tension for the pair.

"So, Léhiona, last time we were all together, you were sharing that you and Aldith were considering starting a family? Do you have any happy updates for us? I bet you could convince Sylvain to stay closer to home with a little niece or nephew," Evienne said, steering the conversation to what she hoped was a safer topic.

"Yes, well, you know it's our duty to continue the Ichornian royal line, and I have always wanted to be a mother. We're planning to adopt next year," Léhiona answered with a smile.

Cecelia squealed and laughed, "Oh, how wonderful, Léhiona! It will be so exciting to have a little one here with you, don't you think? You'll make such a fantastic mother!"

Léhiona smiled at Cecelia, and Evienne grinned too. Léhiona *would* make a wonderful mother; she was glad her friend would be exploring that phase of her life.

"Evienne is right, I won't be able to stay away," Sylvain offered with a wink.

"Enough about me, though, are you two enjoying all the festivities?" Léhiona asked.

"Evi's been enjoying more than just the parties, if you take my meaning…" Cecelia laughed.

Evienne rolled her eyes and blushed, laughing at her friend. "Yes, well, I am making the most of the celebration, I'll say that."

Léhiona laughed and then said, "Cece, what about you? I hope you're taking time away from your dusty old library to have a bit of fun?"

"I've been to a few of the events, but you know I prefer my library to traipsing around with a bunch of dignitaries. Well, except for Jac; I like him. I'll make a few more appearances, but this whole thing is a bit ostentatious for me," Cecelia answered.

Sylvain laughed, "It's just the right amount of ostentatious for me."

"Of course it is, Sylvain. But Cece, I do hope you take some time to celebrate. It won't happen again for a thousand years!"

THE next morning, Evienne and Orion made their way to the palace library. They were in need of information, and Evi knew just the librarian to help them.

They found Cecelia in her cozy study, fully engrossed in the restoration of what was likely one of Ichorna's most precious books. A slight knock on her door frame had her jolting up in surprise; she rarely had visitors back here other than Evienne, and today was not their usual day for tea.

"Oh, Evi, it's you! I thought I recognized your footsteps," Cecelia said smiling. Her gaze shifted past Evienne to Orion as they stepped into the room.

"Cecelia, we're here with a request that is very...delicate. You're my oldest friend, and I know without a doubt I can trust you," Evienne said quietly from where she had taken a seat on the couch, holding her friend's increasingly curious stare. "That *we* can trust you," she added, glancing at Orion.

"Of course you can," Cecelia said, waving a hand as though it was the most obvious thing in the world. "Now tell me how I can help."

Evienne smiled at her friend, always forging fearlessly ahead.

Orion began to explain. "The magic of the Tuanadair is failing. I'm sure you all have some notion of that here, but it's become quite dire. Our King is the only one who still has access to his magic. We don't know when exactly it began, but looking back, we've been able to assess that it was likely about two hundred years ago that our magic began declining. No one but the King has been able to shift for at least fifty years now. I've been at the forefront of our research on this topic, and I have a theory that I've come here to Ichorna to investigate," Orion explained evenly. Cecelia listened intently, so he continued.

"I suspect that Ichorna may be involved somehow in the suppression or siphoning of our magic."

At that, Cecelia's brow furrowed, and she flicked a worried gaze at Evienne.

"You all are the closest geographically to us, and our fading magic likely began around the time we sent our first noble here to become consort," Orion said, glancing at Evienne to see if he should share the most recent update to his theory. Evienne nodded and placed her hand over his, squeezing gently in support.

"I also have reason to believe that our magic suppression is limited to the boundaries of Beitar," Orion added.

"While this is fascinating, I cannot ignore that the implications of what you are saying are very concerning. Evienne, do you believe Aldith knows anything of this?" Cecelia asked, her voice now lower than it had been when she greeted them.

"I do not know. I have to believe she doesn't and that if there is a connection, it is some sort of accident or something that was done before our time," Evienne said, holding her friend's gaze and shaking her head slightly. Sadness at the possibilities sat with her, and she knew she was opening Cecelia up to hurt as well by sharing all this with her.

"What makes you believe your magic suppression is only within Beitar?" Cecelia asked, still worried and processing, but eager to have all the information.

"I was able to shift today. Solon and I are the first Tuanadair to spend more than a few days at a time outside our borders in more than a century. I suspect I am currently free of whatever affliction is draining the magic from my people," Orion said, holding Cecelia's gaze.

The room was silent for a long moment before Cecelia sighed, leaning back in her chair. "Well that's certainly troubling. I do not think we can ignore this, can we?"

Orion relaxed a bit, and Evienne felt the same pang of relief in her chest. Cecelia would help them; she was sure of it. She hated to expose her friend to the same doubts she was having about everything they knew here in Ichorna, but she knew Cecelia would always rather have all the information.

"We need your help in finding whatever we can about what may be happening here, Cece," Evienne said quietly.

"Of course I'm going to help you, don't be silly. If there's something going on here we have to figure it out; it's wrong to just let a whole nation of people suffer. The least we can do is try. I have to believe we will find it's all some misunderstanding," Cecelia said, standing and striding for the door.

"We need to go to the special, secret archive room for this," she said, gesturing for them to follow.

Chapter Twenty-Six

An afternoon spent in Cecelia's secret archive left them with more questions than answers. Most of the texts in that room were from before the first Beitaran consort came to Ichorna. Rare histories to be found in this library, to be sure, but not helpful with regards to their current suspicions.

Evienne had spent the morning engrossed in a book of Beitaran folk tales that told stories of a group of immortals called Contrapensae. They were protectors of balance who seemed to go to extreme lengths to defend the magic of the world. Evienne had never heard of them before, but Orion seemed familiar with the stories when she showed him the book.

"The Contrapensae were said to be immortals, one hailing from each nation of Domhan na Rùin, that wielded unique magic on behalf of the old gods. Sometimes they remained hidden; other times, they served as advisors for rulers or simply wandered the land. We had many stories of them back in Beitar. One, in particular, took to wearing a large floppy hat and enjoyed putting on displays of fireworks for children in the villages he visited," Orion said with a chuckle.

"What sort of magic did they have that was so special?" Evienne asked.

"No one knows for certain, but it was believed they wielded time magic."

The three parted ways after a few hours, promising to continue their search as they were able without raising suspicion. Evienne pondered the implications of all she had learned over the past few weeks as she made her way toward her rooms to dress for the formal dinner this evening.

Her steps slowed, however, as she passed the hall that would take her toward the offices of palace officials who were not high-ranking enough to live in the palace proper, but still required a private workspace here.

She hadn't paid all that much attention to Dominique's career since they had divorced, but she had always been close to the queens' affairs and likely still was, based on comments Aldith made here and there. Hers was one of the dozens of tiny offices, just a few paces down the hall.

She knew Dominique was still in charge of the Sangviere posted at the Centrale Dellumine. After her conversation with Lou the other day, it was worth at least taking a look to see if any of her recent work could help them along in their search. At the very least, perhaps she could find out why Dominique had moved those Sangviere that had been assigned to Lou.

Evienne tried to feel guilty at the prospect of snooping through her ex-wife's things, but she found she couldn't muster it.

Walking with purpose toward Dominique's office door, Evienne grasped the cool metal of the handle and found it locked—annoying but unsurprising. She had hoped Dominique would be arrogant enough to leave her door unlocked, as if she had nothing to hide. She pressed her bladed ring into her palm, a small rush of magic pulsing in her hands, and she willed a strand of physical force to wind its way into the lock mechanism. It released with a click, and she slipped inside as the door snicked shut.

That little trick was one that had taken her a shocking amount of time to learn; and one she did not readily admit to having. Manipulating the physical world with blood magic, which was naturally drawn to living, not inanimate, things, was easier said than done. She had practiced tirelessly to acquire the skill, hating the feeling of being trapped or shut out. Better to let people think their locked doors were safe.

She took a deep breath as she surveyed the small space. It was incredibly sparse compared to the other rooms in the palace. Nearly every corner of Lucinne was filled with rich colors and textures, but this room was all harsh lines and bare surfaces, save for the bronze walls themselves.

The scent of cloves hung heavy in the air; it, too, was everywhere here in Lucinne, but sometimes it felt more concentrated. Dominique must have had her window open at some point.

Evienne stepped over to the bare desk and pulled out the top drawer, full of files, all labeled and organized to clinical perfection.

Most were records of the energy usage of the city, broken

out daily. Some were more general reports, synthesizing the daily data into weekly or monthly charts. Nothing seemed amiss; Evienne had been to all of the official read outs since she took the title of High Sangviere six years earlier.

She continued scanning the files, pulling out one labeled "*Schedule*". Odd—there had been another folder at the front of the drawer that held the full staffing rotation for the Centrale Lumine. She opened the folder, doubting that Dominique had truly left an outdated document in her files, given the rigorous upkeep this drawer clearly underwent.

The document inside was formatted like all the others she had seen, and the dates on the schedule grid were the same that the other file covered. All of the days were the current month. She pulled out the other schedule to compare, and her brow furrowed as she stared at them side by side.

One schedule—the one from the front of the drawer—had the standard two-hour shifts for three Sangviere around the clock to channel magic into the system, with ten supporting guards on duty in the building for twelve hours at a time. The second schedule, however, showed shifts of eight hours populated with a single name each shift.

Something was going on at the Centrale Lumine, and Evienne needed to find out what.

"WHAT year was mage light invented?" Orion asked as he scanned yet another book of Beitaran folklore from Cecelia's secret room.

The three had reconvened early the following morning

to continue their work, and were now settled comfortably around Cecelia's study, pouring over texts in the amber light.

"About two hundred and ten years ago," Cecelia answered without looking up from her book.

"Do you know exactly what year?" Orion asked again, flicking his gaze to Evienne where she sat across from him.

"It was technically invented in 787 Domhan na Rùin Standard, but it wasn't applied more widely until 801," Cecelia answered, finally looking up from her book. "Why?"

Evienne held Orion's gaze as he contemplated, a pit opening in her stomach as she slowly pieced things together. "And what year did the first consort arrive from Beitar?" She asked, her voice barely above a whisper.

"800 DnRS…" Cecelia answered slowly, catching up with the path Orion's mind had taken.

"The train was built in 845 DnRS and was expanded to our outer provinces starting in 895," Cecelia added, her inflection revealing her suspicion.

"When was it *exactly* that you all started to notice a decline in your magic, Orion?" Evienne asked, already knowing the answer, but needing to hear it anyway.

"The first documented account from one of our historians was in 863 DnRS" he answered solemnly.

"Fuck," Evienne swore, standing from the couch to begin pacing. Cecelia heaved a deep sigh, the air puffing up her cheeks as she ran her hands through her already messy hair.

"Fuck is right," Cecelia echoed.

"Alright, so clearly these things are linked—but how are we supposed to find out how exactly? Timing like that cannot be merely coincidence. No one that knew about the connection was writing about it based on how little we've found here in the library," Evienne said as she paced the room.

"It seems like things didn't get really bad until the Rail Dellumine expanded about a hundred years ago. That's when the magic of the Tuanadair really started to disappear, right? Before that it was just weakening?" Cecelia asked.

Orion nodded. "That's right; I agree with Evienne that the timing is too much of a coincidence to be an accident. We'll have to keep searching. We can't do anything without some sort of proof."

Evienne sighed and said, "Unfortunately, we're due for yet another function in an hour, so we will have to continue this tomorrow."

"Not tomorrow," Orion corrected. "Tomorrow is the outing on the Rail Dellumine, remember? The trip to the coast?"

Evienne groaned; she had forgotten. "Right, the outing. Well I suppose you'll at least get a good up-close look at the world-famous Rail Dellumine in all its glory."

Chapter Twenty-Seven

"Blood loss?" Léhiona asked the palace healer incredulously. She had finally relented to Sylvain's pestering and was now certain it was a waste of time.

"Yes, your majesty. Your symptoms are what we would expect to see in someone experiencing blood loss; those we see with it most often are Sangviere who have pushed their magic too far," the healer explained, maintaining his professional demeanor.

"But you see I am not bleeding. I have no scars or injuries. How do you suppose I am suffering from blood loss?"

"It is possible you have an internal injury that is bleeding, your majesty. Have you had any accidents lately? Any falls?"

"No, nothing of the sort," she answered, confused.

The healer's face showed a hint of concern then, and he considered for a moment. "I would suggest as much rest as possible for the next few weeks, as well as increased water intake and an iron supplement. We can check in then to see if your symptoms have improved at all. But please, your

Majesty, if you notice anything at all amiss, please return right away or call us to your chambers."

Léhiona nodded her understanding at the older man, and he turned to leave the small examination room.

Sylvain was waiting for her outside. "Were they able to prescribe anything for you?" He asked as they walked toward Léhiona's sitting room.

She wasn't sure why she felt the need to whisper, but she did. "They said I have symptoms of blood loss. Isn't that bizarre? I have no injuries to speak of."

He looked down at her as they walked, clearly sharing her confusion. "That was all they said? Blood loss? That is very strange indeed."

"They said to rest and drink water and take an iron supplement—but honestly, blood loss? I can't even remember the last time that I bled outside of my monthly cycle."

An unsettled feeling took root in Léhiona's mind that she couldn't quite shake for the rest of the day.

That evening, she sat with a book, waiting for Aldith to come to bed. They hadn't had much time together since the start of the festivities, and Léhiona wanted to talk with her wife about her strange visit to the healer.

The clock had just struck two in the morning when Aldith finally appeared.

"How was the party, my love?" Léhiona asked, setting aside her book and rising from the bed to cross to where Aldith stood removing her jewelry.

"It was alright, dear. How are you this evening? I am sorry you did not feel well enough to stay for longer."

"Sylvain finally convinced me to go to the healer today,"

Léhiona said, watching her wife in the mirror atop the small dressing table, where Aldith now sat.

Léhiona noticed Aldith's shoulders tense ever so slightly at her words. "Well, what did they have to say?" Aldith asked, her tone light, but somehow more intense than usual.

"They said I have symptoms of blood loss, of all things! I told Sylvain, I can't even remember the last time that I bled!" Léhiona said with a laugh. "I know you employ the best in Ichorna, but I must say I have my doubts."

Aldith's shoulders relaxed, and she turned to face Léhiona. "That does seem rather far-fetched. I'll begin a search for a new healer."

"Oh no, you don't need to do that! I don't mean to cost anyone their job. I am certain I'm just overtired and the healer was trying to humor me with a more serious diagnosis."

"Inaccuracy, whether pandering or otherwise, is not something I will tolerate from those in my service. I will find us a new healer. Thank you for bringing this to my attention, my love," Aldith's tone brooked no objection. Léhiona knew not to argue; Aldith always said her input was valuable, but in reality, Aldith had the final say on everything in their lives.

"I am glad there is nothing really ailing you," Aldith said as she slipped a nightgown over her head. "Now, come to bed?"

Léhiona quieted her thoughts and followed her wife to bed.

Chapter Twenty-Eight

The following morning, all of the foreign dignitaries gathered at the station closest to the palace complex. Lucinne had become a hub for travelers since the invention of the Rail Dellumine, but the diversity of this crowd was striking for even Evienne, who had spent many years in the city.

From where she sat aboard the train, she could see a large group of Aphanians, the water-dwellers from the Vaporiad Sea to the south. A cluster of Wellsah stood near them, staring up at the bronze Rail cars in wonder.

Even Daosbor, the realm of necromancers, had sent a delegation. The necromancers stood off to the side looking on, their pale faces expressionless as they took in the scene. Evienne did a double-take as she noticed a tall, striking person she could only describe as…leafy standing with the necromancers. A woman with bright red hair and a radiant smile clung to their arm and looked up at them adoringly. Was that a Dryad? Evienne did not know any of the non-human creatures of Domhan na Rùin had been invited to the festivities, but she supposed stranger things had happened.

Evienne was pulled from her people-watching by a sudden tug of awareness, and she turned just as Orion and Solon took their seats facing hers. A small table sat between them, bolted to the floor.

Before she could open her mouth to greet the two men, Cecelia's laughing voice cut in as she slipped into the seat next to Evienne. "I decided to take the day off, so I get to come too!" she said excitedly.

Evienne couldn't help but smile at her friend. "Oh how wonderful! I'm so glad we'll have your company for the day."

Cecelia settled into her seat looking very pleased with herself. Evienne caught Orion trying not to laugh in the seat across from her and softly kicked him under the table.

Shortly after everyone had boarded their Rail cars, the Rail Dellumine launched into motion, gliding silently over the bronze tracks through Lucinne and out into the rolling fields of Ichora's countryside.

Today's journey would take around three hours each way, with a stop at midday in the harbor town of Brunoy on Ichorna's eastern coast. The bustling port town sat on the shores of the Dalmar Sea.

The journey to Brunoy passed quickly. Evienne let herself forget about the lingering apprehension and stress she felt about their investigation in favor of enjoying her time with her friends. That's what Orion and Solon were to her now: friends. And perhaps, with Orion, something more.

When the Rail Dellumine arrived at the Brunoy station, the horde of dignitaries and nobles disembarked and were set loose upon the small town. The cold ocean air bit at Evienne's face the moment she stepped out into the white light of the afternoon.

Evienne enjoyed the sea on the rare occasions she had reason to see it. The sound of crashing surf echoed through the streets of the quaint seaside town.

Orion offered her an arm, and she accepted it, glancing up into his handsome face to give him a small smile. He smiled back at her, and somewhere in her heart, she knew she wanted to stay with him forever.

AFTER a few hours of enjoying the ocean views and enjoying lunch at lavishly set picnic tables on the beach, the group made their way in twos and threes back toward the station.

Cecelia insisted on taking a detour to have a look around the town square, so the four of them walked in that direction, enjoying each other's company as they went.

The square bustled with activity despite the chill, with market stands selling the day's catch and brightly lit storefronts filled with colorful fabrics, books, and housewares. Evienne was enjoying taking in every detail when, without warning, a siren blared through the general hum of noise in the square.

Evienne knew the sound well from her training, but it was jarring to hear the alarm system here when she least expected it. The system was the same as those that she had overseen the setup of in all of their larger provincial towns; their purpose was to warn citizens of a Gevaud attack.

Evienne's training slammed her into action. She was

nothing if not good in a crisis, and until she understood the scope of this attack, she would treat it as though it were serious.

Evienne turned to her friends, shouting over the now chaotic sounds of the townspeople taking cover as they had been instructed when the alarms were installed. "You have to get back to the station and get on the train; don't wait for me, I'll handle this."

"We're not *leaving* you here!" Cecelia yelled back.

Evienne knew there wasn't time to argue. She looked to Solon, who nodded in understanding. "Please, come with me," Solon said simply to Cecelia, offering her his arm. She glared at Evienne, then took it, not wanting to be rude to Solon. He escorted her quickly out of the square—Evienne only hoped they made it to the train in time.

Orion took Evienne's hand and squeezed. "You know I won't leave you in danger, love," he said. "I'm with you."

She smiled at him then, grateful to have him by her side.

They both turned as a scream sounded across the square, followed by a vicious snarl. Evienne took off in a run, her burgundy dress billowing around her legs as she ran. Orion shifted and ran alongside her. The winter air bit her lungs, and she felt time slow as she neared the scene and took in the sight before her.

Gevaud were indiscriminately attacking anything in their path. There appeared to be around ten of the beasts, but more streamed in to the square from the surrounding streets. Evienne knew only a few Sangviere were typically stationed here, and she didn't see them anywhere yet. Guards rushed into the square, but without blood magic, they stood little chance of neutralizing the Gevaud.

A beast lunged at one of the guards, snapping Evienne back into action. She summoned her most instinctual magic, her blood fire, and hurled it at the beast. It staggered, giving the guard time to fall back.

Orion stood ready at her side, waiting to take his signals from her. Evienne turned to him, holding his piercing gaze, and nodded; her way of telling him to stay safe in the fray.

The Gevaud spread out, attacking without form or reason. Evienne looked around again for the other Sangviere, but saw none. For now, immediacy was key to saving the lives of the people of Brunoy as they tried to find cover. Every second she had spent studying, honing her craft, doubting herself; it was all for this. To help her people.

Evienne strode forward to the center of the square, swiping her ring fully across her palm this time. Her magic roared to life in her veins, stronger, somehow, than she had ever felt it.

She found that place inside herself where she could push her magic to exert her will on another living being. She felt it, focusing on the Gevaud about twenty feet from her. One moment, the beast was lurching forward; the next her magic had taken hold, forcing it to the ground.

She took hold of another beast a mere ten feet away from the first, willing them toward each other. They moved with stilted, unnatural motions until they collided. She forced them to tear each other's throats out, their blood spraying a downed guard trying to scramble away from them.

Evienne didn't lose her focus. Her eyes scanned the square, working to prioritize her next target. Her mind flew over the details as she took them in, strategizing intuitively.

A scream had her turning to the western edge of the square. Two Sangviere had arrived only to immediately be swarmed by a new cluster of Gevaud as they bounded into the open.

At least thirty of the creatures were now running rampant. Evienne had to protect the other Sangviere or they would certainly lose this fight.

She felt for the lifeblood of the two beasts circling the Sangviere where they had been knocked down, forcing her magic into them. Evienne's breath came in heavy pants as she strained with the effort of her casting, before both beasts burst into clouds of red mist.

The other Sangviere nodded at Evienne gratefully and fell back into a formation, covering each other's backs. Each then took control of a creature with their Regne du Sang and disarmed it by whatever means necessary.

She was struck then by how unnerving blood magic could really be. She was grateful she would never know the feeling of someone taking hold of her own blood—the thought of being so completely at the mercy of another was harrowing. Their sort of magic—even without the corrupting influence of the Valsang—was dark enough as it was.

Despite the best efforts of the Sangviere, there were simply too many Gevaud to manage in the way they had planned for, trained for. Taking them out one or two at a time wasn't enough.

The horde had downed at least four guards now. Orion had engaged two of the beasts on the opposite side of the square, and was holding his own against them, swiping his massive paws and deathly sharp claws. She flicked her gaze back to the cluster of beasts in front of her.

Evienne could not allow them to kill anyone else; she had a job to do, and she would see it done.

She sliced her other palm open, power now nearly overwhelming her, and raised her hands before her. Her magic gripped each and every one of the Gevaud that remained, thirty living things falling under her control. She could feel it; the blood rushing through their veins, the life force calling to her soul. Time slowed to a stop as she listened to the chorus of beating hearts, feeling the heat of her own blood on her hands.

Closing her fists, she slammed the creatures down to the paving stones. With a twist of her wrists, a sickening crunch sounded, reverberating off the buildings of the square. Every one of the creatures lay lifeless, bodies twisted and bones shattered from within.

All Evienne could hear was the pounding of her own pulse as she surveyed the scene before her. Her heart clenched painfully; she knew she was pushing her magic too far. Black edged her vision as she scanned the square, searching for a spot of white in what was now a sea of red.

She felt him before she saw him; brilliant pain seared her as her gaze landed on him. Bright red blood marred his beautiful white coat, and Evienne screamed as she watched a Gevaud swipe its massive claws across his ribs.

The beast Orion was fighting lunged, sensing its opponent's weakness, and latched its massive jaw around Orion's neck.

Evienne didn't hesitate, that deeper magic that was her greatest secret rushing out into the world. Every time she had used it, she hadn't known how or why—but it came when she had need of it. Only in her most raw, desperate moments did this gift show itself.

From where she stood, it seemed a trick of the light when her magic first took hold of the beast. But as the seconds ticked by, she could see it. The Gevaud's body was withering, decaying, before her eyes. Its eyes sank in, its skin went sallow and thin, and soon it sagged away from the creatures bones. It became bent, and the colors of rot spread, blossoming across the Gevaud's body. Before ten seconds had passed, the beast was collapsing in front of Orion, its vicious bite long forgotten. Another breath, and it was no more than a pile of dust at Orion's feet.

Orion raised his eyes to her, their gazes connecting across the short distance. Evienne shook her head slightly at him, hoping he understood and would wait until they were alone to discuss what had just happened. Too many secrets had just been laid bare for all to see. The mound of dust blew away on the ocean breeze as they stared at each other.

The few Gevaud that had managed to remain unscathed had turned to flee, running at full speed down the narrow streets. Evienne turned to the other Sangviere, giving them the order to pursue and kill on sight. She could only hope that everyone had been too concerned with the Gevaud to notice a *snow leopard* of all things in the middle of their seaside town. Her heart continued to protest her overuse of her power, thudding painfully beneath her ribs.

One of the town guards rushed over then, wanting Evienne's instructions as the highest-ranking official on the scene. Once she had given all the orders that needed to be given, she turned to find Orion sitting against a wall nearby, back in his human form. The Tuanadair magic seemed to somehow preserve the clothes their human forms had been wearing—a fascinating question for another time. Orion had an awful gash across his shoulder and several sharp punctures around his neck. Evienne quickly forgot the pain in her own chest.

"I need a medic, immediately," Evienne shouted with command in her voice to anyone who could hear her. A medic quickly found her way over to Orion and knelt down to begin her work.

All three were silent as she worked, bandaging up the wounds. Finally, as she was packing up her supplies, she addressed her patient.

"Please take it easy for a while. These wounds were, thankfully, not deep, but there is a risk of infection. Go see the palace healers if anything seems amiss, and change your bandages regularly."

"Thank you. I am in your debt," Orion answered, trying to muster a smile that read more like a grimace. The medic nodded, looking to Evienne.

"Thank you for your service," Evienne offered the medic a slight nod as she departed.

"We need to get back to the station," Evienne said, bending down and offering Orion her arm despite her exhaustion. She didn't let herself pause to think too long on what had just happened.

Chapter Twenty-Nine

THE JOURNEY BACK to Lucinne passed in a blur for Evienne; she could barely keep her eyes open. Expending so much power always took a physical toll.

When they returned to the palace, medics were on hand to treat any minor injuries the delegations had suffered in their flight back to the station. Thankfully no one other than the town guards and Orion had been seriously injured.

"What happened out there?" Orion's voice was full of confusion and disbelief, but not reproach. They had made their way back to his room in the guest wing as quickly as possible when they arrived in Lucinne. Evienne knew she didn't have long before she would need to seek out an audience with the queens to give her report of what had occurred. The attack had been unexpected and was certain to have everyone on edge.

"You remember I told you about how I sometimes see other people's memories?" Evienne began. Orion nodded, but Evienne hesitated.

"You know I'll believe you, love," Orion took her face

gently in his hand and turned her toward him. The certainty she felt in her soul at his statement was…a revelation. It took her breath away.

"Yes," she said, surprised at her own soul-deep surety. "I do know that."

Orion nodded, placing a kiss on her temple and pulling her close.

"Well, a few times it hasn't been memories at all; it's been similar to what happened today. It's as if…" she trailed off, afraid to give voice to the words that had haunted her since that first time in the alley with Cecelia.

"It's as if I've stolen the life right out of someone," she said, barely a whisper. "Like I've taken hold of every moment remaining in their life and yanked it away until all that's left is dust."

Orion considered what she had said, his thumbs tracing circles gently on her shoulders where he still held her.

"Moments. You said moments when describing the way this has manifested," he said finally.

"Yes, I suppose I did," Evienne answered. "That's what it feels like," she continued. "Like I can walk through the seconds of people's lives when I see their memories, or simply rip them away like I did this afternoon."

"You have time magic," Orion whispered, a look of realization on his face.

Evienne was silent, the words sinking into her spirit. She had known intuitively, of course, but hadn't let herself look closely enough at what had happened to name it.

"I have time magic," she echoed. "I didn't think it was real; did you know it was real?"

"It comes up in fables about the Contrapensae and mythological texts every so often, but I don't know of any recent historical accounts that mention it," Orion answered.

"Alright, time magic, then. That's… something," Evienne struggled to adjust to the reality that she harbored some sort of rare, deadly magic.

She knew her blood magic was dangerous, but she had rules and other mages to keep her accountable in how she used it. The knowledge of this secret magic she contained and the implications of its power weighed on her heart.

"I have to go give my report to the queens. We can only hope the news of your shifting didn't make it back to them," Evienne said, pulling the pieces of herself back together. If they were going to get anywhere with their investigation, all needed to appear normal for as long as possible, and that meant giving her report, not lingering here with her lover.

Orion kissed her again. "We'll figure it out together, alright? Thank you for telling me," he said, taking her hand and giving it a soft squeeze. She nodded and turned toward the door.

THE queens' sitting room, which usually felt so warm and familiar, today felt uncanny. Evienne supposed her suspicions about Ichorna's relationship with their northern neighbors had cast an uneasy light on her usually comfortable existence here.

Evienne didn't have to wait long before the heavy wooden door swung open, and Léhiona, always the first to their meetings, glided into the room.

Even she, usually so soft and warm, had an air of worry and tension about her today. The attack had clearly shaken her.

"Evi, are you alright?" Léhiona asked, breathless, as she moved swiftly to Evienne's side at the center of the room.

"Yes, I'm fine. Is all well with you?" She answered, taking her friend's hand. It trembled slightly, and Evienne glanced down, taking in the sight of Léhiona's tattooed wedding band and letting the chill of her friend's hand seep into the warmth of her own.

"I suppose so, yes," Léhiona answered softly. "Though I worry that all our guests do not feel safe here now."

Evienne nodded in understanding, giving her friend's hand a light squeeze.

The door opened again, and the crisp click of Aldith's heeled shoes sounded through the room as she strode over to them.

"Evienne, I'm glad to see you unharmed," she said, voice even.

"Thank you, your majesty. I am here to give my report on the attack in Brunoy," Evienne said, her professional persona taking over.

Aldith nodded, her expression encouraging Evienne to begin her report.

She began recounting the events, focusing on concrete details and providing her assessment of how the guards and Sangviere handled the attack. She left out the part about Orion shifting during battle; she wasn't sure what the queens' response would be, and she preferred to avoid provoking their suspicions as long as possible. She said only that Orion had been injured in the attack, but would make a full recovery.

"Do you have any idea how the Gevaud were able to approach without earlier detection?" Aldith asked, always the pragmatist.

"I do not currently have any theories; only that I assume they are becoming more strategic in avoiding detection from our watchpoints," Evienne offered.

Aldith considered this, her face creasing with worry. "I see. What do you suggest as preventative measures to avoid a repeat attack?"

"Additional temporary lookouts, for the time being," Evienne answered. "Until we understand their motives for attack, vigilance is our only defense."

"I am aware that efforts to determine their motive and origin have been, as of yet, unfruitful, but I would like us to redouble our efforts. We need to understand our enemy, and this unexpected attack would suggest they're not just the mindless brutes we've always thought," Aldith said, pacing her usual route across the center of the room.

"I understand; I will lead the investigation myself," Evienne answered.

"No, you must remain focused on your current task monitoring the Beitarans. We'll have Dominique handle the investigation. Have you managed to learn anything about the Beitarans' motives for being here?" Aldith asked, her dismissal clear. Evienne chafed at the thought of Dominique taking over where she had been unable to make progress.

"Beyond the Professor's desire to access our library for his research, I've not seen anything that would indicate an ulterior motive," Evienne said, the lie rolling off her tongue easily in the wake of Aldith's brusque demand for information and casual mention of Evienne's former wife.

Aldith considered, and Evienne added, "I will continue to ingratiate myself with them in order to learn more."

"And do you, Evienne, think me a fool?" Aldith asked, her tone now icy.

"Your majesty?" Evienne cast a glance at Léhiona, who was staring off into space, clearly not engaged with the conversation.

"There were reports of a snow leopard at the confrontation today. Were you planning to mention that, or did you think it unworthy of discussion?"

Evienne began to answer, but Aldith cut her off. "Don't answer that. I have also heard reports of your nighttime escapades with Professor Doehlan. I take no issue with you seeking your pleasure, Evienne, especially when it is a means to an end. But see that your efforts produce the information we need. I will not have you keeping things from me. This will be your only warning."

She turned to Léhiona then.

"Come, my love, we should prepare for this evening's events," Aldith said, taking Léhiona's hand. Evienne noticed her absently running her thumb over Léhiona's tattooed wedding band. A similar one marked Aldith's left ring finger.

Evienne bowed to the queens as they took their leave, and as she raised her head, she caught Léhiona looking back over her shoulder, worry lining her face.

Chapter Thirty

Orion sat in the quiet of his luxurious room and stared at the flames in the hearth. These were more orange than the scarlet flames Evienne wielded. He preferred hers—more lovely and more deadly, just like her.

The searing pain in his shoulder and neck was starting to subside thanks to his magic; fast healing was one of the strongest gifts of the Tuanadair. He felt very grateful for it now.

The past weeks had been a whirlwind of discoveries and emotions, and Orion was glad to have a moment to himself to reflect on all that had happened. Their conversation with Cecelia in the library a few days ago weighed heavily on his mind now that there was no noise to distract him.

He had known the consorts had something to do with the magic disappearing, but it had just been conjecture. Without more information, it could be dismissed as a coincidence. Lining up the timeline of Ichorna's technological progression with the depletion of Beitar's magic was helpful in understanding the two to be connected, but it still wasn't proof.

They needed to know *why* the two timelines seemed connected. He assumed Ichorna was robbing Beitar of its magic to power its elaborate Rail system, but how could such a thing be possible?

To accomplish such a thing, Ichorna would have had to create some method of siphoning magic from others—he had never read of such a thing—and apply it on a massive scale. They would also have had to keep such a scandal secret for nearly two centuries.

Orion shifted in his seat and felt the stiffness of his muscles. Orion thought about going across the hall to check on Solon, but he was likely with the other dignitaries still. They had been summoned to a meeting to discuss the attack. Moments like this made Orion glad he was no politician—books and lectures would suffice for him.

An image drifted into Orion's mind of the Gevaud that had attacked him that morning—and what Evienne had done to it. He had never seen anything like it. The creature had dried up and fallen to dust before him. It had been incredibly disturbing, and he doubted the image would ever truly leave his mind. To have such power was almost unthinkable.

The fire began to die down and Orion leaned his head back against his chair and closed his eyes. He was so tired and so worried about what the future might hold. He wanted to remain optimistic, but he was afraid. Afraid of what they might discover about Ichorna's intentions, of what the consequences would be if their meddling was found out. He was most afraid of what would happen if they failed; things were not going well in Beitar.

The spirits of the Tuanadair were darkening the longer they were detached from their connection to Domhan na Rùin's magic. He was afraid of watching their health fail, their hearts break. Something told him they were running out of time.

Chapter Thirty-One

That evening, Evienne excused herself from the festivities, citing a need to recover after the attack in the afternoon. In truth, it was the conversation with the queens that had left her shaken. She had never felt such a distance from them in all her years of service. Even before they all stepped into their adult roles, she had never known such awkwardness with them as girls.

The sight of Léhiona's worry as she had left the room hung in Evienne's mind, and now that the adrenaline of the attack had worn off, she couldn't help but ponder her conversation with Cecelia and Orion in the library with increasing anxiety.

There were too many coincidences in the timing to be meaningless. Determining how actively nefarious any connections were would be the real challenge. They needed to find out if anyone currently living in Ichorna knew something, but there was a reason this history—if there was one—was not common knowledge. It was likely if someone did know, they would not appreciate anyone poking around for insight. Evienne knew they had to continue their investigation, but she had a feeling they were about to stumble into a very dangerous game.

Her soul weary with all that had occurred that day, Evienne made her way to Orion's chamber in the guest wing, stopping a maid in the hall to request that dinner be brought up. She rapped her knuckles on his door, and his rich, open voice answered. Evienne found him seated in the armchair by the fire, a book in hand, looking a bit paler than usual.

"How are you feeling?" She asked, curling up on the floor next to his legs. The heat of the fire seeped into her hands; she hadn't even noticed how cold she'd been.

"I've been better, but I am glad you're here with me," Orion answered, his hand stroking Evienne's hair.

"We've had quite a day," Evienne said with a sigh.

"Indeed, we have. I confess, charging into battle in my shifted form is not something I ever thought I would do. It was exhilarating and intense and…sort of awful," he said, considering.

Evienne remembered what it had felt like the first time she had been in a real fight, and she didn't blame Orion one bit for feeling the weight of it. She relished the rightness of wielding her magic, but she did not take joy in hurting other living things. She often pondered how her actions straddled the line between good and evil.

"I do not know if I am cut out for such violence. Perhaps I should leave it to you to be my fearless defender." He smiled at her then. Evienne was so grateful, she realized, that Orion felt comfortable enough to share these musings with her.

"I will happily be your knight in shining armor, Orion," Evienne said, smiling back at him.

"How are you doing?" He asked, giving her space to share her feelings. She looked up at him and saw in his face that he actually wanted to know, that he really cared.

"I'm…" she started, struggling to put words to her feelings. "I'm overwhelmed, I think." Emotion clogged her throat.

"I certainly don't blame you for that, love," he said softly.

"I just," she started again, fighting the tightness in her chest and losing. "The implications of what we were talking about in the library yesterday, and the Gevaud showing up so unexpectedly today, and you getting hurt, and my time magic lashing out, and this strange dissonance with the queens and lying to their faces," the words tumbled out as tears streaked her face. "It feels like my whole life is stained glass, shattering pane by pane," she continued.

Orion remained silent and attentive. She continued, "I know, when it's over, I'll see the true light of day. The colors, however lovely, are lies, it would seem." Her voice broke as the words passed her lips.

As she spoke, Orion joined her on the floor, pulling her close. She rested her head on his shoulder, her face buried in his neck. He didn't say a word, just held her, and she let her tears flow.

After what could have been minutes or hours, Orion's voice broke the silence. "You're the most courageous person I know, Evienne."

"I'm so glad to have met you," Evienne said, her voice now hoarse from sobbing. "I don't know what the future will hold for either of us, or what it really means to be your Còmhanam, but if some higher destiny chose you for me, I can't help but feel honored."

Orion pressed a kiss to her temple, his hand rubbing soothing circles on her back. "I don't know what I did to deserve to share my soul with you, but I will endeavor to be worthy of your love every day of my life. I know what we are facing feels impossible, but the hope of a life with you on the other side..." he trailed off, and Evienne glanced up to find a tear tracing down his cheek. She brushed it away, cupping his cheek in her hand.

"Whatever comes, I'm glad we'll face it together," Evienne whispered. "My brilliant, kind, fearsome Còmhanam."

EVIENNE was unsure if she was awake or asleep as she extended her hand to the luna moth, who seemed so familiar now. It landed on her hand, gently fluttering its wings, and Evienne smiled at it. It was so lovely, so bright even here in the dark.

She looked up from its hypnotic colors to see an expanse of leathery wings filling her range of vision. Its slate gray scales were the size of her hand, and the wind from its landing swept her luna moth friend into the darkness where it danced on the breeze.

The massive beast stilled, and a growling sound filled the space around Evienne. It turned then, and she caught sight of the dragon's massive head, its amber eyes appraising her. She gasped in surprise, but she did not feel fear.

A smaller dragon, this one a vibrant, shimmering blue,

peered around the larger one. It held Evienne's gaze for a long moment before the blinding light Evienne knew too flashed searing red as she woke with a jolt.

The day broke outside Orion's window, a winter dawn kissing Evienne's face as she lay next to him, startled, with a sheen of sweat on her brow. Orion still slept next to her, his breathing soft and rhythmic. She savored these seconds of peace, settling them deep in her mind, calming her breathing.

She had been awake most of the night thinking about what she knew she must do, and her dream made her feel even more sure for some reason. It was the hope of more mornings like this, her Còmhanam peacefully by her side, that gave her the courage to even consider it.

"Good morning, love," Orion's voice greeted her, raspy with lingering sleep. She turned then to look at him, and his beauty truly overwhelmed her.

The sun caught the cool green of his eyes and illuminated every perfect plane of his face. She gave herself a moment to commit the sight to memory, smiling at him.

"I know what I have to do to find the truth," Evienne whispered.

Orion's brow furrowed slightly in question.

"I have to use my time magic."

Chapter Thirty-Two

Léhiona was surrounded by a pulsing blackness. All she could see, everywhere she looked, the darkness encompassed her. Tendrils of it latched onto her skin and pulled, biting at her, burrowing deep into her bones; but she couldn't scream. She could only watch, mute and helpless to pull away.

As more and more of the darkness dug into her, she felt her body relax. She heard the voices of others, softly at first. She couldn't distinguish how many, but the chorus increased in volume as she listened. First, they were murmurs; after a few moments they were screams.

So many voices, screeching in anguish, begging some unseen power to save them. They were lost, confused. They called for help that wouldn't come.

Léhiona could do nothing save bear witness to their suffering, bound as she was by the darkness. Just when she thought her soul could take no more, the darkness swallowed her whole.

She jolted, and felt the weight of Aldith's arm draped

over her. Opening her eyes, she surveyed their bedroom in the early morning light. She took a deep breath, calming her racing heart. These nightmares had become more frequent in the past months, and Léhiona didn't know what to do about them.

She reached down to take Aldith's hand where it lay across her waist, and her thumb brushed against something that felt wet—almost tacky. She brought her hand back up to take a closer look, struggling to see in the dimness. Still unable to see what it was, she carefully got out of the bed and padded over to the window.

She saw then that it was the sticky brown of drying blood. She glanced back at Aldith where she slept and saw that tiny droplets were splattered on her hand and wrist. Her wife was a Sangviere, so it wasn't a cause for panic, but it wasn't like Aldith to make such a mess when working her spells.

Léhiona climbed back into bed, but sleep did not find her again.

Chapter Thirty-Three

Evienne helped Orion change the bandages on his wound, which had healed significantly through the night. He would have his full range of motion back in a few days at this rate. It seemed shifting was not the only magic that had returned to him; the quick-healing gifts of the Tuanadair had found him as well.

After returning to her chambers to bathe and dress for the day, Evienne found Solon and Orion at their usual table in the dining hall for breakfast. There was a tournament today, and they decided it would be as good an opportunity as any for Evienne to use her magic as they'd planned.

"Solon, good morning. I hope you're well and not too shaken up after yesterday's attack?" Evienne took her seat next to the noble and helped herself to a cup of steaming coffee. She tried not to think too much about the magic she would attempt in a few short hours.

"Well, it was certainly unexpected, but I have it on good authority that it was well-managed and that everything is under control," Solon answered, giving her a wry look.

"We've increased lookouts so at the very least, they're unlikely to catch us unawares again," Evienne said, ever the professional.

"And how are you?" Solon asked, his voice softer and full of genuine concern.

"I'm well, thank you. And thank you for taking care of Cecelia yesterday," Evienne answered with a small smile of appreciation. Once this was all over, she'd like to think Solon would consider her a friend.

"So," Evienne continued as she sliced a pat of butter from the communal dish and began spreading it on a warm scone. "Did Orion mention to you how pleasant our ride out to the forest was the other day?"

"He did," Solon answered, his gaze flicking to Orion.

"It really was spectacular, my friend," Orion added, barely managing to contain the smile tugging at his lips.

"Perhaps one morning you'd both show me the way," Solon said, his voice still light.

Evienne smiled and nodded, "We'd be delighted to."

After breakfast, all of the guests that had continued arriving in Ichorna for the festivities over the past weeks began to make their way to L'Arene Lucinne for a Sangviere tournament.

Ichorna held several such events each year, so it seemed only natural to host one as a part of the Millennium celebration. Evienne had loved competing in tournaments as a student, but these days she was mostly a spectator.

Orion and Solon had been invited to sit in the royal box with the queens, and Evienne always had a seat there as High Sangviere. The royal box was on the top level of the arena to afford the queens and their favored guests the best views of the magic duels below. The term "box" was certainly misleading; it was really a suite, complete with balconies, an assortment of seating options, and a table laid with a wide array of refreshments.

The three entered the suite, and Evienne led Solon and Orion toward where the queens were seated with Dominique and Sylvain. Dominique had always loved these public opportunities to flaunt her closeness with the queens; Evienne had counted on this time being no different.

"Your majesties, Dominique," Evienne began, lowering into a full curtsey. "May we join you?" She spoke without making eye contact with Dominique, but even in her peripheral vision, she could sense Dominique's discomfort from her rigid posture.

Aldith's gaze met Evienne's, a bit emptier than usual, though her expression was as calm and regal as always.

"Of course, we're delighted to have you both with us for the tournament today. Thank you for accepting our invitation. Please, do have a seat," Aldith said, gesturing to the empty chair beside Dominique's. Solon took the offered seat, while Orion and Evienne moved to take positions in the row behind them, next to Sylvain.

Evienne knew Orion had told Solon enough of the plan for the Lord to play his part. He would engage Dominique in conversation to distract her from what Evienne was about to attempt.

Evienne had told Orion she'd never used her time magic on purpose, always stumbling on it intuitively. He'd encouraged her to simply try, and she'd had no room to argue when he had suggested it earlier this morning. Their research in the archives was getting them nowhere, and there were only a few days left of the Millennium celebration.

She took a deep breath, steadying her nerves, and Orion's knee bumped hers ever so slightly in silent support. They had decided Dominique should be their target today based on the odd duplicate schedule they had found. It wasn't much, but it was their only lead pointing to anything the least bit suspicious. Likely nothing would come of it, but they had to try. Evienne heard her mentor's voice in her mind, encouraging her to be curious and pull on loose threads.

A cheer rose from the assembled crowd as the first two Sangviere entered the arena below.

Evienne's magic had always manifested as blood red fire. The Sangviere below seemed to have blood ice, while the other crackled with scarlet lightning. Their bolts of magic began flashing across the arena and the crowd continued to cheer.

Evienne shifted her focus back to her impossible task. Solon was talking with Dominique, and she seemed to be giving him her full attention in return—no doubt curious to learn what she could about their unusual visitors. Evienne had bet that Dominique would be charming and attentive to Solon because of his nobility, despite having been so rude to Orion at the garden party. It seemed she had calculated correctly.

Fixing her eyes on a point ahead of her, Evienne began to search herself for the thread of time magic that she had felt when she'd collided with Solon in the hall the other day. The magic of memories was what she needed now, not the more destructive side of her time magic that had made an appearance during the attack yesterday.

She had never consciously done this, so the gentle hum she felt in her mind as she engaged her magic was unfamiliar. She focused on the sensation and cast her mind toward Dominique.

Dominique, who she had thought was her everything. Dominique, who she thought had loved her, but who had loved to control her more.

One moment, Evienne was in the arena surrounded by thousands of people and the flashes of magic below. The next, she was in a dim hallway, not a window in sight.

Chapter Thirty-Four

Red mage lights gave the narrow space an eerie feeling, and Evienne became aware of the feeling of cool metal in her hand. The sound of a door shutting behind her broke the silence.

Evienne's own mind became distant, replaced by Dominique's memory.

Dominique turned to look back at the massive, unmarked door and locked it with a black metal key. The door was made out of the same strange material; Evienne had never seen anything like it.

Once the door was locked, Dominique turned and strode down the hall. Soon, a second set of steps echoed through the sparse corridor, and none other than Aldith rounded the corner. Dominique didn't seem surprised to see the queen.

"Your Majesty." Dominique inclined her head slightly.

"No need for the formality down here, Dom," Aldith answered. "No one here to see." Her words were tinged with annoyance.

"How is our latest addition?" Aldith asked.

"They were one of the more challenging ones, but they've been incorporated. All is well," Dominique answered.

"Good, and you're exploring our next prospect?" Aldith pressed.

"I am. We will likely need to find options outside the city proper to avoid arousing suspicions, but no matter what our time is limited. The power is fading, and taking more from your little pet isn't going to fix your decades-old botched spellwork," Dominique said with a hint of venom.

Aldith glared at Dominique, clearly deciding to ignore her vitriol. "It was ten years ago, Dom. You really should let it go. Just because you didn't take to your wife doesn't mean I can't like mine." Aldith's voice was a hiss. "Let's get back before we're missed; you know we have a special tournament to attend and a suite full of foreign dignitaries to entertain today," Aldith said, turning to head back the way she came.

At Aldith's last words, Evienne began to panic. This memory was from today; the clothes Aldith and Dominique wore were the same. Whatever was going on was actively happening, and she would bet her life that the dark hallway was hidden somewhere in the Centrale Lumine.

Evienne gripped the thread of her magic and ripped herself out of Dominique's memory and back into her own present. Only a breath had passed in the current flow of time. Evienne's sense of foreboding at what she had seen was overwhelming; she couldn't bear not knowing what was happening for a moment longer. More than that, she knew she wouldn't have another chance to look for what she needed.

Acting on impulse, she felt for her magic again, this time throwing her mind toward Aldith's.

Léhiona lay unconscious on the floor of a room lit only by a glowing red light, Dominique standing over her. Evienne oriented herself to the memory more quickly this time, recognizing Aldith's voice as it filled the room.

"We need to be quick. I don't know how long that sleeping drought will last," Aldith said to Dominique.

Dominique nodded and held her hand out toward Aldith, who gripped a silver dagger.

Aldith took Dominique's offered hand, slicing quick and deep across her palm. Aldith's hands glowed a bright red that quickly settled into inky black. The words she spoke were in a language unfamiliar to Evienne.

As she spoke the spell, she grasped Léhiona's left hand and black light condensed, zipping over Léhiona's ring finger. Dominique reached over and pricked Léhiona's finger with her silver mage ring, and the drop of blood that formed floated up to twist around the strands of black magic in the air.

Aldith finished speaking, and the twist of magic and blood tightened around Léhiona's finger in an intricate floral pattern. The writhing black sank into Léhiona's skin, right over where her tattooed wedding band wrapped around her finger, and her face twisted in pain despite her unconsciousness. Aldith drew in a quick breath and rested her hand on Léhiona's cheek. Dominique sliced Léhiona's palm and filled a small bowl with her blood, setting it aside.

Aldith released Léhiona's hand, fighting for breath. Evienne's own mind, distant as it was, reeled in horror at the dark magic she had just witnessed.

Dominique stepped out of Aldith's view, and a loud hissing sound filled the space. When she returned, the bowl of Léhiona's blood was empty.

"Do you think it worked? Is she bound? Did we establish the connection correctly? I thought there were supposed to be tendrils that connected her to it at first," Dominique asked quietly.

"Time will tell, but we followed my father's instructions closely enough. We need to get her out of here before she wakes up," Aldith snapped in a harsh whisper.

"What do you mean *closely enough*? Forgive me for wanting to ensure all of Ichorna doesn't go dark because you did it wrong," Dominique goaded, bending to help Aldith lift Léhiona into a sitting position.

"Of course I didn't do it wrong; I just made a small adjustment," Aldith muttered. "This spell has been in my family for generations. My father trusted me with this, and I will see it done. You know as well as I do, it's the only way to ensure Ichorna's progress."

"Are you sure we shouldn't tell Sylvain about all of this? Just as a backup plan?" Dominique asked, struggling to lift Léhiona's limp form.

"I'm sure; he's too kind to do what must be done."

When evienne's mind retracted into itself, her hands began to shake.

Orion was there, his leg pressed more insistently into hers, but he kept his hands casually folded in his lap. What Evienne had just seen tipped her whole world on its axis, but she had to keep herself composed right now, or she'd risk everything.

She took a deep breath, settling back into her own mind, training her eyes on the tournament below and trying to look engaged. What she had seen was worse than anything she had imagined.

She had been suspicious, of course; the trail of information they had followed had certain implications that she had considered over the past weeks. Her former wife conspiring with the queen to bind Léhiona using dark blood magic had not been on her list of possible outcomes.

Even more upsetting was the scene she had witnessed beneath the Centrale Lumine. It implied that not only did Aldith and Dominique do this awful thing in the past, but they were actively continuing their plot, whatever it may be.

Evienne suddenly understood the duplicate schedule she had found in Dominique's office; it must be for a guard rotation stationed in that room she had seen below the facility. All of the pieces they had unearthed were clicking into place, and Evienne felt her horror solidify in the pit of her stomach.

Léhiona's binding and the secret room were connected, and the fading magic aligned with the consorts' presence in Ichorna going back two hundred years. Aldith had said the binding spell had been in her family for generations…

Evienne's heart was racing and she needed to escape this confined space. Orion couldn't leave with her without raising suspicions, so she would have to make this escape on her own.

She stood and gave her excuses to the group, though

their focus didn't leave the action below for long. When no one made to stop her or ask any questions, she quickly turned to leave, making her way swiftly down the arena stairs and out into the bustling city.

Her breath came in pants now, shallow and unsatisfying. There was a pinching sensation in her chest and her pulse pounded in her ears. Her steps slowed as she became overwhelmed by the sensations of her own existence, and before she knew it, she found herself leaning against the outer wall of a building, just trying to breathe.

She was lost to her own mind when a gentle hand grasped her upper arm, and a familiar face appeared before her—Hestia. Her lovely, kind mentor was somehow here, and Evienne couldn't get enough air down to say hello.

"Come with me, Dove, it's going to be alright," Hestia said quietly, guiding Evienne off the crowded main street.

Hestia pulled her into an alley and looked around; when it seemed she was satisfied they were quite alone, she took Evienne's hand, and the world fell out from under them.

Chapter Thirty-Five

WHEN EVIENNE OPENED her eyes, she found herself—rather inexplicably—in Hestia's sitting room.

She was laid out on one of the plush sofas with a cool cloth on her forehead. Hestia stirred in the armchair across from her and looked up.

"How are you feeling?" Hestia asked, closing the book in her lap.

"Well I've been better, I suppose, but I've certainly been worse," Evienne answered, her voice a rasp. "What happened? Did you carry me here?"

"Don't be ridiculous, of course I didn't carry you here. We glanced," Hestia said matter of factly.

"Glanced?" Evienne didn't feel well enough to try to decipher what that meant.

"Yes, we bounced from one spot to another in the world; just popped back here to my home. I thought it would be better that we discuss whatever upset you so in private. Also, you were having a panic attack, and that's never pleasant when out on a crowded street, now is it?" Hestia answered.

"Right...well ignoring the fact that you just told me you can hop around from place to place with some sort of magic..." Evienne began.

"Glancing, yes," Hestia interjected.

"Glancing, sure. Aside from that, how did you know I was upset?" Evienne asked, sitting up.

"I felt you use your time magic, Dove," Hestia said and Evienne's blood ran cold. She had never told anyone but Orion about that facet of her magic.

Hestia held a hand up to stop her as she started to protest. "Don't try that with me, Dove, I know what it was and it was the longest you've ever used it at once, so I had to assume you'd done it on purpose. Memory walking is no easy feat, so you must have had a good reason to attempt it purposefully today."

"Memory walking?" Evienne asked, her voice belying her disbelief.

"Yes, Dove. I think it's time we had a talk about your future," Hestia said, not at all concerned with Evienne's confusion. "I'll start and then we can talk about what had you so upset, alright?"

Evienne just nodded, not even knowing how to respond to her mentor's declaration. She had known this woman for fifteen years; she knew Hestia was no-nonsense, but this was drastic even for her.

"We will start with the Gevaud that you've been so diligently managing all of these years. They're not *ours*, per se, but they were created by the wild gods as a sort of backup for us. When the world's magic is out of balance, the Gevaud can sense it, and they pursue the source of the imbalance with mindless ferocity, as you've witnessed first-hand. In this case, they've sensed some sort of imbalance originating here, but we haven't been able to determine what it is."

"I'm so sorry, I don't believe I'm following you—who do you mean by *us*?" Evienne asked, wondering if she was, in fact, having some sort of fever dream.

"The Contrapensae," Hestia said as if it were the most obvious thing.

"The Contrapensae…from the folktales?"

Hestia nodded."The very same. Other Contrapensae have positioned themselves closer to the leadership of their respective nations; it seems keeping my distance has been my greatest mistake. I've been unable to truly investigate because of how tight a grip Aldith keeps on everything, and I thought we had more time," Hestia finished, leaning back in her seat.

"Hestia," Evienne said, a bit exasperated. "Are you trying to tell me that *you* are a Contrapensa?"

"Well, yes, Dove."

Evienne stared at her, truly beyond words now.

"You, Evienne Elodie D'Auclaire, have been elected to take my spot on the Council of Contrapensae. Before you go asking what that is, I'm going to explain it all to you, so just relax and try to take it all in."

Evienne nodded again.

"Good. The Council of Contrapensae was established ten thousand years ago by the now forgotten gods of this land. It is a group of nine immortals—one from each magical territory—that are tasked with maintaining balance between the magical forces in our world. We have several tools at our disposal to accomplish this task. One of them is glancing. Another is the memory walking you've experienced. We can discuss all of your abilities later, but suffice it to say, all of the non-blood magic you've been experiencing is a result of your election to the Council ten years ago.

"We select new members about a decade before their training begins. Sometimes the gifts manifest early in times of heightened emotions, but yours seem to be stronger than usual. We will sort it out during your training. You should also know that I nominated you, but the entire Council voted to select you. We choose successors from each territory based on their competence and integrity, and, as immortals, we have the luxury of time to wait until the right person comes along."

Evienne just stared at her mentor and found herself fighting the urge to laugh. But no, Hestia was not the sort to make something like this up as a joke. So Evienne paused, reviewing the facts that had just been laid before her.

"So you're truly a Contrapensa?" She asked.

Hestia nodded.

"And I've been… elected… to be one too?"

"To replace me one day, yes," Hestia answered.

"What happens to you when I replace you?"

"Then I am finally allowed to fade from this world knowing I have done right by its magic for the last thousand years," Hestia said, not missing a beat.

"You're a thousand years old? Wait, you're going to *die* when I replace you?!" Evienne couldn't keep the tinge of panic out of her voice.

"In a sense, yes, but it will be a relief after so many years of life, Dove. I am looking forward to retirement," Hestia said, a gleam in her dark eyes.

"The Gevaud are yours?!" Evienne asked as it sank in.

"No, they're not ours, they're like our…cousins. Sent by the same gods for the same purpose should we fail in our duty," Hestia said.

"Well if they're here, then what's wrong? Why haven't you all fixed whatever imbalance is at play?" Evienne asked.

"As I said, we don't know what it is. We can tell there's something wrong, but we've not been able to identify the cause. We know something is off with the Tuanadair's magic, but our efforts to correct the imbalance have been…unsuccessful," Hestia answered with a sigh.

"I think I may be of some help on that front," Evienne said slowly, her brow furrowed as she rose and began to pace.

HESTIA insisted on making a pot of tea before she would hear what Evienne had to say. It left her with a moment to herself to figure out what, exactly, had just happened.

One moment, she had been in Aldith's mind, Léhiona's unconscious face before her; the next she was hearing about forgotten gods and balance-keeping immortals, of which she was now one, apparently. This was not how she had expected today to go.

But the lack of balance, the presence of the Gevaud over the years, and everything Hestia had told her about the Contrapensae made sense when combined with what she had seen in Dominique and Aldith's minds.

If Ichorna was truly responsible for the loss of the Tuanadair's magic, that would certainly throw things out of balance. What Evienne still couldn't comprehend is *why*. Why would Ichorna want to steal Beitar's magic?

When Hestia returned, Evienne tried to start explaining what she had seen, but again Hestia silenced her, saying, "Please, Dove, calm yourself and have a cup of tea first. At least pour it before you start, just to humor me."

Evienne poured her tea, the earthy floral scented steam kissing her nose as she took a sip.

"I saw what Dominique and the queen did to Léhiona after she arrived here," Evienne began. Her mentor, if she was surprised, didn't show it. She just sat in her chair, sipping her tea, her eyes locked on Evienne's.

"They bound her, Hestia. With her wedding band tattoo. I thought Aldith loved her, but she used her, Hestia. I saw the dark magic they worked, and Dominique said something about Ichorna going dark? And some sort of connection? I heard Aldith say the Valsang she worked had been in her family for generations," it all came tumbling out now.

"They meet under the Centrale Lumine still; I saw them there just this morning in Dominique's memory. There has to be something going on there...I know there's a secret guard rotation at the facility, so it must be for whatever is held in that room." Her mind raced, trying to piece it all together.

"And I know the Tuanadair's magic began to fade around the same time their first noble came here to be our consort." Tears gathered in Evienne's eyes as she spoke; it all made sense.

"I see," Hestia said, sighing and turning to look into the

flames in the hearth. "So Aldith did something—and presumably her forebears did as well—to her consort that has caused Beitar's magic to go out," Hestia said softly, deep in thought. "I think, Dove, that you ought to make your way to that secret room; seems like it shouldn't be a secret any longer."

Evienne had known from the moment she saw Dominique's memory that she would have to infiltrate that space somehow. It was unlikely Aldith or Dominique would expect her to go poking around, but regardless, Evienne knew what she must do was incredibly dangerous.

"Let this be the start of your training as a Contrapensa, Dove. You must face this danger not only because it is the right thing to do to free the Tuanadair, but because balance must be maintained at any cost. You will go to any lengths necessary to achieve this goal. Do you understand?" Hestia's intensity was unsettling. She had always been an unwavering teacher, but Ichorna's rules had centered their blood magic training in the past. This was different.

"I understand, Hestia," Evienne said quietly. Her tea had gone cold but she took a sip anyway, not sure what else to do with herself.

"You'll teach me about my time magic though, right? It seems like it's actually quite dangerous." The thought occurred to Evienne and was out of her mouth a split second later.

Hestia laughed, "Of course, Dove, we'll hone your memory walking, your husking, glancing, and even spell-cleaving when this crisis has passed. For now, trust your intuition to get you through; finesse will come with practice, as it does for all things."

"So the horrible life-draining thing I've done has a name too?" Evienne rubbed her temples, all of this new information overwhelming her.

"Most certainly," Hestia answered with a chuckle. She rose from her seat then. "Well, I think it's time you go find that Tuanadair mate of yours and restore balance to Ichorna."

Chapter Thirty-Six

Evienne made it back to the palace in time to dress for the evening's formal events. The crowds had grown larger as they edged closer to the final day of the year; tomorrow night, the celebration would culminate as everyone gathered to ring in the new millennium.

Tonight's ball was truly a spectacle—a show of Ichorna's abundance and elegance. Despite the night chill, the ball was to be held outside in the palace gardens. A warm glow was cast in puddles here and there throughout the rows of hedges and graceful evergreens; Queen Aldith had arranged for a network of temporary mage lights to be constructed across the garden. Her intent was, no doubt, to show off to all the foreign dignitaries in attendance.

Evienne wore a black velvet gown that had a corset built into the bodice. It hugged her waist, but the skirts floated out away from her hips, moving gracefully as she walked. The neckline was a pronounced sweetheart, and she wore black diamond earrings. Her hair was swept back away from her face only on one side, her natural curls on full display tonight.

She casually began to scan the garden for Orion and Solon, but instead found Queen Léhiona floating toward her with a tired smile on her face. Prince Sylvain was at her side, looking dashing as ever. He steadied the Queen Consort on his arm, providing her support in more ways than one.

Evienne would never get bored of watching her friend move through the world; she had such a delicate grace about her, even in her exhaustion. The world could never be all bad if something as lovely as Léhiona was in it. Images of Aldith's memory, of Léhiona's binding, flashed through Evienne's mind, and sadness for her friend nearly took her breath away. She wondered if she should tell Léhiona what she had seen, though she knew she couldn't say anything here amongst all these people.

"Evi, are you quite alright?" Léhiona asked as she stepped up to Evienne's side. "I was so very worried when you disappeared this afternoon so suddenly," she added.

"Yes, thank you my friend, I'm quite well." Evienne smiled at her reassuringly. Léhiona didn't look convinced, but she wasn't one to press. She glanced up at Sylvain, who clearly shared her skepticism but decided to change the subject.

"I think I'll be quite glad when this is all over," Léhiona said quietly. "I'm so tired these days, Evi. I just don't have the energy for all this."

"I understand. It's all a bit overwhelming," Evienne responded, her heart breaking; she now suspected the true reason for Léhiona's exhaustion. How someone who supposedly loved Léhiona could use her so was beyond Evienne's comprehension.

"Did you enjoy getting to sit with the Beitarans this afternoon at least? You haven't seen anyone from your homeland since you left, right?"

Léhiona's face flashed a sad expression before she recovered her detached, pleasant mask. "Yes, they're very kind," she answered.

"Léhiona?" Evienne asked, her voice barely a whisper. Léhiona looked into Evienne's eyes, her brows creasing slightly with concern and curiosity at what her friend might say. "Do you ever wish you had been able to use your magic and shift? Do you feel like something is missing?"

Evienne could see the tears spring to Léhiona's striking eyes, and she wondered if she would be able to speak of it, even if she wanted to. "Oh Léhiona, I'm so sorry, I didn't mean to upset you; please do not hurt yourself because of my clumsy curiosity," Evienne added, taking her friend's hand and squeezing gently. Her hand brushed over the tattooed wedding band on Léhiona's slight finger, and Evienne nearly recoiled. Sylvain watched the conversation quietly; Evienne knew that he had no notion of what his sister had done to Léhiona, and she trusted his kind heart.

"No, it's quite alright," Léhiona said, laughing a bit as she delicately dabbed at her tears before they could escape. "No one has ever asked me that," Léhiona said, thoughtful. "I do feel like something is missing, every day. The deepest longing of my soul is to know my magic. But it's not to be, I suppose," Léhiona said, looking at her friend.

"I am glad to know you, Léhiona," said Evienne. "I am glad you are my friend."

"Me too, Evi." Léhiona gave Evienne's hand a gentle squeeze in return before letting it go.

Sylvain finally spoke then. "I am very happy to be here at home with both of you—it's been too long," he said, emotion coloring his voice.

"We missed you every day you were gone; it doesn't quite feel the same when you're not here," Evienne said, giving the prince's arm a supportive pat.

"Well, I suppose I ought to be off to find my wife. I can't very well leave her to all the diplomats alone, can I?" Léhiona said.

Sylvain smiled at them both, and turned with Léhiona to guide her through the crowd.

Evienne's heart felt so heavy; she knew her friend's magic had been bound, but why? Should she have told her? Told Sylvain? She knew in her heart the prince would help. He had always been good and warm and kind where Aldith had been stoic and prickly. She just didn't understand why Aldith would do something like this to the woman she loved. For all her stern nature and ambition, she believed Aldith did really care for Léhiona. Evienne had watched their love grow over years as they'd grown up together. It had been arranged from the moment they were born, yes, but what was between Aldith and Léhiona was at least somewhat true; Evienne was certain of it. Aldith loved Léhiona in her own imperfect way.

She was interrupted from her thoughts by the sound of Solon's voice close beside her.

"Good evening, High Sangviere," he said, his voice as deep as the night sky was dark above them.

"Solon, you know you don't need to be so formal, I've told you a hundred times this month," Evienne said with a laugh.

"Silly me to keep forgetting," he said with a wry smile. "I may have had more important things on my mind," he continued.

Evienne raised a brow at him in question.

"What do you know of dragons, Evienne?"

Evienne's heart stopped at his question. She quickly gathered herself, remembering that eyes and ears surrounded them.

"They are only legend, Solon. Have you been at the folklore books in our library today?" She said, trying to sound teasing.

"I have, in fact," he said, eyes shining with the mischief of their exchange. "I read something about a dragon in Assombrie Forest; do you know anything of it?"

Evienne couldn't help the smile that captured her features. "It is an ancient place, to be sure. I wouldn't be surprised if a dragon had haunted its mossy depths."

Solon smiled back at her, a wicked gleam in his eye. A dragon, of all things. Solon's animal soul suited him.

"Do you happen to know where Orion is this evening?" Evienne asked, not wanting to dwell too long on the topic of dragons with so many others around.

"He said something about a hedge maze," Solon said.

"Ah, of course. Well, if you happen to see him before I

do, let him know to find me, will you?" Evienne said, smiling at him. Solon nodded, grinning, and Evienne turned away to make her way to the hedge maze. She had no intention of just waiting around for Orion to find her; they had a lot to discuss.

Chapter Thirty-Seven

Léhiona let sylvain escort her through the crowds that filled nearly every inch of the gardens. It was truly a magical sight; warm lights dotted the inky darkness, the smell of warm cider on the air.

She felt so very tired.

"Sylvain, why is it that you stay away so much? Evienne was right. It doesn't really feel like home without you here."

He looked out over the gathering with an air of regret coloring his features.

"To be honest, it became difficult to sit by silently and watch Aldith rule. I know she is respected by our people for all she has done for them, but I found myself often disagreeing with the way she treats people. I didn't agree with her pursuit of so-called progress at any cost. I would have done things differently, but you know she doesn't listen to me. It was easier to leave and explore the world."

Léhiona felt sorrow deep in her soul over Sylvain's admission. She had thought he left only to see Domhan na

Rùin, happy to be free of any responsibility to Ichorna. She had not realized he felt so strongly about how Aldith ruled.

"What would you do differently?" She asked.

Sylvain looked at her and considered for a long moment.

"Many things, but to start, I would be kinder to the palace staff and not force them to obey simply out of fear. I believe a ruler should be loved, not only feared. I would stop trying to force our Rail onto our neighbors, and I would put our resources into resolving the Gevaud Crisis, which actually affects our rural population."

Léhiona was surprised to hear Sylvain had these ideas at the ready. She had always seen beyond the shallow façade he put on for others, but she realized now how truly great he could be.

"I'm sure if you talk with her and explain your desire to be more involved she would be happy for the assistance," she said encouragingly. Sylvain only smiled ruefully in response.

"Since when do you know Aldith to be open to assistance from anyone other than you, dear sister?"

She knew Aldith had her faults, but this conversation gave her pause. She wasn't quite sure what to make of it, but she hoped Sylvain would stay after the celebration ended. It was good to have him home.

"I'm very glad you're here, Sylvain. Will you at least consider staying when all this is done?" He looked down at her with a fond smile.

"How can I refuse when you ask? I will consider it."

Chapter Thirty-Eight

As a close friend to Ichorna's heir and her intended, she had grown up near this palace. They had spent countless nights in this garden getting up to all the nonsense seventeen-year-olds could muster. Evienne knew the hedge maze like the back of her hand.

Back then, this had been the best place on palace grounds for a midnight tryst. Evienne supposed it still was, but the hum of voices that filled the garden reminded her how many people were nearby.

Though people lingered close to the maze, it didn't seem to be the most popular spot at the party. The mage lights only stood near the entrance, the darkness discouraging people from getting lost in its winding rows. This hedge maze took up nearly a full acre of land, its paths lined with seven-foot-tall yew bushes.

Evienne didn't hesitate, striding into the vast maze. A massive oak tree stood in the clearing at the center of the maze, ancient and twisting. It was visible from anywhere in the maze, meant to taunt those trying to solve the massive puzzle.

She walked the paths of this maze she knew so well, not faltering in her path as she made her way toward the center. After about ten minutes of walking, she arrived at the middle clearing. She paused and took a deep breath of cold night air, looking up at the darkened sky in all its majesty.

"Hello, love," Orion's gentle voice drifted to her on the night breeze. She closed her eyes as his arms wrapped around her waist from behind, his body pressing into her back. "Are you alright? I was so worried this afternoon," he continued.

"Yes, I'm well. I…Orion, I saw what we needed," she whispered into the night. She felt his breath catch where his chest was pressed to her back. His hands splayed across her soft waist, and his arms tightened a bit.

"You're certain you are alright? I've never seen you so shaken, and I…" he trailed off, considering. "I felt your fear and chaos in my own soul."

Evienne turned in his arms to face him, and she felt tears spring to her eyes. "I feel very overwhelmed, but I have to be strong," she said, her voice breaking.

His hand cupped her cheek as he wiped away the tear that fell. "You're the strongest person I know—but part of having a Còmhanam is sharing your burden with me. I'm here for you. Whatever you need," he said quietly.

Evienne didn't know what the future held for them, tonight, tomorrow, next year. But she knew she wanted him one more time before they plunged into the danger ahead.

"I need you," she said, pulling him down into a kiss.

He kissed her back, meeting her tongue stroke for stroke. His touch lit up every nerve ending in her body and heat trailed down her spine to the apex of her thighs. She felt the tips of his fingers pressing into her waist, his kisses growing more urgent.

"Orion, we don't have to if you don't want to," she started, breathless.

He cut her off by slipping his hand between her legs over the fabric of her dress and pressing, the friction exactly where she needed it.

"You said this is what you need, and I will always give my Còmhanam whatever she needs. I am yours, body and soul," he whispered against her neck. She moaned as he scooped her up with an arm under her rear, and her legs automatically wrapped around his waist.

He walked them backwards, never ceasing his trailing kisses and bites against her neck. He stopped as Evienne felt the bark of the great oak pressing into her back.

Evienne looked up at him, both of them out of breath and flushed, and he smiled at her wickedly. "I intend to have you here against this tree, Còmhanam, and knot you in the light of the full moon," Orion said, his eyes roving over her.

Evienne knew they shouldn't, out here in the open where anyone could find them, but she found she didn't much care for what they should or shouldn't do. She knew they were about to risk their lives to find the truth of Beitar's suffering; all else seemed unimportant in comparison.

"Then take me," Evienne said, the challenge in her voice echoed in her gaze.

Orion didn't hesitate. He hiked her skirts up to expose her legs and found her bare, fully exposed to him with her legs still wrapped around his waist. He groaned at the sight, running his hand from where it had been cupping her face down over the curve of her breasts, across her rounded stomach, finally coming to rest between her legs.

She could feel how wet she was for him; she needed him to touch her, now. She ground her hips against his hand, and he smirked at her, enjoying how needy she was.

"Look at you, begging me to touch your pretty cunt," he purred.

She whined, and let her head fall back as he pressed two fingers into her.

"Fuck, you're so tight on my fingers," he said as he found and stroked that spot deep inside her that made her whole body tense with pleasure.

"Fuck me, Orion," she moaned. "Please, don't tease me like this." She continued grinding hard against his hand, the friction driving her mad. "Fuck me and knot me and mark me so the whole world knows you're mine."

Orion stilled his hand, and she felt a wave of love and awe strike her soul; it was his response to her words.

"Evienne, if I mark you, it will be very hard for us to go our separate ways, you understand that? The pull between us will be too strong."

"I understand," she breathed. "I want it. I want you," she said, looking up at him through her lashes. The moonlight kissed his high cheekbones, and it looked for a moment as if tears were glistening in his green eyes.

The next moment he was kissing her again, somehow even deeper now, almost reverent. She reached between them and unfastened his pants, gripping his hard length in her hand and stroking. He moaned into her mouth before breaking their kiss. For a moment they just stared at each other, time suspended between them, taut and fragile and endless.

Evienne moved first, guiding him to her entrance. She panted at the feel of him against her opening and Orion growled, pushing his hips forward to enter her. Evienne couldn't breathe around the stretch of him at first; he filled her so completely.

The small broken noise Orion made in his throat as he bottomed out inside her had her on the edge of her release. He began thrusting into her in short, deep strokes that kept the base of his cock rubbing against her clit. She felt the first flutter of her orgasm; a few more strokes of him inside her and she would be lost…

The next thing she knew, Orion's mouth was on her neck, and a violent pain filled her mind, followed almost instantly by a flood of pleasure. She felt the waves of her release all the way to her finger tips, her legs numb, her breath coming in shallow pants. Orion continued rutting into her, his tongue lapping at her neck while his teeth still broke her skin.

After a few more thrusts of his hips, Orion released his bite on her neck, smoothing over the mark with kisses. The place on her neck felt like a cold breeze over flushed cheeks, like winter's first wind. Orion found her gaze, and what she saw in his face would have brought her to her knees if she'd been standing. This man would go to the ends of the earth for her. He trusted her, admired her, respected her. He was her Còmhanam.

Evienne shifted slightly to lean forward and kiss him, and gasped at the sensitivity she felt where their bodies were still joined. Orion moved then, pulling her away from the tree and laying her down on the grass. He was still inside her, still hard and throbbing.

He thrust once and they both groaned at the sensation. Then he drew back slightly, making room to push Evienne's legs toward her chest. The angle immediately deepened the feeling of him inside her, and she cried out in pleasure. He pushed forward, his weight pushing her legs even further, and he began to thrust again in long deep strokes.

Evienne couldn't think beyond the feeling of him inside her, the pressure of his hard cock rubbing against that deepest spot that had pressure building in her lower back. He kept going, the same even pace, his green eyes fixated on her. She watched him, too, and saw when his gaze drifted down to where they were joined; she noticed the way his jaw flexed and a vein pulsed in his neck as he watched himself pushing into her body.

"Evi, I know we haven't talked about it, and I don't want to overwhelm you. I know you are protected, but by all the old gods, what it *does* to me to imagine breeding you," he rasped, eyes now fixed on hers.

"You want to breed me?" Evienne asked, breathless. Her contraception was still in effect as Orion said, but she found the thought appealing.

"Yes," he ground out, never losing his rhythm. "I want to fill you and watch your lovely waist swell with the life we create."

Evienne moaned, clenching around his cock at his words. With anyone else, this sort of talk would have been off-putting, but with Orion, it felt safe. She wanted it, even if it was only imagined.

"Breed me, Orion. Knot me and bury your seed in me, please," she begged.

"Fuck," he whispered, his thrusts picking up in pace slightly.

"Come for me first, love," he said, his hand reaching between them and stroking tiny circles around her clit.

The pressure Evienne had felt in her lower back spread down through her body and she held her breath, every inch of her felt hot and tight. With one final thrust against her sensitive spot, she felt a rush of wetness as she came. She screamed and Orion swore, letting go of her legs so they fell down to his sides. He rutted into her, short, deep strokes, until she felt his knot locking them together.

When the tightness became almost too much, Orion came with a moan, and she could feel his hot release filling her over and over again. Evienne came again at the sensation, her inner walls fluttering against Orion's hard knot.

He leaned down on his elbows and kissed her then, sweetly, rolling his hips a bit and moaning into her mouth.

"Orion?" Evienne asked, still catching her breath.

"Yes, my love?"

"No matter what's ahead, I'm grateful to have had this time with you," she said, stroking her hand down his back.

"We will have an eternity together, my love," he said, nuzzling his face into her neck. "I will fight to my last breath for every moment I can have with you."

Chapter Thirty-Nine

An hour later, Orion sat with Evienne, their backs against the ancient oak tree, still hiding away from the world in the middle of the maze. The moon was starting its descent, the hour late.

Evienne had recounted everything she saw in Dominique and Aldith's memories and had given Orion an overview of all that Hestia had revealed as well. He had listened silently—engaged—but gave her space to fully explain before he started asking questions.

Now they sat in silence, the heaviness of the facts hanging in the night air between them.

"So, you have been chosen as a Contrapensa? I thought they were no more than legend?" He asked finally.

A small laugh bubbled up from Evienne's chest; out of all the things she had told him, that's what he asked first?

"Yes, I suppose I have. Though admittedly, that's very low on my list of priorities right now. I am relieved to know that my memory walking and my husking—as it's apparently called—are normal abilities for a Contrapensa," Evienne answered.

"Alright, so you're a time-wielding immortal balance-keeper that is not, in fact, just a folktale of my people, and we know now that something is going on under the Centrale Lumine. Oh, and that Aldith and Dominique colluded to bind Léhiona's magic through her wedding band," Orion said, laying out the pieces. He continued, "I had wondered why Léhiona isn't able to shift like Solon and me; but why would they bind her magic like that?"

"Maybe to keep anyone from being suspicious? It would be odd if it was generally known that Tuanadair were losing their magic, but the one that lives in Ichorna still had hers," Evienne reasoned.

"Well if that's the case, it doesn't bode well; they're trying to hide something."

"I think we need to find that room under the Centrale Lumine and see what they're hiding. I don't want to do anything rash, but we need to understand what we're dealing with," Evienne said as she stood, brushing grass from her skirts. "And there's no time like the present…the queens will be distracted with this party until the wee hours. We should go now."

Orion stood as well, bending to kiss Evienne's cheek. "I'll follow your lead."

He trusted her instincts. However this played out, she was grateful to have him by her side.

ORION went to quietly tell Solon to make sure the queen stayed occupied for the next few hours before slipping away from the party. Evienne had left separately. They met back up at Evienne's door, and she handed Orion a dark cloak, twin to the one she now wore. He followed as she led them through the winding passages of the palace, down several levels, and out a service door into the night. Orion found himself feeling both anxious and eager; they must be close to uncovering the truth, surely.

They made their way through the darkened streets of Lucinne, staying out of the bronzy pools of mage light that dotted the busier streets. The train's gentle whir floated through the quiet of the night as it passed through this part of the city on its elevated tracks.

Orion caught sight of the great gilded dome of the Centrale Lumine peeking out above the tangle of buildings as they wound their way closer. Finally, Evienne turned onto an unassuming alley and made her way about halfway down to an equally unassuming door.

"Ideally, I won't have to announce myself and use my title to gain us access. If this side door doesn't work, we'll have to come back at a time that would make more sense for me to give you a pretend tour of the facility..." she said as she pricked her palm with her ring. Her brow furrowed in focus as she willed her magic into its more physical application.

Orion held his breath as the seconds stretched on, but finally, he heard the bolt slide open with a snick. Evienne grinned up at him in satisfaction, and the sight of her, smiling and proud of what she had accomplished, nearly took his breath away.

She didn't miss a beat, however, and quickly turned back to the door, turning the handle quietly and opening it just enough for them both to slip inside.

He took in their surroundings. They were in a hallway with no windows, but plain doors dotted the hall at equal intervals. Posters hung on the wall in the spaces between the doors, all illustrations of various sights in Ichorna with text advertising the merits of the Rail Dellumine.

Evienne signaled for him to follow her to their right as she whispered, "These are all offices, but one of them must conceal some kind of staircase to a lower level. There isn't any officially documented basement here, and I can't think of anywhere else in the building they could hide it. The rest of the facility is one huge room under the dome."

"Any idea which door?" Orion asked, keeping pace beside her.

Evienne paused beside a door with the name *Dominique Malinois* on the plaque. They shared a glance, and Evienne twisted the handle. All of the office doors stayed unlocked here; they only kept the front entrance open, and it was guarded at all hours of the day. They weren't too concerned with break-ins here.

They stepped into the room quickly, closing the door behind them. The office was sparse, just a desk, a large bookshelf on one wall, and a mage lamp in the corner that was currently turned down to give off only a slight glow. Orion felt on edge but tried to remain focused on the task at hand. He owed his people that much.

They both began to search the room for some sort of door, or anything that could lead them to the stairs they sought. Orion combed the drawers of the desk to no avail, but when he ran his hand down each of its legs, his finger caught on what felt like a switch. He flipped it. The clicking sound it made was abrasive in the silence, but a lump appeared under the large rug that covered the center of the room.

Evienne moved to pull the rug back, and they both gasped when a hatch of sorts was revealed. A handle now protruded from one side of the trap door in the floor. Orion gripped the handle and pulled back the heavy door as quietly as he could. He felt his heart pounding in his chest; surely finding a concealed doorway boded well for their search.

They both climbed down the small ladder that was revealed into the dim hallway below. Evienne's breath caught as she stepped off the ladder and took in their surroundings.

"Orion, this is the place I saw," she whispered.

He nodded, watching to see what she would do next. He was here to support her; she knew what she was doing, and he would take his cues from her. Taking a silent step, Evienne squared her shoulders and pushed forward into the inky dark of the passage. Orion followed, checking behind them as they moved. It did not escape his notice that Evienne *wasn't* checking behind her; she trusted him to have her back.

The love and respect he felt for this woman, his mate, nearly took him to his knees. She must have felt it, because she glanced back at him with a small smile, her gaze intense and knowing. Orion knew, even if this was the only time he had with her, he would cherish the memories for as long as he lived.

As they moved silently down the long hall, Orion noticed the smell of cloves becoming stronger. It was everywhere in this city to a certain degree, its spicy-sweet edge not unpleasant; but here, in this enclosed space, the scent became cloying and unnatural.

They finally came to a plain door, and Evienne's shoulders tightened slightly, her back going straighter. Orion realized this must be the place she had seen in Dominique's memory. She turned and nodded to him, her face a mask of determination. He dipped his chin in response, bracing himself for whatever they might find behind that door. Evienne's finger dug into her palm, readying to wield her magic if needed.

With her other hand, Evienne grasped the door handle and turned the knob. It didn't budge, so Evienne forced her magic into the mechanism of this door, too, and Orion held his breath, waiting for it to turn. After a long moment, it did, and the door drifted open, heavy but silent on its hinges.

Orion couldn't see fully into the room, but he heard a rustle of movement. A Sangviere was rushing at them, a blast of red ice released in a split second. Evienne expertly dodged the icy blow as Orion shifted into his snow leopard form.

Before he had even finished shifting, blood-red flames filled Evienne's palm. She didn't hesitate, launching them at the other mage, who lost their balance dodging and fell to one knee. Evienne turned to glance at Orion, and he understood her need instinctually. He leapt from his position at her side, tackling the mage to the ground, pinning their shoulders with his massive paws. This form, while still new to him, felt as natural as breathing.

Evienne approached, quickly summoning more fire, and asked the mage, "What are you doing down here?"

"It's classified," the mage said, grunting as they attempted to break free of Orion's hold.

"I am your High Sangviere, and you will answer me," Evienne said, her voice that of a commander, demanding obedience. This woman was a force of nature, and Orion thought that he would never tire of watching the way she moved through the world with such passion. It was no wonder her magic came to her as fire; it burned as brightly as her soul.

"I can't tell you because I don't know. Commander Malanois stations us down here in this little room, but I don't know what's past that second door, and she said she would hurt our families if we look," the mage said, closing their eyes in resignation. Evienne's features tightened. Orion felt his apprehension rising.

"If you don't have details, we need you out of the way so we can look around." She scanned the room for something they could use to restrain the mage, and found nothing. The tiny room was bare, save the door on the far side that the Sangviere had mentioned.

Evienne thought for a moment, then summoned what Orion recognized as one of the hard defensive shields the mages had used in the arena, but this one was the size of her hand and no larger. She shoved her hand forward, and the shield launched into motion, slamming into the other mage's temple. They lay still, unconscious from the blow.

Evienne nodded and Orion returned to her side. She wasted no time; they were now on the clock.

She strode to the second door, feeling the lock on the door. She focused, sending her magic spearing into the mechanism, and the bolt flicked open. She pushed open the door without hesitating and her eyes widened at whatever she beheld.

Orion stepped up beside her and took in the sight. His blood ran cold at the sheer *wrongness* of it. A choked sound broke from Evienne's throat as she stared at the great red mass that sat on a low pedestal at the center of the chamber.

"*What is that?*" Orion asked, unable to keep the words from slipping from his mind into hers.

"It's…" Evienne started, then stopped, swallowed. Her lip trembled, and a tear traced down the curve of her cheek as she turned to look at him. He had never seen her so distressed; he knew this had to be something truly evil.

"It's alive, Orion—so many lives, so much stolen time, all tangled and forced together," her voice broke. "I've never seen anything like it."

Chapter Forty

It was too much.

It was too much, and too wrong, and the scent of cloves scorched her throat as she heaved in air, desperately trying to get her feelings under control. Whatever this was, it was so much worse than anything she could have imagined.

Orion stood by her, his furry body pressed against her hip in support. She put her hand on his massive feline head, digging her fingers into his thick coat, grounding herself in the sensation against her fingertips.

She lifted her eyes again to the monstrosity sitting across from her. The red mass pulsed with energy, solid but not, shifting under her gaze. It sat on a low silver pedestal, and thick copper wires came from above the mass to connect to the base.

She didn't know how she could tell, but she knew without a doubt that dark magic had been used to create this abomination. It called to her power, her senses picking up the horrible thing as if it were many living beings crowded into this small room.

Evienne, for once, had no idea what to do. They had found this awful secret, whatever it was, but she still didn't understand how everything connected. It was too risky to do something rash like destroy this *thing*—no matter how awful it was. They needed to understand the implications.

In spite of her horror, Evienne ran the logical choices through her mind, calculating possible outcomes, pitfalls. After a moment she decided the best option to mitigate risks was to simply walk away. They had seen it; they knew what Dominique and Aldith were hiding down here. They knew Léhiona's binding was connected somehow, and they suspected it would all lead to understanding what Ichorna had done with the Tuanadair's magic. But right now, they needed to get out of here and regroup.

"*What are we going to do about the Sangviere?*" Orion asked into Evienne's mind.

"I think it's time to put my Contrapensae gifts to the test, and see if my memory walking can get us out of this bind," she responded, steadying herself now that she had a purpose.

"We'll deal with the mage, and then we need to get out of here for now," she said quietly to Orion. He shifted back into his human form and took her hand, squeezing lightly in encouragement. Evienne was grateful to have him by her side in this moment.

They stepped back into the entry room and found the other Sangviere still unconscious. Evienne stepped up to them and focused, spearing her mind toward them and focusing on her own face as an anchor to the memory she sought. Suddenly, she was looking at herself through the other Sangviere's eyes, fire in her palm and cold determination on her face.

Time moved slowly as Evienne took control of the moment; she acted on instinct, her will pulling at the corners of the memory. It began to peel back, disintegrating as Evienne pushed, focusing on emptiness, darkness. Slowly the scene before her fell to dust and only all-encompassing darkness remained.

She retreated then, thinking of her own mind from where she stood in the nothingness, her own seconds ticking away. Her eyes opened and she was back in her own body, staring down at the still unconscious mage.

"I think I did it," she whispered to Orion. "I think I stole the memory," Evienne said with a tinge of horror on her face. She didn't know what the Contrapensae had seen in her to make her worthy of these abilities, but she was quite glad there were not many others with the same magic. Orion only said, "Good, now let's get out of here before anyone else sees us."

They retraced their steps through the facility, barely making a sound. Evienne's mind swirled with all that she had seen, that horrible *thing* beneath them. She knew they had to pull on this thread until the whole miserable truth unraveled.

Evienne closed Dominique's office door behind them, and as they turned to make their way down the hall, they heard it. The sharp clicking of heels echoing down the hall, moving toward them.

Evienne felt Orion tense next to her, readying for a fight, but she caught his gaze and gave him a look that assured him she would handle this, not to panic.

Evienne did panic, however, when Dominique herself rounded the corner at the end of the hall, a vicious smile on her face.

"Right on time, it seems," Dominique sighed as she continued toward them. Before Evienne could get a word in, Dominique continued, "Don't even try to talk your way out of this, I know why you came snooping down here. Too curious for your own good, and too stupid to avoid getting caught."

Evienne had long since let go of her grief over the end of her marriage to Dominique, but her harsh words still stung. She had known Dominique since they were both children; did their past friendship, at least, mean anything at all?

"I saw the alternate guard rotation document in your office, and as High Sangviere, I felt I needed to know what it was about," Evienne said evenly. She could at least try to salvage this.

"Oh I know you found it; I saw you leaving my office that day. In your rush to flee, you left the paper sticking up slightly out of the file. I would *never* do that. I value order and precision in a way you never did, and it will be your downfall," Dominique spat.

"What *is that thing?*" Evienne asked, not taking Dominique's bait. No point in avoiding the topic at this point;

she wasn't about to ask further questions and give away that she had been rifling around in Dominique's memories of all things. Evienne's abhorrence at the monstrosity she had just seen was turning into a simmering rage in the pit of her stomach, and she fought to keep herself composed, alert.

Dominique smiled. She *smiled* and said, "The Sangroche is the legacy of our people; our greatest secret, our greatest triumph, the source of our progress. For generations, our royals and those closest to them have guarded this secret. It is the cost of our innovation. We owe everything to Bastille du Pont. Without his creativity and cunning, Ichorna would still be in its dark age," Dominique explained.

Evienne's mind spun to process each of Dominique's words, but alarm bells clanged in her head, drowning out everything else. Dominique shouldn't be telling them this without a fight, especially not Orion. Evienne's blood ran cold with the realization that Dominique did not expect them to leave this place with their lives.

Dominique continued, not noticing Evienne's shift in demeanor. "The Sangroche acts as a sort of… funnel? I suppose that's the closest thing, a magical funnel. It's crafted with the truest blood magic—the art of Valsang—created originally by King Bastille and maintained by each subsequent monarch feeding it lifeblood. Its sister stone sits far beneath the capital of Beitar, in the catacombs, and has yet to be discovered or disturbed all these years. The sister stone calls to the magic of the Tuanadair, pulling their power into itself and portaling it here, to the Sangroche, where we channel it into Lucinne's power reserves."

Dominique was being reckless, so convinced that she

could control this situation. Evienne had to get answers while she could; she would worry about getting them out of here later. She didn't hesitate before she asked, "And how exactly does binding Léhiona come into this?"

Brow furrowed slightly, Dominique looked as if Evienne had caught her off guard for the first time in her life. "Isn't it obvious?" She began, her bravado winning over any misgivings. "In order to keep the Sangroche connected with its sister stone, we need to regularly feed it with Tuanadair blood. What better way to keep one on hand than to have them here publicly, in a position so far removed from the every-day people of Ichorna that no one will ask questions? We have to bind their magic so no one is suspicious. If we hadn't she would have gained her magic back being so far from the sister stone in Beitar that is keyed to harvest her magic. The stone here only releases the captured resources; it wouldn't have done the job."

"You and Aldith have kept that horrific thing here, right under our noses, practicing forbidden magic using blood sacrifice and slowly draining the life from our friend, all for what? The fucking Railway?!" Evienne lost her composure, yelling the last part as she took a step toward Dominique. Orion shifted at her side, ready in a moment to pounce.

"No no, don't come any closer—and keep your cat away from me as well. It was a kindness to you for me to explain; consider it my last favor to you as your *wife*, though I never truly chose the role," Dominique raised her hand as she spoke, and Evienne spotted a small vial of red liquid clutched tight in her palm.

"What do you mean you didn't choose?" Evienne froze.

Dominique laughed, her tone pitying as she answered, "Oh Vivi, you always were so gullible. Of course I didn't choose. Aldith knew even when we were children what she would one day have to do, what was her father's legacy to protect. As you rose in power, she knew she would need to keep a close eye on you, and who better than her dearest friend and confidant? My family has been aiding the royal line of Ichorna in this endeavor since it began, the secret passed down through our line to ensure loyalty and silence. You were alright, I suppose, but I never wanted to be with you romantically. It was my duty, and a Malanois never shirks her duty," Dominique said, so casually that it sounded as if she had just commented on the weather.

Evienne's heart shattered. Everything she had known had been a lie. Ichorna wasn't some bastion of innovation and progress; it was built on forbidden magic and the blood of innocents, allowed to flourish on its theft of a whole nation's power. They were parasites, feeding off of the Tuanadair's magic to achieve their own advancements.

Aldith was not the stoic but virtuous queen she had thought. Dominique was not her domineering former wife, but a liar who had taken a torch to Evienne's self-worth, who had never even wanted her to begin with. Just like her parents when they sent her away, this woman Evienne had planned to share her life with hadn't wanted her at all. It had all been a horrible lie.

The rage hit Evienne swift and hot, searing through her veins as her lips curled into a snarl. She punctured her palm, calling her magic, but before she could even think her flames into existence, she felt every muscle in her body locking up.

Her knees hit the cold hard floor with a crack, and she couldn't move, couldn't breathe. She fought down the panic curling through her. They would make it out, somehow.

Orion leapt then, a graceful arc toward Dominique. Evienne looked at her then, and noticed blood running down her wrist and forearm. Ringing filled Evienne's ears as she realized what was happening; the smell of cloves, sickly and sweet, filled the hallway.

Orion landed a split second later only to drop to the ground, his legs splayed around him unnaturally, trembling.

Dominique chuckled and said, "Oh no, you two won't be touching me, and you certainly won't be leaving."

Evienne began to feel lightheaded, her vision going hazy. She noticed Dominique's fingers making a downward motion and realized, in horror, that Dominique was forcing the blood out of her brain. Blackness edged in. The last thing Evienne heard before the darkness claimed her was Dominique laughing, saying, "Have a nice nap, you two."

Chapter Forty-One

Orion's head pounded his pulse in his ears as he slowly became aware of his body again. The floor was hard against him, and he could tell before he even tried to move that every muscle would scream in protest the moment he adjusted.

He gradually became aware of the fact that, despite his position on what seemed to be the ground, he wasn't cold. He slowly opened his eyes to find his own massive white spotted paws in front of him—still shifted then.

He pulled air into his lungs, grasping desperately at a memory that seemed just out of reach. He moved then, pulling himself into a sitting position, his paws finding purchase on the cold ground and carefully took in his surroundings as he tried to recall how he ended up here.

A small, plain room with one tiny door, no handle, and not a window to be seen. A cell, then.

Orion recalled the sound of Evienne's knees cracking against the stone floor of that awful hallway. The memory shattered Orion's cautious quiet. It shot through his mind as his rage filled him again at seeing her overpowered.

Evienne—brave, powerful Evienne—his Còmhanam; she needed him, and he was caged here alone. They were in over their heads with Dominique and Queen Aldith. He saw that now, but he thought they had been so careful to avoid detection as they sought answers. What a costly mistake.

Orion's heightened hearing alerted him to approaching steps long before the cell door slid open with a groan. None other than queen Aldith stood in the doorway, her face a perfect impassive mask.

In this form, he couldn't speak to her, so he attempted to summon his magic to shift. Despite his weakened state, it poured through his veins in a rush, and in a blink he stood before her on two feet.

"It's truly fascinating to see the shift up close; it's really a shame that wild magic was the cost of progress," she said, her voice casual but firm. Orion remained silent.

"I've known since you arrived in my palace that you were up to no good, *Professor*," she continued. "You and your noble friend wouldn't have come here after all those years for nothing. I had hoped our High Sangviere would be loyal enough to come to me with any concrete proof of your meddling, but she proved to be a disappointment. Though, you do not seem to find her so. I hear you've grown rather *close*, hm? You can't have thought I'd be so naïve as to not have noticed your poking around in my affairs and *bedding* my closest advisor? You wanted the truth, Tuanadair, so you shall have it—alone in this cell where you can do absolutely nothing about it.

"You and your friend are powerful, so fortunately we have a use for you. The Centrale Dellumine has been slowly failing since my lovely queen consort took over as our link to the Sangnoyau, the Sangroche's sister stone in Beitar. We had a contact in the Beitaran court that helped us establish the link centuries ago, but no one is there to help us now. When Léhiona arrived here, I developed a soft spot for her; I cared for her. In a moment of weakness, I decided to alter the binding spell so it would not…drain her so. But now, her regular donations of lifeblood aren't enough to sustain the connection. We had no idea how much magic our two sister stones could really drain from Beitar, but we want to see how far we can take our progress. What are a few lives here and there when the whole of Ichorna can shine bright as a beacon of innovation for all of Domhan na Rùin?"

Orion listened with vicious hatred simmering in his heart. This woman, and all her forefathers, had thought it acceptable to rob his people of their magic; it was the most heinous crime in the history of Domhan na Rùin.

"Don't worry, dear, you won't have to bear the burden of this information for long. You and Solon have both been contained and will be incorporated into the Sangroche shortly," Aldith said coolly.

"What will become of Evienne?" Orion asked, his voice hoarse.

"Why do you ask, dear? You can't have been so stupid as to fall in love with her? I thought at least you were savvy enough to use her and her lust for your own gain without getting your feelings involved," she answered, observing as Orion clenched his jaw in an effort to restrain his fury.

Orion knew he couldn't tell Aldith that Evienne was his Còmhanam; he would protect her to his last breath, and snapping to indulge his anger wouldn't help Evienne, wherever she may be.

In answer to his silence, Aldith considered him before sighing. "Fine, I suppose you'll be gone soon, so I may as well tell you. She'll be sacrificed as well, but more slowly. I intend to feed her lifeblood to the Sangroche over time to strengthen the original Valsang that brought the stone to life. Sangviere blood is the most potent, you see. Her new home is next to the Sangroche," Aldith said, turning as the door opened again and Dominique stepped in.

She nodded a greeting to the queen as she closed the door, her eyes flicking briefly to Orion where he stood in the corner. Even in that split second of eye contact, Orion could read the hatred in Dominique's gaze.

"Alright, the other one is unconscious next door. Ready to fix your mess, your majesty?" Dominique laughed derisively as she spoke.

"How dare you speak to me that way in front of another," Aldith hissed, her eyes lighting with anger now, her mouth drawing into a snarl.

Dominique rolled her eyes and said, "Aldith, he's about to die, it doesn't matter. I just hope all of this works and we don't have to go to the trouble of getting a new consort just because of your botched spellwork. How are you feeling about your *love* for her now? Was it worth all the trouble it has caused us?"

Aldith's gaze flashed to Orion's, clearly attempting to see if he was understanding the implications of Dominique's words, her disrespectful tone. Orion didn't let anything show on his face, holding his body as still as possible. He knew they wouldn't forget he was there, but he could do everything in his power to make them think he was in shock and not absorbing what he heard.

"We have to go, dinner is soon, and we have to be on time," Aldith snapped at Dominique.

"Fine, fine—it's only upstairs, calm yourself. We'll deal with these two after the closing ceremony?"

Aldith nodded and turned to leave with Dominique close behind. Neither of the women spared him a second glance as they left the cell; he was already dead to them, alone here beneath the palace.

Chapter Forty-Two

Evienne sat alone in the gloom with the wrongness that was the Sangroche. Every time she breathed, pain seared through her palm where the massive silver spike was shoved into her hand. It dripped blood slowly down the sides of the spike into a tiny collection dish with a delicate dropper coming out the bottom. Emptiness consumed her mind with its vicious darkness.

Her hand was strapped in tightly to the arm of a chair that seemed to have been designed for this purpose exactly. The whole rest of her body was strapped in too for that matter; she couldn't move an inch.

Every few minutes, a drop of her blood would release from the dropper and slide down a tiny silver channel and onto the Sangroche. It would hit the seething stone with a hiss and a flare of black shadow before it disappeared quickly into the shifting, matte surface. Numbness was better than the phantom voices that called to her from its glowing red depths, tiny remnants of all the lives bound up inside it.

She stared at the mechanism slowly draining the life from her, bolstering the magic of this atrocity. She felt exhausted, drained, weak. She stared and stared, her soul opening into a void. In the darkness of her inner world, her thoughts started drifting.

Failure. Unwanted, unloved. Useless. Stupid. Of course it would end this way. How could she have thought otherwise? She was only a success because she had followed all the rules; of course it would all crumble the moment she stepped out of line, pursued something *she* thought was right. Of course she would make a mess of it.

Her parents had known she wasn't worth their time. Now she knew Dominique, too, had never really cared for her. That was a coarse grain of salt in the wound of Evienne's self-loathing.

She already thought herself stupid for not seeing sooner how unhealthy their relationship had been; for letting herself be controlled and spoken down to. She felt immense guilt for the years she had lost to Dominique—so much remorse it would suffocate her if she gave it more than half a thought.

Learning that it had all been a farce? That she had gone through that darkness for no true reason, that it had been a lie from the start? Evienne felt hot tears sliding down her face, dampening her neck.

Aldith, one of her oldest friends, had wanted her to succeed, but only enough to be useful to her. She had put Dominique, her friend, her lover, her wife, on her tail to keep her close, to keep her from shining too bright. Aldith had never wanted anything good for Evienne, had never trusted her. She just saw her as a resource, something to be used.

Evienne had tried and tried to make people love her, to be enough for them. She did everything she could for them, emptied herself for them, and it was never enough. She wasn't enough.

And her mate—her beautiful, strong, noble mate. She had only just found him, only just opened herself up to the possibility of a future with him. And now he was gone from her, likely dead, because he got entangled with these people she had thought loved her.

She didn't deserve to be Orion's mate. She couldn't do anything right or true or good, couldn't be anything more than a disappointment. She wasn't worth the space she took up.

Her breaths came in shallow waves, her tears tracing salty stinging lines down her cheeks. She couldn't sob, couldn't move, couldn't take her eyes off the slow dripping of her blood.

She didn't know how long she sat and stared. How had it come to this? She wished they would kill her quickly and get it over with instead of this slow, agonizing draining of her lifeblood. Why did they need her anyway if she was so useless?

It started small—a spark of doubt in her seemingly endless dark. If she was so useless, why would they need her for this? The spark flared. If her blood was so potent it could power this centuries-old magical abomination, was she really so useless? Deep in her soul, she knew the answer.

She had been chosen as a Contrapensa—chosen by her

mentor, who knew her well, and by others who only knew of her character. Not by luck or some random divine mandate. No, she had been chosen *because of who she was.*

That's what Hestia had said. It was because of who *she was*, who she chose to be, every day. The person she had hammered and forged herself into, through pain and mistakes and misery and joy and laughter and hope.

All of those people she had emptied herself for, had practically begged to love her; they were the ones not worth a second thought. She had herself, and she had her Còmhanam, who had shown her what it means to be truly accepted for what and who you are.

Maybe she wasn't worthless at all. Maybe they wouldn't need her if she wasn't the most powerful thing they could get their hands on. Evienne decided that for herself, for everything she had survived, she would hone her rage into a blade and slice away all the doubt that had held her back. She was a force of nature, and she would free herself—and the people of Beitar along with her.

Chapter Forty-Three

Evienne felt her rage building in her soul, a death knell for those who had wronged her. These people she had loved would not continue this parasitic existence; sucking the magic from innocents, without consequence. She didn't care if it made her a villain. She would bring the full force of her wrath against them for what they had done not just to the Tuanadair, but to her as well.

Her mind sharpened, and she focused, closing her eyes, searching for the pulsing power that rested in her core. If this horrific stone was formed of lifeblood, it was, very technically, alive. If it had moments to be stolen, she would rip those years of existence from it without a shred of remorse.

Her blood magic was constantly attuned to the stone and its wrongness, but she felt for a deeper awareness. After silent moments of concentration, she felt it. The pull of every second of energy, of life, the stone had in it. She took hold of it with her power and pulled, gently at first. Once she was sure she had a hold of it, though, she ripped at it ruthlessly.

The stone fought her the harder she pulled, and her eyes

flew open as she screamed, tearing at the stone's life force with everything she had. Flashes of the lives bound into the stone crashed through Evienne's mind—smiles, and laughter, embraces with loved ones, sorrow, and pain, and jealousy—every human experience, exploding out of the Sangroche.

First it cracked, a deep crevice forming on its surface. Then it began to shift from red to black until the whole stone seemed to suck in every bit of light from the already dim room.

She didn't let up, forcing her Contrapensa magic into the stone, ripping its time from it by the strength of her will.

After what felt like an eternity, the stone suddenly crumbled, pieces falling to the ground, quickly turning to a fine black dust.

Evienne panted, beads of sweat rolling down her temples as she stared at the remains; she had done it. Her heart squeezed painfully in her chest in response to her great expenditure of magic. She had stolen the life from that horrible stone just as she had that man who had attacked Cecelia all those years ago, just as she had drained that Gevaud when its jaws had been around Orion's throat.

Now she needed to free herself, but her exhaustion weighed heavily. She already felt drained from the loss of blood, and the Sangroche had fought her for its continued existence. Despite the deep ache throbbing in her temples and the straining of her heart, she had to get loose before anyone came to check on the stone. She knew the Centrale Dellumine had a mechanism to store excess energy, which she realized now was because they siphoned more than could be channeled out into the system at once—greedy leeches. She guessed that she had a bit of time before the city mage lights actually went out, but she needed to move.

Evienne took a deep breath and sank into that sharp, logical place that her mind went in a crisis. Without movement of her arms, her blood magic should be impossible to wield; the art was built on gestures to direct the power.

But she had to try. She had managed to master the physical aspects of blood magic when so many others hadn't; why not this, too?

Blood still leaked from her palm where it was pressed onto the silver spike. She felt the tired hum of her power, and she called to it, envisioning a tiny tendril of her magic slicing through the leather restraint around her wrist.

Nothing happened. So she closed her eyes, gathered her magic to her hand and raised her pointer finger as much as she could. The pain was blinding, but she continued breathing and curled her finger in toward her palm, again imagining a precise cut with a tiny flare of her magic.

This time, a gentle rip sounded through the silent chamber, and she looked down to find her wrist free.

With the use of her hand, freeing herself from her remaining restraints was straightforward, and she found herself unbound and standing after only a few moments. In the next breath, her magic was spearing toward the locked door, forcing its way into the mechanism. Evienne was glad now that she had never told anyone but Orion of her mastery of the physical aspects of blood magic.

Her body screamed in protest as she moved toward the door, exhaustion pulling her down. Her rage and adrenaline were the only things that kept her standing.

Evienne's fury took her into a cold, calculated place, and she easily sent small, forceful blasts of her power at the temples of each of the guards in the antechamber. They fell to the ground, unconscious, as Evienne strode past, fighting for breath.

She made her way through the underground hallway, memories of Orion's snow leopard form prone on the ground vivid in her mind's eye. Her rage was a song in her soul and ice in her veins.

Chapter Forty-Four

When evienne exited the side door of the Centrale Dellumine into the dark alley the sounds of a city celebrating greeted her. The music and laughter of Ichorna's people felt garish in comparison to the intense silence of her focus. Fury pulsed through her in time with her heart, her pain a song echoing through her mind.

She walked calmly through the streets, drifting in and out of the pools of mage light that painted the streets in a warm glow. No one spared her a glance despite her disheveled appearance and bloodied hand, too preoccupied with the revelry around them.

With the millennium celebration in full swing, she must have been locked in that room for a full day. She could only imagine what they had done to Orion; she didn't have a single second to waste.

She had another gift at her disposal—one she would have to use for the first time now if she had any hope of getting her Còmhanam out of this alive. She would need to glance to make it in time.

Evienne let every moment she had spent with Orion flood into her mind, feeling the sense of rightness that always burrowed into her soul when he was near. She thought of his striking eyes, so full of caring and intelligence. She thought of the warm sound of his laugh, the feel of his thick fur beneath her fingertips, the feeling of his voice in her mind. She ignored the burning sensation of the blood in her veins.

One moment, she was on the crowded street; the next breath she took filled her nostrils with the scent of damp, stale water and a tinge of blood. Her eyes adjusted to the darkness to find Orion sitting against the wall, eyes wide and trained on her in shock.

"Evi, how are you here?" His voice was a whisper as he rose and rushed to her.

She was too stunned to answer; she couldn't believe it had worked.

"Orion, we don't have time; we need to get Solon, and you both have to leave *immediately*," Evienne said, her voice even.

She took his hand in her uninjured one and squeezed softly.

"I don't know what will happen to me tonight, but over my cold, dead corpse will they take your life. You have to run, to survive, and if I make it out, I'll find you wherever you are."

Orion shook his head, brow furrowed and denial on his lips, but before he could speak, Evienne kissed him. She kissed him as if it was the last time she ever would. Then she took his hand and sent her magic spearing for the door mechanism.

They found Solon in a cell down the hall, much worse for wear. They had sent the guards for him, and he hadn't come without a fight apparently. Bruises marred his handsome face and his left eye was nearly swollen shut.

"How..?" He began, trying—and failing—to get to his feet as they barged into the cell.

"No time to explain, old friend. We have to get you out of here," Orion said quietly, striding to Solon's side. Orion looked to Evienne.

"You have to get him away from here, Orion. And you have to stay away as well. If Aldith sees you again, she will kill you. I won't be able to live with myself if I don't keep you safe from this," Evienne said, voice breaking.

"Evi, not leaving you," he said.

Evienne knew they didn't have time to argue, so all she said in response was "I love you, Orion, and I am proud to have been your Còmhanam, even if this was all the time we had."

She didn't wait to hear his response, but glanced out of the dungeons beneath the palace to the hallway just outside the great hall, where she knew the queen's grand finale to this whole cursed celebration was taking place. Her heart was breaking to leave Orion behind, but his safety was more important than having him by her side. She loved him, and she would protect him to her dying breath.

The music and joyful chatter of the streets was echoed in the palace as Queen Aldith's final ball raged on, the minutes until the new Millennium dripping away in a haze of alcohol and dancing.

Evienne took a deep breath and steeled herself for what she knew she must do. Aldith had to be removed from power tonight, one way or another. Her plan was simple: make the truth known, no matter the cost. She would have to intuit the rest as she went. Her anger kept her mind sharp and pushed any doubt out of her mind.

She strode into the great hall, head held high, and made her way to the very center of the room. A few surprised exclamations rose from the crowd as she passed—blood still dripped from her hand—but no one stopped her.

When she was only twenty paces from the dais, she let her voice ring out clear as a bell on a winter morning.

"Aldith of Ichorna, I condemn you and your forebears for the atrocities you have committed against the nation of Beitar. You have robbed the Tuanadair of their magic, crippled them, to power our technology. You have bound our queen's magic and preyed upon her to work your Valsang. All in shameful secrecy! You are not fit to bear Ichorna's crown any longer!"

Silence had fallen across the hall the moment Evienne began to speak, and now the only sound was the rustle of skirts as guests shifted anxiously, unsure what to do.

Léhiona sat frozen on the throne next to Aldith's, eyes wide with horror and fixed on Evienne. She wished that Léhiona, who had been a true friend to her all these years, had found out about this another way; there just hadn't been time. Her shock and devastation broke Evienne's heart. Anger for her friend was a keening wail in her soul.

After a moment of horrible, tense silence, Queen Aldith spoke, not even deigning to rise from her throne to respond to Evienne's accusations.

"Guards, remove this traitor from our celebration immediately."

Evienne glared at the guards, her labored breathing the only sound she could hear. No one moved. Léhiona slid her eyes to her wife at her side and said quietly, "Aldith, my love, what is she talking about?"

Without tearing her gaze from Evienne, Aldith replied, "Nothing but traitorous delusions, dearest, I'm sure."

If Aldith continued to play the fool, Evienne knew she would have to strike her down and become Ichorna's villain in the process. It was something she was prepared to do.

Sylvain stepped forward from the crowd then, moving with grace toward the front of the hushed room.

"Your Majesty, I have never known our High Sangviere to harbor delusions. I would not dismiss her so lightly."

The crowd began to murmur at Sylvain's declaration. Even he did not usually dare to speak so publicly against the queen. Aldith's placid expression hardened into cold anger at her brother's defiance.

"I will unbind Queen Léhiona and you will all see for yourselves Queen Aldith's deception!" Evienne spoke surely, taking another step forward. Despite her body's protests, she would have to put another facet of her Contrapensae magic to the test tonight.

"Guards! Remove her!"

Evienne's magic lashed out of her; it came as naturally to her as breathing, though she didn't consciously understand what she was doing. Her power bore down on the dark magic binding Léhiona, rending it, forcing the dark magic wound into that black band around her finger to disintegrate bit by bit.

Léhiona screamed and doubled over as the magic was torn from her, and Aldith leapt up to take her wife's hand. When she realized what was happening, though, it was too late. Léhiona's scream halted as quickly as it had begun, and she darted her gaze to Evienne.

Evienne nodded to her friend, emotion nearly overwhelming her as she realized Léhiona was free for the first time in ten years. Tears streamed down Léhiona's face—she knew, too.

The moment Léhiona began to shift, unbound, time slowed to an ethereal drip. Her magic shimmered and her graceful human form dissolved. Out of an opalescent mist, a jewel-toned luna moth the size of a raven materialized, each beat of its massive wings an eternity.

Seconds slipped back into place, and Evienne heard sounds of awe rise from the crowd around her at Léhiona's second form. She fluttered down from the dais, and Evienne extended a hand toward her. Léhiona came to rest on Evienne's finger as she said, "This is proof of my condemnation. Bear witness to your wife's oppression and answer for your crimes, Aldith of Ichorna."

Sylvain rushed to Evienne's side as she spoke, offering his hand to Léhiona. She fluttered over to him, and he stared at her in awe, running a finger over her downy wing. She was so beautiful it nearly took Evienne's breath away.

Dominique's strident laughter cut across the soft murmurs of the crowd as she slithered toward the dais from wherever she had been hiding. Evienne's exhausted body tensed at the sound of Dominique's voice. She addressed Aldith with open derision.

"You imbecile, how could you think you could contain her? I bet her Tuanadair friends are halfway home by now. You should have killed her when you had the chance and fixed your spell, but you can't do anything right can you, *your majesty?*"

Aldith stood frozen, her jaw slack at Dominique's words. Evienne and Sylvain watched, both on edge and ready to protect Léhiona. Sylvain was no great Sangviere, but he had some basic defensive training. Léhiona was now perched on his shoulder, her wings flitting nervously.

"Nothing to say for yourself?" Dominique asked before turning to address the crowd.

"The truth is, my friends, your queen does not have the strength to do what must be done to ensure our progress—to solidify Ichorna's greatness, our place in this world. Aldith had one task to carry out to ensure Ichorna's needs were met for her lifetime, and she put her own desires above the needs of her country. That little Tuanadair wife of hers was supposed to give us access to power for decades, but she couldn't bring herself to do it right—didn't want to hurt her as much. Take me as your ruler instead, and I will not suffer anyone to stand in the way of our dreams! I will not stand for imperfections or weakness or sentiment!"

The crowd inhaled a collective gasp at her words, and before Dominique could even turn back to Aldith, she lurched, her body seizing. Evienne glanced at Aldith, who now had a trickle of blood running down her wrist. She had used another of those cursed vials of another's blood to perform her Valsang. Evienne watched as Aldith took hold of Dominique's body and held it at her mercy.

A few people in the crowd screamed as the sound of snapping bones echoed through the hall. Dominique's arms and legs now bent at unnatural angles. She shouldn't be standing, but Aldith's grip on her kept her upright. She had no control of her body now. She couldn't even scream.

"You disloyal, grasping, *traitor*!" Aldith screamed, and a trickle of blood ran down from Dominique's nose to her chin. She did not look afraid. She stared back at Aldith with hatred in her eyes. Evienne made no move to interfere; if these two wished to destroy each other, she would gladly let them.

Aldith didn't let Dominique go, clenching her hand into a fist around the blood and broken glass in her palm. A sickening crack sounded, and a mist of blood sprayed where Dominique's body had been.

Chapter Forty-Five

Chaos broke out in the hall. A few people ran, screaming, from the room. Some were sick where they stood. Most looked to each other, unsure of what to do. Despite the confusion, everyone invariably stayed clear of the space in front of the dais where Evienne still stood, facing down Aldith with Sylvain by her side and Léhiona, in her shifted moth form on his shoulder.

"You," Evienne said, pointing at Aldith. "I will teach you to regret what you have done."

Evienne's body cried out in protest as she shifted on her feet, her heart clenching. She knew she had pushed her magic too far, but there was no other choice. If she gave her life for this, so be it. At least Orion was safe.

Several other Sangviere rushed into the room then, looking a bit unsure. They hesitantly gathered into a formation behind Aldith. Everyone stilled then—the tension in the room was razor-sharp.

Evienne heard the rustle of clothing to her left, and

turned to see Cecelia elbowing her way through the gaping nobles.

"Evi, what's going on?" She made to run toward where Evienne and Sylvain stood, but Aldith bent to swipe her hand through the spray of Dominique's blood that now covered half the dais. Evienne realized what was happening too late.

The next moment, Cecelia lurched to a stop and Sylvain tensed where he stood. Aldith laughed cruelly, her right hand held out and splayed wide, shaking with effort.

"I will not suffer this insubordination a moment longer. You must reckon with my Valsang, the magic that only true Sangviere dare to wield."

She forced Cecelia and Sylvain to the ground, and Evienne felt the pressure of Aldith's magic trying to take hold of her. It took every ounce of her focus, but she resisted this time, her will like iron. Evienne barely noticed Léhiona shift before she was in her human form screaming, running toward Aldith.

"Aldith, you mustn't! They're innocents, they're our family!" Léhiona yelled in horror as she rushed toward her wife, her silk gown tangling around her long legs.

Almost too quickly to see, Aldith flicked her other wrist and a blade of pure blood cleaved the air, piercing Léhiona's chest.

Léhiona gasped, and Aldith's face twisted in shocked horror. Time again seemed to slow as Léhiona fell. Evienne felt, more than heard, herself scream. Her dear, soft, kind friend collapsed slowly to the marble floor, her skirts billowing out around her on a phantom breeze. Aldith was crying out too, refusing to release her hold on Cecelia and Sylvain, but in obvious agony over what she had just done.

Evienne rushed to Léhiona's side, taking her hand. Aldith, now with tears streaming down her face, was fighting to keep Cecelia and Sylvain restrained with her dark magic. She struggled with the effort of controlling them. Evienne knew she had only seconds before Aldith's attention turned back to her and Léhiona, where she lay bleeding. Everything felt distant, like this was some fever dream and Evienne would wake up any moment to find none of it had been real.

"Evi, it's alright, I," Léhiona began, her breath coming in harsh pants. Her eyes flicked over to Aldith on the dais.

"Thank you. Thank you for even just a moment. I thought I'd never know, never feel what it was like. Thank you, and please...make it right for my people," she said as her eyelids grew heavy.

Evienne sobbed and nodded, leaning down to kiss her friend's forehead. "I will," she whispered. "I'm so sorry, Léhiona. Thank you for being my friend."

Evienne lifted her head when Aldith's screech of effort sounded from where she still stood near the throne, struggling to maintain her hold.

Aldith finally lost her fight to hold both, and they collapsed to the ground, attempting to recover from the effects of her control over them. She turned her gaze toward Evienne; hatred and death darkened her face. Evienne was nearly overwhelmed by all the emotions biting at her soul. She would end this.

"You have ruined *everything*, Evienne D'Auclaire! I

curse the day you came to my city!" Aldith yelled on a sob, truly beyond herself.

Evienne tracked Aldith's gaze as it darted to the back of the hall. Evienne turned and felt terror like she had never known as she watched Orion rush into the room. She was exhausted, her blood like fire pumping through her body, but she saw Aldith gripping another vial in her hand. Evienne knew she had but a moment to stop whatever she planned to do next.

Evienne glanced down to Léhiona, still fighting for breath; she held up a bloodied hand for Evienne to take. Evienne understood what her friend was offering, what she had to do. She knew it would corrupt her soul somehow, but Hestia's words rang in her ears. She would do whatever it took to restore balance, no matter the cost. More than that, she would not let harm come to her Còmhanam. She would sacrifice her soul to bring Aldith down. Her evil could no longer be allowed to taint the world.

Evienne gripped Léhiona's bloody hand in her own and felt the deepest part of her magic, her Valsang, scream to life in her veins. She didn't hesitate, gripping every drop of blood in Aldith's body, holding her perfectly still. The world narrowed and all Evienne could see was Aldith, frozen, eyes wide with terror.

She could feel Aldith fighting her, but she held fast, her hand tight around Léhiona's.

"No more," Evienne screamed, and her Contrapensa magic poured out of her. It grabbed onto Aldith's lifeforce, every moment of her future at Evienne's fingertips. Darkness edged Evienne's vision—she had gone much too far, but she didn't care.

Evienne held Aldith's gaze as she slowly unraveled each second, hour, year of her life. Aldith's skin wrinkled, her back hunched, a hundred years of decline all in a moment as Evienne continued to scream.

Evienne released her at last, withered creature that she now was. Aldith collapsed on the dais, unmoving, and Evienne shifted her gaze back to her lovely friend still bleeding out on the cold floor.

Evienne fell to her knees and tried desperately to summon a shred of healing magic, but her power lay silent, her body drained. She could feel her own heart on the verge of giving out. Léhiona squeezed her hand gently, unable to open her eyes, and Evienne sobbed as she watched her friend's breathing grow shallow.

Orion had made his way to her side, and he took her arm, helping her slowly to her feet. Evienne's voice was hoarse as she addressed the shriveled shell of a woman now cowering on her throne.

"Aldith of Ichorna, you will die for your crimes. I am Evienne Elodie D'Auclair of the Contrapensae, and I will see balance restored to this world."

She didn't hesitate before reducing the queen to a mound of dust.

Chapter Forty-Six

Orion had gotten Solon far enough out of the city that he could rest and shift safely without being seen. The great dragon had taken to the skies not long after Orion departed, flying to Beitar on swift wings to report on all that had occurred.

Orion knew Evienne had left so suddenly to protect him, and he could understand her reasoning. He likely would have done the same in her position. His mate was here, though, and he was going to get back to her.

He shifted and ran as fast as his four legs could carry him back into the city. He didn't stop, not caring about the gasps and screams from revelers crowding the streets. He bounded straight up the palace steps and didn't hesitate to run into the grand hall.

He could feel that she was here, and he called to her mind, "*Evienne, my mate, where are you?*"

She didn't answer, so he rushed into the throne room to find her standing alone against Aldith's rage. What happened next was a blur. Evienne's scream of rage still filled his mind as the silent aftermath of the confrontation settled over the room. Now he watched as she knelt with Léhiona's head cradled in her lap, Cecelia and Sylvain close beside her.

Tears traced down her cheeks; he could smell their salt on the air.

"She's not quite gone, but," Evienne said through her sobs. "I can't do anything, I don't know what to do," she said as she looked up into his face.

The great hall, still full of nobles, observed in shocked silence.

They all looked up at the sound of footsteps clicking on the marble floor, and an older woman who Orion realized must be Hestia stood before them.

"Well, Dove, you certainly handled things."

Evienne started at the sound of Hestia's voice addressing her.

"Hestia, I," she began, her voice a broken rasp.

"It's alright, Dove, we're here to support you. I know it feels like a mess, but you're showing us why we chose you," Hestia said, leaning down to give Evienne's shoulder an encouraging squeeze.

"We'll have time for introductions later, but these are some of your new colleagues," Hestia continued, her voice lowered.

Orion watched Evienne look up to see the several rather regular-looking people gathered around her mentor. She seemed too overwhelmed to really take in their faces, her eyes glazed over. Hestia began speaking again, pulling his attention back to her.

"You'll need to stand up with us and join hands if you

want to save her," Hestia continued, beckoning Evienne to stand. Orion took her arm and helped her up, wrapping his arm around her waist in support.

"We'll hold her in stasis while her healing gifts do their work. She will be alright. Come here, Dove."

Orion helped Evienne into position between her mentor and a kind-looking man who bowed his head slightly to her in greeting. Hestia closed her eyes in focus and Orion felt the rush of power filling the room.

Léhiona lay perfectly still, her body now covered in a gentle glow; the white light made her look otherworldly. Orion stood behind Evienne, steadying her as she worked with the other Contrapensae for long moments.

After what felt like hours, Hestia took a deep breath, and the hum of power ceased. Léhiona still lay unconscious, but the ghostly pallor of blood loss had left her features. She breathed easily. The palace healers rushed forward then, lifting her gently onto a cot and carrying her to her rooms. Cecelia hurried after them. Evienne leaned fully on Orion in exhaustion.

Once they were gone, Hestia's voice again cleaved the tense silence to address Evienne. He honestly couldn't believe she was still conscious, but she seemed determined to stay awake. Orion wanted nothing more than to take her out of this room and take care of her.

"Here's your second official lesson as a Contrapensa, Dove: when dealing with transfers of power, time is of the essence."

"I think I understand, Hestia. You mean we need a new

ruler. As soon as possible," Evienne said, her voice a bit hoarse.

Hestia nodded. "Where is Prince Sylvain?"

"I just saw him leave with Léhiona," Orion said, caressing Evienne's waist where his hand supported her.

"Very well. You will rest, and then you will talk with Sylvain, Evienne. There will be a coronation in the morning. We will keep order for the rest of the night," Hestia said.

Orion didn't need to hear anything else—he scooped Evienne into his arms and made his way to her rooms.

Chapter Forty-Seven

As the first light of dawn kissed the land the following morning, all of the nobles and guests had reassembled in the great hall. Frost tipped every blade of grass outside, and the air was still, clinging to the early morning peace. Evienne stood on the dais, Orion still supporting her in her weakened state. Hestia and the other Contrapensae were gathered nearby. The gathered crowd was nearly silent, waiting for their new king.

Evienne had sought Sylvain out before the dawn, as soon as she was well enough to walk to Léhiona's room on Orion's arm. Despite his grief and shock, he had taken the news of his impending coronation gracefully. As Aldith's only sibling, he had known all his life that this was a possibility. Knowing and experiencing were very different things, though, and Evienne admired Sylvain's resolve in the face of such unexpected responsibility.

Léhiona was resting comfortably in her room, and Cecelia insisted on staying to keep watch over her. She would awake to a new world, and though Aldith had wronged her so greatly, Evienne knew the loss would ache. Her heart broke for the grief Léhiona would feel.

Evienne's attention returned to the gathered crowd, and she saw Sylvain step through the massive doors at the end of the great hall. The sun was now high enough in the sky that it sent a kaleidoscope of colors glimmering across the room through the panes of the stained glass. It was the first dawn of the new millennium and a new dawn for Ichorna, as well.

Sylvain du Pont made his way down the long aisle. Evienne stood at the center of the group, holding Ichorna's crown. She watched the crowd and saw all of her varied emotions reflected on the faces of those gathered. Grief, surprise, hope—the people of Ichorna felt it all.

Sylvain reached the dais and lowered to his knees before Evienne, head bowed. Evienne placed the crown upon her friend's head.

"Ichorna, this man is your new king, his power vested by the Council of Contrapensae."

At the mention of the Council, a wave of surprised exclamations rose from the crowd. Hestia nodded to Evienne, so she continued.

"He is responsible not only for your care, but for the care of the balance of our world. I charge you all, in turn, to be loyal to him, and to partner with him in the pursuit of balance and justice. Sylvain du Pont of Ichorna, rise as king."

The crowd applauded as Sylvain turned to face them. A single tear escaped down his cheek as he addressed the gathered audience.

"People of Ichorna, and all those gathered here from near and far: I vow that our memory of this night will not be distorted. We will move forward, but we will not forget those who suffered. We denounce Queen Aldith, and vow to move forward into a new era of peace. The Contrapensae of legend are real, and they have uncovered the imbalance and injustice hiding in the shadows of Ichorna. I will serve you all loyally as we set about correcting our path. I do not know all that will fill the days ahead. I do not know what our Beitaran neighbors will do when they hear of the truth, but we must be prepared to atone for the harm we have caused. The road ahead will not be easy—our entire way of life has been built on the backs of others—but we will be innovative, and brave, and we will never again harm others in our pursuit of progress. As we begin this new millennium, we ring in a new era of truth and balance in Ichorna."

The people bowed to their new king, and Evienne could not have been more proud. Sylvain's words gave her hope for the future of Ichorna.

AFTER the coronation, Evienne and Orion had slipped away to her rooms. She still felt on the verge of collapse; her use of magic the night before had truly taken its toll on her.

"Are you well, love?" Orion asked as they settled down under the covers of her bed.

"I am grateful to be here with you, and grateful that we have freed your people," Evienne said, her throat tight.

"And?"

"And I fear my soul is now ruined by the taint of dark magic. I do not regret what I did—I saw no other way forward—but I fear I am now no better than Aldith herself," Evienne whispered, letting her thoughts out into the world.

"Oh, my love," Orion said, folding Evienne into his embrace. "You are nothing like her. You did not steal Léhiona's blood for your magic; it was freely given. You did what you had to do to save your friends and all the people of Beitar. You were willing to take on the burden of that magic for the good of others. Some with more rigid mindsets may say that makes you a villain, but you know the truth of your spirit. That magic only makes you evil if you let it," Orion said and pressed a kiss into Evienne's hair.

"I love you, Orion. I am so, so happy to be yours. I don't ever wish to be parted from you."

"I love you too, lovely, deadly Evienne. My fearsome, bright, exquisite Còmhanam. I will love you with every breath until my very last."

LATER that afternoon, Evienne sat with Orion, Sylvain, Hestia, and Cecelia in the sitting room adjoining Léhiona's bedchamber. They had all barely rested for a moment since the coronation that morning, but they managed to gather here around a pot of tea, as if not much had changed in the world.

Lucinne had power reserves that, despite their ill-gotten origin, would keep the city from total chaos for a short time. They expected they would have power for about a week if residents were careful with their usage. Determining a plan for the Centralle Dellumine would be one of Sylvain's first great challenges as a ruler.

While Ichorna's future weighed heavily on Evienne's mind, she couldn't help but think of all that Aldith and Dominique had revealed in their recklessness. They had said there had once been an ally in Beitar, that they had lost contact.

"I think we need to get to Beitar," Evienne said, and conversation amongst her companions halted.

"What makes you say that?" Orion asked, no challenge in his voice, only genuine curiosity.

"Aldith said there was someone in Beitar who helped establish the Sangroche and its sister stone long ago, that the other stone is still there, in Sgùrdruid's catacombs. If that's true, isn't it possible this could happen again?"

"Whoever helped King Bastille then could have installed some sort of successor, similar to the pass down of the knowledge we had here. I just don't understand why someone in Beitar would have helped him with this; though, whoever it was may not have been from Beitar themself," Hestia said.

"I think your instinct is right, Evienne, and I believe our king is likely to be amenable to a visit from the woman who is our savior," Orion added, giving her hand a supportive squeeze.

"If there is any chance the conspirator or their ilk are still around, they must be rooted out," Sylvain said. "We can handle things here, Evi."

Cecelia nodded in agreement at Sylvain's words.

"Take your fluffy mate to Beitar, Dove, and set things right. Oisín Treun is the Contrapensa in Beitar. They are a quiet sort, but they will help you," Hestia said and took a sip of her tea.

Silence fell, each of them too tired and wrapped up in their own thoughts to continue the conversation. Just as Evienne was about to excuse herself to go rest, the door to Léhiona's bedchamber creaked open.

"Sylvain? Evi?" Léhiona's voice was hoarse, and everyone turned as she stepped carefully into the room.

"What happened?"

Epilogue

Solon's wings were spread wide as he flew across the border and into Beitar. He hadn't quite believed that the magic was really free; he thought perhaps he would fall to his death in his human form the moment he re-entered Beitar. He waited for it to happen…but it didn't.

The mountains of his homeland loomed ahead of him, and he pushed toward them. He was exhausted, but he had to make it back to tell the king of all that had occurred in Ichorna.

After another hour of flight, Sgùrdruid appeared perched on the side of a mountain. He would never stop feeling awe at the sight of it. He looked around for a place to land—no easy feat given his size in this form—and decided on the city square.

People screamed as he slowly descended, scattering and taking shelter. When he landed, he shifted as quickly as possible so people would stop panicking.

As soon as he did, a hush fell over the square. He looked

around at his fellow Tuanadair and smiled, giving them a quick wave. Before he could be bombarded with questions, he took off walking toward the castle.

Solon thought he was going to keel over in exhaustion by the time he was admitted to the throne room. It was early morning, and the king looked as if he had just sat down on his throne. His clothes were off-kilter, as though he had thrown them on in a rush, and his hair was not in its usual slicked-back style.

"Solon, I was not expecting you back from your little vacation until tomorrow at the earliest," the king said, distracted with adjusting the positioning of his crown.

"Your majesty, I come with the most incredible news," Solon began, unable to hide his smile.

"The hold on our magic is broken. Beitar is free at last."

The king froze and finally looked at Solon. His expression was blank save for the very slight pinching of his brow. He lowered his hands from his crown and said, "What makes you think that?"

Solon didn't answer in words, he just felt for his magic—and shifted.

The king's eyes widened as he took in Solon's dragon. He didn't look… happy. Or relieved. Or any of the things Solon was expecting. Instead, he almost looked angry.

His words did not at all match his demeanor as he said, "What incredible news you bring, Lord Solon; I am eager to hear how this all came about, but you must excuse me for now. I find I am in need of a moment to process what you have shared."

The king rose and Solon shifted back to his human form, the pinching pain and rush of power that came with the shift still foreign, but somehow natural.

"Of course, your Majesty. I will remain at the castle," Solon bowed at the waist as the king hurried out of the throne room.

What a bizarre encounter. Of all the possibilities Solon had considered, veiled anger and dismissal were the furthest from what he had expected. There was no point in waiting here in the throne room, he supposed, so he made his way up to the chamber he kept in the castle. Most nobles from across Beitar had accommodations here due to their frequent visits.

As he passed through the main hall, he heard someone shouting in the distance. He turned to examine the source of the noise, and one of the castle servants came running across the open space.

"Whatever is going on? Is someone hurt?" Solon yelled after the servant as he ran by.

"It's the king, my Lord! He's ill! He's dying!"

Content Warnings

- Attempted SA, non-graphic, not happening to the main character
- Gore related to blood magic
- Discussion of past emotional abuse by a romantic partner
- Negative self-talk from the main character
- Breeding kink but no pregnancy
- Knotting
- Panic attack on page

About Emma Elizabeth

EMMA ELIZABETH IS an Indianapolis-based author of LGBTQIA+ Romantasy and Monster Romance. She loves escaping to fantasy worlds in her free time, and is passionate about representation in fantasy media. She enjoys spending time at home with her husband and her little dog, runs a monster smut book club, and likes chocolate croissants entirely too much.

More by Emma Elizabeth

The Songbird & The Forest is a spicy sweet novella featuring a non-binary Dryad and their feisty necromancer lady-love, Dahlia. It's available now on Kindle Unlimited, Kindle, and paperback.

If you'd like to keep up to date with Emma's writing adventures, join her newsletter or connect with her on social media.

Printed in Great Britain
by Amazon

55963039R00178